HARDIMAN SCOTT, for many years the BBC's political editor, was a familiar figure on British television screens. After covering assignments at home and abroad, the last five years of his career with the BBC were spent as Chief Assistant to the Director General. He took a leading role in negotiating the radio broadcasting of Parliament, and his last assignment before leaving the BBC in 1980 was as a member of the four-man team to help organise Zimbabwe's broadcasting system. Since then he has become a successful thriller writer.

BECKY ALLAN has worked in advertising, PR, the print industry and publishing. She moved around quite a lot. Between raising two sons and taking a theology course, she has written several religious books.

Bait of Lies

Hardiman Scott and Becky Allan

'. . . See you now,
Your bait of falsehood takes this carp of truth:
And thus do we of wisdom and of reach,
With windlasses and with essays of bias,
By indirections find directions out . . .'

Hamlet, Act II, Sc.1

HEADLINE

First published in Great Britain in 1986
by Brechinset Publications
First published in paperback in Great Britain in 1987
by Headline Book Publishing PLC

ISBN 0 7472 3008 0

Printed and bound in Great Britain by
Collins, Glasgow

Headline Book Publishing PLC
Headline House
79 Great Titchfield Street
London W1P 7FN

For
Sue & Keith

Acknowledgements

A number of people have helped the authors with information and advice, and they would like especially to thank Joyce Board, David and Wendy Brooks, Richard Gates, Jan Kavan, David Peck, Keith Roper and Richard Taylor.

1

In the last hour the place for the meeting had been changed. Perhaps that should have warned her. But Josef had said that, in Prague, it was only a sensible precaution whenever a small group of Charter 77 got together.

'It's not dangerous then?' Carolyn had asked, although she knew that would not have made any difference. A sudden feeling of gratitude for the young Czech, and the feeling of escape from her own past, ensured that she would go.

She thought of him as young perhaps because of the unexpected happiness that had linked them together. In fact, he was probably six or eight years older than her twenty-four, and he certainly had the confidence and self-possession of an older man. A month ago she had not even known him. Now she adored him. Who wouldn't? He was tall — over six feet — with dark, slightly curly hair, deep brown eyes, and with the classic swimmer's body — broad shoulders and chest, slim waist. How could she be so lucky?

'Dangerous?' he smiled. 'Every moment of this country's history has been dangerous.'

'I'm not aiming to make history.'

He patted her strawberry-blonde hair reassuringly. 'You don't have to worry.' There was the tolerance of experience in his manner. 'It's a precaution. It always works.'

'And even if I agree to take something back to London for you — don't I have to worry about that?'

'You're a privileged visitor. Not everyone gets a visa to spend about six weeks studying art and picture restoration. The Czechs — even the government — put a high value on our art.'

He had gone on to explain to her how the leaders of Charter 77 were tailed all the time, but not even the plain-clothed members of the STB bothered with all the Chartists. They couldn't possibly. They didn't know them all anyway, and the STB frequently behaved so obviously that they might just as well be wearing the peaked cap and plum-blue uniforms of their SNB colleagues.

'Do they know you?' she asked.

Josef shrugged. 'They've left me alone.'

That had not answered her question, but the way he had said it even made her question seem unimportant. Perhaps, she had reflected, it was because of his job. He had proudly told her that he taught English at Charles University. Apart from at her tourist hotel, the Zlata-Husa in Wenceslas Square, she had not found many people speaking English. Maybe the authorities were prepared to be tolerant or perhaps, as she hoped, they didn't know about his other activities.

It was in Wenceslas Square that she had first met him. She had been standing high on the steps of the National Museum, the great plinth and mounted statue of Saint Wenceslas, in cloak and armour, looking, as she was, down the dual lanes of the broad street that, incongruously, was called a square. On the edges of the wide pavements the trees were in bright yellow-green leaf. Set like teeth down each side, cars were parked at right angles. Behind her was the great columned and decorated facade of the museum.

'You must be English.'

She turned to face the owner of the barely accented voice and found herself looking up into tanned features with laughing brown eyes.

'How did you know?'

'The designer jeans,' he had replied knowledgeably.

'And you?' She saw that he was wearing slacks and a light sports jacket — neat but dull.

'Oh, Czech.' Then seeing the way she looked at him, he had added, 'We're better at designing glass than clothes.'

She laughed. 'Your English is good.'

'It had better be. I'm paid to teach it.'

'Have you been to England?'

He paused, almost as though considering the question, and then briskly replied, 'No. I should like to. Are you on holiday?'

'Yes and no.' She surprised herself at already feeling that she knew him well enough to tease.

'Oh, the enigmatic English,' he smiled.

'I'm learning to restore pictures.' She saw his sudden interest and was pleased. 'I've come here to look at your art, and study some of your restoration. I've been lucky.'

They walked down Wenceslas Square together, chatting easily until they reached her hotel on the right-hand side. Then with a polite, 'Do enjoy your stay,' he was gone. She stood beneath the hotel canopy feeling disappointed. She almost called after him, but he didn't even look round. Why should he? She was just a girl he had met on the steps of the museum, and he had taken the opportunity of a little English conversation and . . . well, he had his own life. Why should she have expected him to do anything but walk away? Wasn't that what usually happened with casual encounters? Yet, she now realized, that was not what she had expected.

Her hotel room was large with two single beds and two tall windows that looked down on to the 'square' below. The accommodation had obviously been designed for tourists. The carpet was thick, a beige-brown mixture that toned with the varied apricot and cream of the curtains, the bed covers and the walls. A wide panel of hardwood was fixed round the room at hip height. There was a small bathroom en suite, and the whole thing, she thought, was meant to impress. She felt very alone. They had not even exchanged names.

That, however, was an omission that was repaired two days later. She had gone to the Convent of the Blessed Agnes, a collection of buildings that had been skilfully restored and reconstructed as a national gallery to hold the permanent exhibition of Czech painting of the nineteenth century. At the time she was standing in front of a painting of St Vitus Lake by Antonín Chittussi. The foreground of water, the reeds, the bank beyond, the darker hedgerow and single tree, all had a pearly opalescence that reminded her of similar scenes by Corot.

'He spent some time in France, you know. That accounts for the influence.'

Carolyn sighed with pleasure as she turned round to face him.

'I . . . I thought I might not see you again,' she said awkwardly.

'Hardly possible in Prague.'

Carolyn thought that was rather chancing luck, but decided that it would be indiscreet to admit it. 'Well,' she said, suddenly happy, 'if we're going on meeting like this, oughtn't we to know who we are?'

'I'm Josef Foerster, and I teach English at Charles University. It is the oldest university in central Europe.'

She noted his pride, and acknowledged it with a nod, as she said, 'I'm Carolyn Hailston, and you know what I'm doing here.'

They stood looking at each other.

'I know, too,' he said, 'that you have very bright blue eyes, and a nose with the merest tilt at the end. That might make it difficult knowing when you are being serious.'

He spoke with such assurance that she didn't know whether to laugh or to take him seriously.

'Well, I can't straighten it out,' she said.

Josef laughed and put his arm round her shoulder.

'I think you're a bit of a romantic, too.'

'Oh, why?'

'I don't find you in front of one of our realists like Pinkas. I find you — what is the word? — drooling over a romantic.'

'Chance,' she replied. 'That seems to be playing quite a part in our meetings.'

'Then, shall we put a stop to it? Chance, I mean. Then we shall *know* when we're meeting.'

'I think that's a good idea.'

'I was hoping you would. So, when you have finished here, I will take you where you can eat some good Czech food.'

'That'll make a change. I haven't found any yet.'

'Too many dumplings,' he laughed. 'Every single Czech eats one hundred and fifty-six kilograms of them a year.'

Josef took her hand as they went slowly from room to room in the gallery.

That had been almost a month ago. Since then there had been days of dreamlike happiness. Prague, she decided, was conducive to it. The city had something of a dreamlike quality itself. Maybe it was the way that centuries of fine buildings had somehow survived and been preserved in the narrow streets and the great squares, the twisting alleys and flights of steps. From the top she could look down on the enormous huddle of peg-tiled and pantiled roofs, with trees and gardens that seemed to erupt between buildings and palaces that stepped up the hillsides. Through it all, with the sheen of mother-of-pearl, flowed, in a silky movement, the river Vltava. Literally like a crown, high above the west bank, were the white walls of the castle with its huge courtyards; and out of the centre of that, like the peak of the crown, rose the great tower and spires of St Vitus Cathedral. Oh yes, it was magical, especially with Josef.

It had been a fortnight before he even mentioned the work of Charter 77 to her. They were walking hand in hand across the Charles Bridge at the time.

'There's an old legend,' he said, 'that Wenceslas is not really dead. He's just waiting for when we need him most. Then he will rouse up the old knights from under Blanik Hill, and as he leads them across the bridge, at this very point where we are now, his horse will stumble. That's the sign that he has reached the spot where the knight Bruncvik hid the magic sword. Wenceslas recovers the sword and rides into Prague to destroy the enemies of the people.'

'Sounds a bit like King Arthur,' Carolyn mused.

'Ah, but you don't have need of him. Some of us think that, like your King Charles adying, old Wenceslas is an unconscionable time arising. We certainly have need of him.'

Then, as they wandered on into the rising streets of the Little Quarter, Josef spoke to her about the secret meetings, pamphlets clandestinely printed and circulated. And he recalled the first day of the Soviet occupation — 21st August 1968.

'I was only a kid,' he said, 'but I helped build the barricades near the radio station. That's where we set fire to three Russian tanks. "Brezhnev is Hitler" the students chanted. But after that there was not much violence. We just sat down in front of the tanks, took down road signs, argued with the troops, refused them food. They couldn't understand why we were not pleased to see them. The old democratic spirit is still there now — the demand for human rights. It does not die. Like Wenceslas, it's only sleeping.'

Carolyn felt she had almost been transported back in his own memories, sharing his sadness, his conviction. It was the same with everything, as they walked and talked: his joy in swimming — he had been champion at the university; her art studies. She had never before been so aware of this feeling of identity with another person.

He took her to a small restaurant near the castle where, he promised, she would not have to eat indigestible dumplings. By the time they returned to her hotel it was quite late in the evening.

As he approached the desk, the receptionist looked up from the newspaper he was reading. Half turning in his chair he reached for her key and, without a word, unsmilingly handed it to her. She turned towards the lift. Josef had already pushed the 'ascend' button and the doors were opening as she quickened her step to join him. At the second floor they got out into a spacious landing, furnished with armchairs, settees and potted plants. They stepped off into the empty corridor and, as he had done for the past few nights, he gently took her hand. Giving it a squeeze, he smiled at her with that half-amused half-conspiratorial smile of his. At the fifth door on the right-hand side she stopped, placed the key in the lock and eased the door open.

In what was now a familiar ritual he held on to her hand and raised it to his lips. The game they conspired to play was familiar and safe. He kissed her hand, wished her sweet dreams, and promised to collect her from the hotel the next day.

This time only one of them was abiding by the old rules. He raised her hand to his lips, kissed the backs of her fingers, then very slowly but with determination, turned her hand over and gently kissed the palm. Following along the heel of her thumb with his tongue he expertly located the pulse point in her wrist and with more urgency kissed her again.

Clumsily Carolyn withdrew her hand and backed into her room. There was a nervousness in her voice as she said, 'Goodnight Josef. Thank you for a lovely evening.'

Quickly he had taken a step into the room and was casually leaning against the door jamb. His eyes teased. 'Must it really be "Goodnight Josef"?' His tone was slightly mocking.

'Yes it must.' She backed away from him, trying to put as much of the room between them as fast as possible. Her voice was trembling. Even from the other side of the room he could see she was shaking.

He moved from the door towards her.

'Carolyn, I'm sorry, I didn't mean to . . .' He stopped, as she again backed away from him.

Now the two single beds were between them. Her eyes

darted from the door, which led into the bathroom, to the one through which they had just entered, which led back into the corridor.

Escape signals? he wondered. 'I apologize, please forgive me.' Quickly he turned on his heel and left the room.

The door closed behind him. For a moment she stared at it, then wearily crossed the room and turned the key, pressing herself against the locked door. As the tears started to run down her cheeks she thumped her clenched fists hard on the panelled wood. Furiously she shouted, 'Bugger . . . bugger . . . bugger.'

After two days of not seeing Josef she had begun disappointedly to consider the possibility that they might never meet again. She wished she had had the opportunity to say something to him — but what? She supposed she had been naive, but he had surprised, even shocked her. It was the shock that worried her, always had worried her. The time they had spent together had been filled with laughter and gentle teasing. She had thought they were both playing the game by the same ground rules. Now, somewhat bitterly, she realized it had been different for him. Why the hell hadn't he given her advance warning?

She missed him terribly, and she couldn't remember anyone having made her laugh so much. 'Women,' he had confided, 'more than anything else like to laugh.'

'Oh, do they indeed, and how did you become such an expert on the likes of women?'

'A grandmother, mother and two sisters all living under the same roof. My father died when I was very young. I was the only male in the family. Believe me, when the house is filled with female temperament and hormones, you very soon learn that, if you want to lead anything resembling a tranquil life, you keep them laughing.'

Thus she had laughed, and continued to laugh, until two days ago.

Whenever she went into an art gallery she hoped and half expected that he might suddenly appear behind her, as he had at their second meeting. He never did. Then, just when she had sadly convinced herself that she was unlikely to see him again, he arrived at her hotel with the largest bouquet of gold-coloured roses she had ever seen, and two tickets for a performance of *The Bartered Bride*. Her pleasure in seeing him was utterly transparent.

Smiling sheepishly from behind the flowers he asked, 'Am I forgiven?'

'Completely,' she whispered. 'But where on earth did you get them? They're not in season.'

He smiled. 'There is a saying in Czechoslovakia, "Patience brings roses".'

Within days their old friendship had returned. Josef Foerster was attentive but not familiar; he was charming, kind and amusing. Oh yes, she had missed him. She also became aware that he was the recipient of many an admiring sidelong glance from other women. Sometimes the glance was not so much sidelong as full frontal. She was cross with herself that she hadn't noticed it before. She found herself taking his arm with a show of proprietorial right. If he noticed he certainly didn't let on.

Since his return he had not again gone with her to her room. He merely waited for her to collect her key, wished her goodnight at the lift door, and left.

Carolyn had come to the reluctant conclusion that time was not on her side and that the next move was definitely hers.

Returning with him to the hotel after a boisterous evening of folk song and dance, she collected her key and walked purposively towards the lift where Josef was waiting. Her next act was difficult for her, but she had made up her mind. When he raised his hand, instead of placing her own in his to be kissed, she breathlessly dropped the key into his open palm.

For a second she thought he was going to let it slip to the floor. Then looking her straight in the eyes, he asked, 'Carolyn, are you sure?'

She hesitated. 'No. No, I'm not.'

He held the key before her, inviting her to take it back. 'So, you are not sure,' he said. 'And I'm not in the business of laying young women visitors, however beautiful, particularly beautiful virgins. Understand?'

She nodded, feeling tears pricking at the back of her eyes. She said with difficulty, 'It's not my virginity — alleged virginity. That's not the problem.'

The lift had arrived, the doors opened. Carolyn stepped inside and pushed the button for the second floor. Josef managed to jump into the lift just as the doors were closing. They reached the room without exchanging another word. Once inside she did not turn on the lights but instead pulled back the curtains which draped the tall windows. Enough light flooded in from the street below to illuminate the room.

She motioned for him to sit in one of the modern wooden armchairs. On a small table were two tumblers and a bottle of cognac. She unscrewed the cap and, raising the bottle slightly, she asked, 'Will you? I'm afraid there's nothing to go with it.'

He nodded. 'Please.'

She poured two very generous measures into the glasses, handed him one. She wasn't sure she was going to be able to manage this, but resolutely she sat in the other armchair and took a large gulp of the brandy. 'It would help if you would say something,' she muttered nervously.

His voice was gentle, no longer any hint of amusement in his words or manner. 'What should I say? I got it wrong. I thought it was because . . .' He sighed, pausing for the right words. 'Well, that it was the first time. But if that's not the problem, what is? Me?' He sipped at the brandy, but before he could continue she interrupted.

'It's not you.'

He watched her take a long draught of the cognac. 'Do you want to tell me?'

This was it. She could feel herself trembling inside and wondered if he noticed. She took another mouthful of brandy, grateful for its comforting heat in her throat. Last time it had been disastrous, made everything worse for her. She gripped the bowl of the glass so tightly she thought she would crush it. Dare she? Suddenly, her voice harsh, unrecognizable, she blurted out: 'My father!'

Josef looked mystified. Then he said cautiously, 'I can guess he would not approve. You have never mentioned your father. You are very close to him?'

'No, I'm not. What's more, he wouldn't give a damn.'

Josef shook his head. 'No — I'm sorry, Carolyn, I don't understand.' His voice trailed off.

In the half light she could see his anxious face. He half leaned towards her, willing her to speak. His eyes pleaded with her to let him help.

Then the tears began, hot and scalding they ran down her cheeks. Now she was committed. She had no alternative. Desperately she wanted his understanding, his love.

'Ten, no eleven years ago,' she began between sobs, 'Mummy was away for a few days. I was home from school for the holidays. I hated her being away, travelling without me. I suppose I was at the age when parents suddenly become mortal. Anyway, I was having nightmares.' She paused, wiping her cheeks with the back of her hand. 'One night the nightmare was so vivid I woke up screaming. I ran to their bedroom. Of course, Mummy wasn't there, and my "devoted" father had not heard me cry out. I could smell whisky on his breath as I shook his arm to wake him.' Her voice faded beneath her tears, and her whole body was shaking. She still could not bring herself to describe how he had taken her into his bed.

Swiftly, Josef moved from his chair and knelt before her. He tried to put his arms round her to comfort her, but she pushed him away, roughly.

19

'Afterwards, I felt dirty, unworthy. I remember I washed again and again. I tried to scrub myself clean. My skin was raw with the scrubbing. The feeling of betrayal was so awful I just wanted to die.' Her sobs had subsided into a pitiful moan.

Josef leaned back on his heels. He stared incredulously at the young woman before him. Anger flooded through him. The bastard — The Honourable Stanley Hemingford Hailston MP — the perverted bastard, had violated his own daughter.

It was past midnight before she fell asleep. Josef had wrapped her, fully clothed, in one of the apricot and cream coloured bed covers, and had sat holding her hand as she lay quietly crying herself to sleep.

He awoke first the next morning, and hardly dared to move lest he disturbed her. He needed a few minutes to himself, to get himself together. How was he going to handle the situation in the cold light of day? More to the point, was he going to be able to cope? In the silence he watched her sleep, the reddish gold of her hair like a halo on the pillow. Poor, lovely Carolyn — she deserved to be loved. It would be so easy to fall quite hopelessly in love with her . . .

When she awoke he was speaking on the telephone, ordering breakfast for the two of them. They ate silently, exchanging half-smiles of gratitude and understanding. He looked out of the window and said he thought it was going to be another nice day. Then he left her to get a change of clothes, promising that he would be back within the hour to take her out.

He returned promptly, and they spent the day in a frantic round of visiting galleries and museums. It was collusion, and they both recognized it as such. The activity obviated the need for anything other than a kind of professional conversation.

Eventually Carolyn said, 'You know, you're the first to believe me.'

They were sitting in a coffee bar near the towers and spires of the Týn Church, and could glimpse the Old Town Hall between the pillars. Pigeons were puffing their chests on the uneven setts.

'You've told others?'

'One other. For a long time I thought that it had never happened to anyone else, that there must be something wrong with me, that I must be a freak. I even thought I would go mad. There was someone on the staff at school who was very popular with all the pupils. I just knew she would understand and be able to help me.' Carolyn paused, even now inwardly shuddering at the recollection. 'What she actually said was: "You're an evil, lying, attention-seeking child, and if I hear any more of this I shall report you to the head". I was devastated. That bitch will never know what it had cost me to summon up the courage to confide in someone. I never did again — until last night.'

For some time they were both silent. Josef was the first to speak. 'I'm glad you did. I was afraid I had ruined our friendship. And that's very important to me.' He sought refuge in a light-hearted tone. 'I think, young woman,' he said, 'I might be a little in love with you.'

'I'm also glad.' There was an unfamiliar firmness in her voice. Then mimicking his own tone, she added, 'Because I think, young man, I am quite a lot in love with you.'

The hotel receptionist sniffed loudly as he handed over her key that evening. Carolyn and Josef giggled with relief as they made their way to her room.

Once inside she switched on the small table lights. A soft apricot glow embraced the room. Carolyn turned towards him, and very slowly and deliberately, Josef bent and kissed her. After a few moments, just as slowly and cautiously, he began to undress her. She moved away to turn off the lights.

'No — leave them,' he insisted.

He kissed her again and again as he undressed her, and when he took her to one of the beds, she was quite calm — calm, that is, except for her desire to hold him closer to her. He loved her slowly and with painful gentleness — as if she were an unexploded device which might suddenly destroy them both. When finally she did let go her eyes were wide open, and she whispered over and over , 'Josef . . . oh Josef.'

Carolyn had less than a fortnight of her stay left when Josef said he would take her to a meeting of a small group of Chartists. There was something she could take back to London for them. He sounded so confident, so authoritative, almost as though she had no choice in the matter. Perhaps she had not. She felt so grateful to him that . . . no, it wasn't only gratitude. It was much more than that. She was in love with him, of course. She accepted that. But she felt somehow a different Carolyn Hailston from the girl who had arrived in Prague a month previously. He had released her, untangled a web of years and enabled her to escape their subtle imprisonment.

He showed her the house where they would meet. It was in a narrow street not far from the Old Town Square. People still lived in houses in the centre of Prague, houses that rose sheer from the pavement with their signs carved above doors and windows.

Just an hour before the meeting was due he told her there had been a change of plan. He took her instead, in his little Skoda car, scurrying out to a modern housing development in the suburbs. He parked his car a couple of streets away, and they walked back to an undistinguished block of flats.

They went to an apartment on the third floor and joined five other men and two women seated on a variety of chairs in one large living room. There was a central table with coffee pot and cups, a couple of bottles of wine and glasses. They all jumped up, smiling their greeting as she and Josef entered. He introduced her with a long explanation in Czech but, judging by the warmth of their individual greetings, she had the impression that she was expected. Only two of them attempted to speak to her in English, but Carolyn saw Josef smiling at her reassuringly,

22

and she felt surprisingly at home in spite of the unfamiliarity of her surroundings.

One of the other English speakers, a wiry, alert little man with leathery features, asked her about England, and where she lived and what she did. Then, almost unnoticed, they slipped into speaking Czech. Carolyn found she was still listening, although she had no idea what they were talking about.

The wiry, leathery man appeared to be the leader, and Josef took no greater part in the discussions than any of the others. The coffee had been passed round soon after they entered the room, and now one of the women poured out glasses of wine. The whole occasion took on a fresh earnestness, even an urgency. There was an occasional gesture in her direction, and a smile from Josef as he replied. She began to feel part of the group, sipped at her wine and waited expectantly to learn what was wanted of her. She no longer worried about the danger. Indeed, looking at Josef leaning forward, talking with a sense of purpose which pervaded the whole company, even the idea of danger seemed invalid. Adventure — yes, but successful adventure. She felt invigorated, excited, and she looked at Josef with undisguised longing.

She could tell by the atmosphere, the good humour as they took a second glass of wine, that the meeting was fruitful. The wiry little man had a brisk efficient manner and bright eyes, and he was evidently moving the meeting along swiftly from subject to subject. Sheets of printed paper were produced, and pamplets, fingers pointed, pens scribbled, they discussed, they altered, they sat back with satisfaction. Carolyn smiled. The leader smiled back, and lifted his glass of wine. They all looked at her and drank, then plunged into further discussion with the enthusiasm and purpose of swimmers diving into a pool.

Perhaps it was because of this purposefulness, and sheer concentration, that none of them heard anything. Carolyn didn't, until the door burst open. Four men stood there in plain clothes, guns in their hands. There was immediate confusion.

Papers were scrabbled, scattered, people jumped to their feet, hurled themselves towards the door. She couldn't see if any of them reached it, or if they were all simply hauled back into the room. Josef, however, did not move. He simply reached out and took her hand. He whispered to her, 'The STB.'

One of the four who had entered was waggling the pistol in his hand and shouting.

'What's going to happen?' Carolyn whispered nervously.

'Don't worry,' he said, as he pressed her hand, and then he turned and spoke rapidly in Czech to the leader of the four security police.

After that, Carolyn was not sure what happened — whether all of them were arrested, or only a selected few. For a moment, several people seemed to be talking at once. Then there was quiet as the police officer snapped his instructions. Two of the Chartists were led away. Josef was pulled from her grasp, and she felt a firm but not rough grip on her shoulder. She was hustled out and into the corridor.

Outside there were several members of the SNB in their plum-blue uniforms. One of them propelled her down the stairs. In the street was a collection of beige-coloured cars with yellow stripes outlined in red and bearing the words VERAJNA BEZPECNOST. She looked round for Josef, but couldn't see him anywhere. She called his name. There was no reply. A plain-clothes officer took her elbow and levered her into a car. It sped back towards the city, other cars following behind.

The man sitting beside her appeared stern, humourless. He looked straight ahead at the neck of the driver.

'I'm English,' she said. 'English.'

He glanced at her, unsmiling, but said nothing.

'Do you speak English?' she asked.

He made no reply.

She began to notice familiar buildings, and at last the car turned into a very narrow street, which she remembered Josef had translated for her as Bartholomew Street, and she knew that the buildings on one whole side of it were occupied by the State Security Police. The car screeched to a standstill. A van and other cars drew up behind. It suddenly occurred to her that probably the others had been huddled into the van; she had been accorded the luxury of a car. She looked back, hoping to see Josef. But no attempt was made to open the van doors until she had been taken into the building.

She was led down a corridor that she guessed ran parallel with the street, and then into a small room, sparsely furnished with a table and three or four chairs. They were joined by a young uniformed officer who, at least, looked a little less severe.

The plain-clothes man indicated one of the chairs near the table. Carolyn sat down. He snapped some words at her in Czech.

'It's no good,' she said. 'I'm English — English.'

The man looked at her, took a pocket-book and papers from his jacket, pointed at her and then at the papers.

Carolyn knew very well what he meant, but she merely shrugged and spread her hands in incomprehension. He snatched the strap of her bag from off her shoulder, threw the bag on the table and opened it. He extracted her passport and the duplicate half of her visa, which she had been told she would have to return to the immigration officer at the airport when she left the country.

The STB man grunted, turned crisply on his heel and left. The door of the room slammed shut.

2

The headquarters of the Czech State Security Police (Statni Tajna Bezpecnost) in the narrow street standing back from the river Vltava, was formerly one of the old city's monasteries. Josef had told Carolyn about it on one of their dreamy explorations of Prague. So monks had also known this silence in such a room. It was little consolation. Once or twice she had tried to break it by speaking to the young uniformed policeman. He had merely smiled, nodded, and stared back at her. She noticed, from time to time, an undisguised look of pure lust. Once she got up from the table and walked across the room to stretch her legs. He was instantly alongside her. His hand stroked round the curve of her bottom to redirect her, and then he gripped her upper arm, so that the back of his hand was pressing against her breast, and led her firmly towards the table. When she was again seated, he immediately went and stood, very properly, against the opposite wall, and merely watched her.

She sat feeling very alone, wondering what was going to happen to her. She began by reminding herself that she was a visitor, and had thought she was simply going to meet friends. She had no desire to break their laws and had not done so. She would ask them to inform the British Embassy immediately, and that would be that. She had no doubt that they would appreciate their mistake, and would not wish to interrupt her studies.

After half an hour this explanation was less satisfactory. Suppose they couldn't understand her? None of them seemed to speak any English. Moreover they had taken her passport. Perhaps they were getting in touch with the British Embassy, making inquiries about her. That would account for the delay. When the STB man returned he would give her back her passport and release her.

Nervously she opened her handbag. The policeman was watching her closely. She extracted the small mirror, looked at herself — the reddish-blonde hair, the bright blue eyes, the little tilt to her nose adding humour to her features — and tried to assure herself that she was not looking too attractive. But, as a morale booster, it was not altogether successful. She was troubled by her guard's insinuating glances.

After fifty minutes had passed she was not sure that her earlier conclusions were convincing. How could she be certain that they were getting in touch with the British Embassy? Perhaps they had no intention of doing so. And how would she be able to convince them that she had meant no harm; that Josef was her friend, and she had no idea that she was doing anything illegal? How could she? She didn't understand the language. They might not accept ignorance as a defence. She began to remember stories in the papers of people being held in East European countries for weeks, even months; she was sure she had read of people who had simply disappeared. But that wouldn't be possible for her — would it? She was the daughter of a government minister, and she was in Czechoslovakia to study their art, and especially their techniques of restoration. Dr Vladislav, at the National Museum, would be able to confirm this. But supposing they were not interested in confirmation? Supposing they . . . ? No, that was unreasonable. They wouldn't behave like that.

She began to fiddle with the clasp of her bag. She was conscious of the young officer watching her. She felt a nervous smile coming. He took no notice. She started to say, 'How long will I be here?' but only got as far as 'How long will — ?' when she broke off, knowing that she was wasting her time. The man ignored her words. He merely stared at her.

Carolyn became aware of the grain of the table-top. It ran in lines that disappeared over the edge. Her eyes began to follow it. Then she put her bag decisively on one side, planted her feet firmly together and sat upright.

The silence continued. Yes, she told herself, I'm simply trying to give myself confidence, convince myself that I have nothing to worry about.

She looked at her watch. It was an hour and ten minutes since she had been brought into the room. What could they be doing? Why were they not questioning her? Ah, perhaps they were trying to find an English speaker. That would explain the delay. Ridiculous to think that they didn't have anyone in an organization like this who could speak English. That was no good. There was a reason for this. They didn't care about her.

Maybe they were questioning Josef. They were going to force information out of him first . . . out of all of his friends too perhaps. Then they would come to her, and . . . She thought of Josef. Would they ill-treat him? She couldn't bear that. It was unthinkable. She would do anything rather than let them hurt him. She put her hands flat on the table, as though trying to steady herself. She had read about torture. Would they torture Josef? Or her? What would happen? What would they do?

Carolyn looked up desperately at the young man opposite. He stared back at her, but did not smile. He was SNB, the uniformed branch. Perhaps that was a good sign. Perhaps the STB were going to leave the questioning to their colleagues. Perhaps there were not as many of those who spoke English, and that was the reason for the delay.

No, no — that wouldn't do. She knew it would be the STB who would deal with her. But when? How? Even the thought, 'deal with her' — what did it mean? What would they do? What were they doing, this minute, to Josef?

Carolyn shuddered. She knew the man opposite had noticed. She sighed. Oh God, what was going to happen? Josef . . . herself. Surely they would come soon? They must come soon. There were rules about these things . . . international conventions. No, that was absurd. They wouldn't care about such things. They wouldn't care. About Josef, about herself. This wasn't a British police station. It was no good demanding to see her solicitor. She was behind the iron curtain. My God, anything could happen. Charter 77 would not exist were it not for the injustice, the oppression, the lack of respect for human rights. That's what it was all about. And now she was trapped.

She sighed again, looked at her watch. She had been there an hour and a half. The man opposite still stared at her, expressionless. She wondered what he was thinking. Probably that she would make a good lay, and he was looking forward to it. Did they do that kind of thing too? She began to feel panic. Her breathing became more rapid. He was watching, watching her breasts rise and fall, quickly, more quickly. She felt like screaming. Her hands gripped the sides of the table until her knuckles showed white. She tried to still the panic, slow her breathing. Her knuckles were white as moons. Her nails dug into the wood of the table. She gritted her teeth together, held her jaw tense. Now she was holding her breath. She felt her lungs would burst, burst in a scream of sheer terror and panic. He was watching her, just staring, not a flicker of understanding or sympathy. Very deliberately she steadied herself, relaxed her grip, let her hands fall away from the table. Her body slumped.

It was hard to think at all, let alone clearly. Her mind was now a confusion of thoughts and images, superimposing one upon another. Josef, the cars screeching to a stop outside the building, being led to this room, the man opposite, torture, imprisonment, questions, not understanding, nobody understanding. She jumped to her feet. The young officer moved, took her arms firmly, forced her back into her chair behind the table.

She must try to be calm. Try . . . try . . . try . . .

The door opened. She looked round. There were two men in plain clothes, STB men. She saw one of them nod to the uniformed officer. He went out. The men drew two wooden chairs noisily across the room and sat down opposite.

They were both big men, broad shouldered, square, grey features. They could have been brothers. One of them sat back, relaxed, almost bored. The other leant forward across the table, looked at her fiercely. He spoke to her in a loud voice, a stream of incomprehensible and angry Czech.

Carolyn was struggling to calm herself. She was nervous, feeling the edges of fear and panic that had grown into her during the hour and a half of waiting. She mustn't show this, must be calm, puzzled and reasonable. She did her best to smile.

'I'm very sorry,' she said, gesturing with her hands at the same time, 'but I do not understand your language.'

The interrogator snorted, clamped his lips into a straight line and stared at her. Then he began again. It sounded like sheer vituperation.

'It's no good,' said Carolyn. 'I'm happy to answer your questions, if someone can speak English.'

The man opposite banged the table, and made a gesture of angry impatience. He tried again — a short burst of Czech.

For the first time the other man spoke. He was still leaning back at the end of the table. He turned to Carolyn with a similar angry stare.

'Your name? Your address?'

It sounded as though he had broken the words off a longer sentence. She breathed a sigh of relief, tried to smile again, and gave her name and the address of the flat off the Bayswater Road in London, which she shared with another girl, Toni, a secretary at the House of Commons. The second man wrote it down carefully, showed it to her. She nodded.

Then began the stilted interrogation. The first man in Czech; the second man in bitten-off English. His accent was as harsh as his manner. He looked at Carolyn, and then at his large hands in front of him on the table, then at Carolyn again. Immediately she was convinced that he would think nothing of clasping them round her throat and strangling her. She was now giving her whole attention to him, and not to the first man.

'What are you doing here?'

Carolyn answered slowly and clearly. 'I am studying Czech art, and restoration. I have been working with Doctor Vladislav at the National Museum. I am sure he will tell you.'

'You are a spy.'

'No.'

An enormous fist cracked down on the table. 'You are a spy.'

'No. I am studying art. My father is a minister in the British government.'

Both men snorted with an indignation close to fury. There was no mistaking the anger in their eyes.

When the first one shouted again, she did not even have to wait for the equally fierce translation. She recognized the same phrase.

'I am not a spy,' she repeated, trying to sound quiet and reasonable. 'I have been working at the National Museum, and visiting your art collections in Prague. I am most grateful to your government for allowing me to do this.'

There was another grunt of contempt from the interrogator.

'You were at a Charter meeting. That's against the interests of the State.'

'I am very sorry. I went with a friend. I did not understand.'

'Liar.'

Carolyn tried to look puzzled. 'I thought they were just his friends. I did not know what they were doing. They all spoke in Czech. I had no knowledge — '

'That's a lie. What you have done is illegal. It is against the

31

State. The punishment here for that kind of thing is severe. It is in your country — isn't it? — for traitors.'

'Look,' she said hopelessly, 'I have done nothing to harm Czechoslovakia. I don't want to. I have no need to. I am here studying your art.'

'You are here to spy. You knew that meeting was illegal.'

'I did not.'

'Then why was the meeting place changed?'

'I . . . I don't know.'

'So you knew it was secret?'

'Truly, I did not.'

'Lying will not help you. You make it worse for yourself.'

Carolyn felt the panic returning. God, what was going to happen to her? She gripped her hands tightly in her lap, and looked back at her interrogators, innocently.

'Could I please see someone from the British Embassy?'

'No.'

'You have told the British Embassy that I am here?'

'No. Why should we? Has nothing to do with them. Our government gives you permission to study here. What do you do? You conspire with enemies of the State . . . '

'No, I promise you, I — '

'Don't contradict. Chartists act illegally . . . against the State. You take part with them. You are an enemy of the State . . . a spy.'

Carolyn tried to explain, but was shouted down, as both men leant across the table and glared at her. They now spoke almost simultaneously. Behind the shouted English translation she could hear the jagged sound of Czech.

'You will have to be punished. Men, women — makes no difference. It is . . . ' There was a long pause as the two men stared at her. Then the English speaker said, 'Painful. It is painful.'

Now she was frightened and, at the same time, almost

'But, if you really believe that, am I not going to be charged — tried?'

'Yes . . . in time.'

'And the British Embassy will explain to you . . . represent me.'

They both snorted. 'Why should we believe them? They won't admit you're a spy.'

'But I can be represented — a lawyer?'

'In time. These things take time. Often a long time. We shall have to hold you — a prisoner.'

'But — '

'Yes, we can,' he snapped. 'You have offended against our laws. We can hold you as long as we like. Who can stop us? The British Embassy?' he added contemptuously. 'We cannot allow you to act against the interests of the State, Miss Hailston.'

Carolyn felt exhausted. She didn't know what to say. Nothing she said was going to make the slightest difference.

The two men got up from the table.

'There is paper. Write your confession. It will help at your trial . . . eventually. If you don't write it down now, we shall have to force it out of you.' He paused. 'You won't like that, Miss Hailston. The human body can only stand so much pain. Meanwhile, you will be held in the cells, as long as we want to keep you.'

The two men strode out of the room. The uniformed officer returned and stood against the opposite wall. He looked at her with the merest smile.

It was the first time she had seen any hint of humanity since her very first attempt to speak to him. Now she felt too exhausted to respond. She sat staring at the pad of paper in front of her. She was dazed, confused. None of this could be true. It wasn't reasonable. It didn't make sense . . . Oh yes it did. It made horrible sense, frightening. They were going to hold her prisoner. They would torture her, force a meaningless confession under pain. Afterwards there would be an equally meaningless trial. She would be found guilty. Back to prison again. The British Embassy would protest. The Foreign Office would protest, perhaps even the Foreign Secretary himself. None of it would make any difference. There was nothing anyone could do. These people would behave just as they wanted to. There was nothing to stop them.

She fingered the ballpoint pen beside the white pad of paper. What was she meant to write? Confession. Confession to what? 'I went to a meeting with my friend. I did not know it was a meeting of dissidents.' Is that what she was going to write? She just sat staring. She was no longer conscious of the man opposite. She was alone . . . empty.

Somewhere she heard a door slam. She looked up, saw the uniformed man moving away. Again the door shut. This time it seemed to shudder her back into focus. Another man, in an ordinary lounge suit, was sitting on the chair opposite. Only he did not lean across the table; he leant back, relaxed. He was smiling, a full friendly smile. He was not big, strong-looking like the others. He was even a little plump — homely looking with a rosy, clean-scrubbed face.

The man fumbled in his jacket, then held a packet towards her.

'Cigarette?' he asked.

For a moment she couldn't reply. She looked at him, bewildered.

'Cigarette?' he repeated.

'No. Thank you. I . . . I don't smoke.'

'Ah, that is sensible, eh?'

A nervous smile flickered at her lips and disappeared.

'I am not so good,' the man continued. 'But I won't smoke now, eh?'

Carolyn breathed deeply, straightened up and looked at him directly in the eyes. 'What is going to happen to me?' she asked.

The man shrugged. 'I apologize for my colleagues,' he said. 'They get a bit rough. They are not used to dealing with young women.' He uttered the gentlest of laughs, as though to excuse them and establish his own friendly credentials. 'Now,' he began, as though he were wiping the previous slate clean, 'you are Carolyn Hailston. You are studying the restoring of paintings. Your father is a Member of Parliament, a minister in the Defence Ministry of the British government. Eh?'

'Yes, that's right. But that doesn't make me a spy,' she said.

He laughed. 'No, of course not. But you have done wrong, Miss Hailston. Dissidents are enemies of the Socialist Republic of Czechoslovakia.'

'I meant no harm.'

'Perhaps not. We have to be sure, you understand.'

'Your — ' she paused, wondering what word to use, and then settled for colleagues. 'Your colleagues said they would not be telling the British Embassy that I am here.'

He shrugged again, and then nodded thoughtfully. 'That could be so,' he said. 'You see, there is nothing they can do. We *can* hold you as long as we want to. You can be charged and tried, and I would think — yes, found guilty. You were arrested at the scene. You convict yourself, h'mm?'

She thought it had all sounded too good to be true. She couldn't disguise the alarm in her eyes as she looked up at him.

'But,' the man continued, speaking very slowly, finding his words, 'but . . . I . . . I would not want that . . . to happen, Miss Hailston.' He paused again, putting his hands together judicially, as though considering. 'You are not one of them . . . not like Josef Foerster. Now he is . . . '

But Carolyn didn't hear any more. She felt suddenly guilty that her own anxieties had momentarily driven thoughts of Josef from her mind. God, what would happen to him? Would she ever see him again? Was the happiness, their happiness, all over?

The man finished speaking. Her eyes pleaded with him. He looked back as though he recognized her pain, her fear.

'Josef — where is he? What will happen to him?'

'He is here. He will be tried. There is, I am afraid, no doubt about his guilt. He will be punished. It will be . . . not nice.'

'I am sure he does not mean harm,' she said, 'no more than I did.'

'Ah — you . . . you love him, eh?'

Carolyn didn't know what to say. The tears were pricking behind her eyes. She was thoroughly confused. The man looked kind, understanding.

'I couldn't see him, I suppose?' she asked, her voice faltering.

'Ah.' He paused. 'Yes, yes, of course you may.'

'Oh . . . oh, thank you,' Carolyn smiled.

He led her to the door. In the corridor was the young uniformed officer and another of his colleagues. The man spoke to them in Czech, and they walked her to the end of the corridor where they took a lift to the basement.

When the lift doors slid open again, they emerged into a stone passage. It was cold, flagstones on the floor, and was lit only by small bulbs in the ceiling. On each side were cells with heavy steel doors. They stopped by one of them about fifteen yards along. The two men appeared to confer, and the one who had guarded her nodded at the blank steel door. He slid back a small panel at head height. He held her upper arm, again pressing the back of his hand against her breast. His companion grinned. He moved her to the door. Carolyn peered through.

Josef was in the far left corner. He crouched there like a wounded animal. He gave no indication that he had heard the observation panel slide back. He was staring at the floor. His face looked blotched, his clothes dishevelled.

The cry trapped in her throat. 'Oh God, they've beaten him up.' She called his name. He didn't even look up. Perhaps he had not heard her. She called again. He remained staring at the floor, almost cowering. She turned away, dabbed at her tears with the back of her hand. No one said anything. They led her to the lift and back to the interrogation room.

The same man was there. He rose to greet her, smiling, and then instantly looked sympathetically sad. As she resumed her seat behind the table, he handed her his handkerchief. She wiped away the tears. Then she put her elbows on the table, her head in her hands. The man waited patiently, saying nothing.

At last she looked up. 'He's been ill-treated,' she said.

The man spread his hands, despairingly. 'I do my best. I can't control them all. Some are . . . you know.'

Again she felt the utter exhaustion of hopelessness. There was nothing . . . nothing she could do, nothing to be done. She looked up at him imploringly.

'He is not one of your enemies of the State,' she said simply. 'He is so proud of his country.'

The man shrugged. 'We shall see,' he said. 'First, we have to consider what to do with you, Miss Hailston.' His tone was firm but not unkind.

'I haven't done anything. I went to see some of Josef's friends . . . '

'Yes, I know. It was . . . unfortunate you were there, eh? These things happen.'

'How long will you keep me?' She thought with horror of Josef in the cell below them. 'What will you charge me with?'

'It may not be so bad. Perhaps I can — ' He broke off, looked thoughtful, and then added, 'Well, I will do what I can. Perhaps if you were to sign a document, saying that you understand what you did, it was an illegal act, against the interests of the State, and you apologize to the people of Czechoslovakia . . . perhaps then I could persuade the authorities to release you. You could not remain for the rest of your stay. You would have to leave for England at once.'

'Oh, could you?'

The rosy, scrubbed face broke into a smile. 'I'll see if I can persuade them. There might be conditions. I'll do what I can.'

The man got up, summoned the uniformed officer back into the room, spoke to him briefly in Czech, and left. The young man took up his accustomed position, and then smiled at her as though he were welcoming an old friend. Carolyn shook back her hair, and almost laughed with relief, but decided it was prudent not to be too friendly. She feared that might be another offence. When, however, she got up from the table to walk about the room, he made no attempt to restrain her, but instead rewarded her with a nod and a smile.

She had only just resumed her seat, when the door opened and another uniformed young man brought her a cup of coffee and some biscuits. She thanked him. The two men looked at her, exchanged glances, and it was obvious to her what they were thinking. The newcomer patted her hair and left.

Carolyn sipped at the coffee. It was good. Then she nibbled on a biscuit and, with a sudden ache of despair, thought again of Josef crouched in the corner of his cell. If only there were something she could do for him. Her relief at the prospect of her own escape had momentarily dulled the pain of knowing how he had suffered and the anxiety of not knowing what they would do with him. She felt guilty as she drained the last of the coffee. Only yesterday they had been so happy, and she had begun to hope that Josef might be allowed to come to London. Anything had seemed possible, as they stood hand-in-hand among the crowd of sunlit tourists watching the astronomical clock on the Old Town Hall. Everything had been believable. She had never known such happiness. Yet now . . . she still could not believe that she might never see him again. How long would they keep him there? What would they do? She began to hope that the second, more kindly interrogator might be able to help. She clung to this doubtful hope.

It was an hour and a half before he returned. By then the anxieties had begun to recur. Perhaps they had no intention of releasing her after all. And Josef would disappear. No one would hear of him again. Such things had happened. And if they were not going to release her, what would they do? The next evening she was expected at a reception at the British

Embassy. Maybe, when she failed to turn up, they would start to make inquiries. And where would that get them? Or her? She was startled out of her musing by the sound of the door opening. And there was the slightly plump, fatherly interrogator, clutching a sheaf of papers and smiling at her.

He came and took his seat opposite her at the table. 'I have it here. Your confession.' He looked pleased with himself and, at the same time, reassuring.

Carolyn shuffled the pages he handed to her. They were not numbered, and no sentence was carried over from one page to another. It took her ten minutes to read them. They were written in tolerable English, and began with her name, age and address, and the purpose of her visit to Prague. There was a lot of stuff about being mindful of her responsibilities as a privileged visitor to the Czechoslovak Socialist Republic, and her duty to respect their conventions and their laws. It went on to admit that she had deliberately made contact with Josef Foerster and had conspired with him to abuse the laws of the State by attending a meeting of a proscribed organization. The statement then went into considerable detail about the work of disaffected and dissident groups, and how it was not consistent with the socialist aims of the republic, and declared that she was aware of all this and, in spite of it, deliberately chose to break the laws of the State and conspire with the enemies of Czechoslovakia. There followed a most involved apology for her abuse of the hospitality of her Czech hosts and for knowingly breaking their laws in a way that cast suspicion upon the real purpose of her visit to Prague. That was the nearest the statement got to suggesting that she had been employed as a spy. With fulsome apologies and regrets she undertook to leave the country immediately, never to return. She also agreed that her confession should be published.

Carolyn laid the papers on the table and looked up into the round smiling face of her interrogator. 'It's not all true,' she said.

'Truth is a troublesome thing. You want to go. I give you the means. You can refuse, but . . . Then, I could not help you.' He gestured as if in disappointment and dismay.

'I'm worried about Josef. This makes it worse for him,' she said ingenuously.

'I'm sorry. It is that, or nothing.'

'I don't mind about the rest,' she said. 'It's not all true, but perhaps that doesn't matter. But about Josef, I don't want to — '

'I understand. You think this . . . ' He paused, trying to find the right English word. 'Incriminates him,' he said, triumphantly.

'Yes.'

He shrugged. 'You have your laws,' he said. 'If your people break them, they are punished, eh? Josef Foerster has broken our laws. He will be punished. You must see that is just.'

'But — he's been beaten.'

He threw up his hands in disapproval. 'It should not have happened. I shall deal with it personally.'

'But he will still be — what?'

'Imprisoned, I expect.'

Carolyn clasped her forehead. She didn't want him to see tears again, and she strove to calm herself.

'If I didn't sign this,' she asked, 'would it help him?'

'No.' He leant forward to emphasize what he was going to say. 'And it would be worse for you.' He spread his hands on the table. His forehead wrinkled in a frown. 'I have done all I can for you. I have tried to help.'

Carolyn sighed. She was ready to believe anything. 'I know.'

'I can't tell you what will happen to you — you understand? They can do what they like.' He seemed to be dissociating himself from his colleagues. 'Imprison you . . . anything.'

Carolyn hesitated. She felt the trap had closed upon her. She had got to sign the thing. She knew that. She clutched her head between her hands, thinking of Josef in that cold miserable cell beneath them.

The silence lengthened. It was interrupted by a gentle drumming of the interrogator's fingers on the table. 'Of course,' he said, speaking so slowly that it emphasized the tension of the silence. 'Of course . . . yes.' He paused. 'There is a way you might be able to help him.'

Carolyn looked up hopefully. 'Oh, please!'

He studied her, almost benevolently. 'If,' he said, 'when you return to London, if you could be of some help to us, it might mean that we can treat your friend better, eh?'

'Help — how do you mean?'

'Your friend is in big trouble. You understand?'

Carolyn nodded. All she really understood was the horror of that cold cell.

'But,' the man continued, 'we can be — ' Again, he searched for the word. 'Lenient,' he said. He gestured with his hands. 'He can be treated quite well, eh? That is, if you would agree to help us. Otherwise . . .' He threw his arms wide, and his voice tailed off despondently.

'You want me to spy for you?'

He shrugged. 'Help us, perhaps, with a little harmless information, eh?'

Carolyn fiddled with the papers thoughtfully. It was obvious that, if she did not sign them, they would not release her. But surely it was extraordinary that they should trust her to provide them with some kind of information in London without any sort of guarantee whatsoever? And if she did, could she trust them? Would they fulfil their side of the bargain? She really didn't have an alternative but to trust them. If she thought better of it in London, and refused to co-operate — well, at least there was nothing they could do to her. But Josef — ?

'It might,' said the Czech, 'even be possible for you to come back to Prague to see him. Who knows?' He jerked his head towards the door. 'They are not the only ones, eh? I have been able to help you. I might be able to . . . well, you understand, eh?'

Carolyn drew the final sheet of her 'confession' towards her and signed her name at the bottom of the page.

The man opposite smiled. 'That's right,' he said. 'Now you will be free to go. And in London — well, it is up to you. If you help us, I have told you I will do all I can for your friend. If not — ' He shrugged.

Carolyn got up, and half turned towards the door.

The Czech put out a restraining hand. 'No, no — not so quickly. We have to take you to the border. It is too late today. You will stay here tonight. We drive you to the border tomorrow.' Then seeing the look of despair and alarm in her face, he added, 'No — not in a cell. We have a room for you. It is quite comfortable.'

He gathered the papers together. 'Come with me, eh?'

'But, my things . . . '

'They will be collected from your hotel, and brought to you here. Your passport will be returned. Come.'

He led her away to a different part of the building, and into a room which was indeed much more comfortable. It was carpeted, had a divan bed, a wash basin, and easy chairs.

As the Czech prepared to leave her, he said, 'Food will be brought to you here. Then, tomorrow morning, you will be driven to the West German border.'

'Not to the British Embassy?'

The man laughed and shook his head. Then he stretched out his hand. 'I may not see you again,' he said. 'Good luck, Miss Hailston.'

Carolyn dazedly shook his slightly podgy hand, and then watched with a mixture of relief and disbelief as he closed the door behind him.

At eight-thirty the next morning, two men in the plum-blue uniform of the SNB called to collect her. They were tall, tough-looking police officers. One of them carried her two suitcases, which he passed to her. The other handed back her passport and the remains of her visa. They spoke to her only in Czech, but their instructions were obvious. She followed them, carrying her suitcases herself.

Outside, the day was overcast, but Carolyn breathed the air deeply and gratefully. By the kerb was parked a Volga. One of the men threw open the boot lid and nodded. Carolyn loaded in her cases. He gripped her firmly by the elbow and urged her into the back of the car. He followed beside her. The other officer slipped quickly into the driving seat, and with a loud click shut the central-locking system.

She gave a little shrug and turned to her guard with a smile. He did not appear to notice. His face was drawn taut from high cheek bones, his jaw set firm.

Once they had left the centre of Prague behind, Carolyn noticed they took the road signposted Plzen. Between Prague and Plzen the countryside was flat, but once they had left the industrial town behind, the landscape was more undulating, and the nearer they got to the border the hillier it became, the slopes more thickly wooded. After about three hours they came to the border near the West German village of Schirnding, and she looked out to see mountains on the horizon.

Neither of the policemen spoke a word during the journey. The car eventually pulled to a stop near a complex of grey, functional buildings surrounded by barbed wire and overlooked by watch-towers. Border guards were standing close by with sub-machine guns slung in their hands. Barbed-wire fences stretched into the distance. Ahead of her the road was no-man's land, and at the end of it was another group of squat buildings patrolled by the West German border guards.

Her cases were taken from the boot of the car, handed to her, and she was hurried into a customs building, where a uniformed officer demanded in Czech that she open her cases. He went through them diligently, and then emptied the contents of her shoulder bag. Eventually he appeared satisfied, and she was passed on for her passport to be inspected and the duplicate visa retained. Judging by the vigorous head-nodding of the khaki-clad official, her accompanying policeman provided a satisfactory explanation. The passport photograph was studied carefully; so was her face. The officer half smiled and nodded approvingly. Her passport was returned to her, she was taken outside by her two guards and led to the gate that closed on the stretch of no-man's land. It was swung open, the policeman said something to her in Czech, and indicated with his hand that she was free to go.

Carolyn looked nervously at the guards standing nearby with their sub-machine guns resting across their bodies. Ahead of her she could see other uniformed border guards. Clutching her cases, she stepped out into no-man's land. In the distance one of the West German guards focused his binoculars on her as she walked steadily towards him.

3

David Rackham had an office on one of the higher floors of Century House, the twenty-storey building of steel, concrete and glass that housed Britain's Secret Intelligence Service (MI6). From it he could see down the Thames to the towers of Westminster.

He was no more than average height, but his wiry, sinewy frame was the clue to an earlier prowess on the athletic track when he was at Cambridge. His freckly face and sandy-coloured hair gave him an almost boyish expression, and his light-hearted manner tended to persuade the unwary that he still had not grown up. This was certainly the view of his father, whom the Conservative Party had rewarded with a life peerage. He had invariably found his son's manner irritating, and they now saw very little of each other. Rackham readily admitted that he was not prepared to take life too seriously, and that in itself disguised the seriousness and efficiency with which he tackled his job.

At the moment he was considering a report he had received from GCHQ at Cheltenham, telling him about the arrest, detention and deportation from Prague of a twenty-four-year-old English girl, Carolyn Hailston, the only daughter of Mr Stanley Hemingford Hailston MP, a minister in the Ministry of Defence, and of Mrs Esme Hailston, with addresses in Chester Square and Sussex. The British Embassy in Prague had not been informed and consequently had not had access to the girl. He noted with interest that she was arrested with one Josef Foerster at a meeting of a Charter 77 group. At present she was at the British Embassy in Bonn and would be returning to London tomorrow morning. All of which meant, he supposed, that he would have to postpone the completion of his article for *The New Yorker*.

He had begun scribbling humorous pieces for *Punch* at Winchester, followed it up while he was at Corpus Christi, Cambridge, and became a regular contributor while working for the British Council in the Middle East. Success with *The New Yorker* came later. He wrote under a pseudonym, and no one, especially in SIS, had any knowledge of his clandestine journalism — a fact which appealed to his sense of humour. Of this humour, some of his colleagues wearily considered that they had too much knowledge.

Rackham looked at the colour photograph of the strawberry-blonde, and decided this was something he was going to deal with personally. After all, he rationalized, she was the daughter of a government minister. Moreover, she was very attractive. Oh definitely, one for him.

'You know, I shall never understand why you stick it out here. You could make far more money as a model — with those looks, that figure. Oh . . . '

Stanley Hailston drew in air appreciatively through his teeth. He had come in early during the afternoon from the Ministry to his office at the House of Commons, and had surprised his secretary, Jane Bacton, as she was standing before the mirror drawing a fine line with her lipstick brush.

She methodically finished the stroke, then turned round, her grey eyes looking up at him from beneath well-arched brows. 'Then,' she said, 'I shouldn't see so much of you, should I? Besides,' she added tantalizingly, 'there are compensations.'

'Compensations? I call it something else,' he said. He cradled her head in his hand and kissed her warmly. He was instantly aroused by the pressure of her body against him.

'I can feel you do,' she smiled.

He stroked her reddish-blonde hair. It was lovely — just like his daughter's. He winced at the thought. The coincidence was something he never liked to dwell upon.

'Hey, I shall have to take time off for a hair-do if you go on like this.'

He held her close and kissed her neck. 'In office time then,' he murmured, 'not in our time.' He moved himself pleasurably against her.

Hailston was lucky, he knew that — having her there to provide what his wife had contentedly opted out of. There was almost twenty years between him and Jane, and she seemed to ask no more than to give him pleasure. That was enviable, he guessed. For his part, he was quite proud of his sexual prowess. Of course, he had kept himself fit, and that early SAS training had laid a good foundation; it had paid off in his maturer years. He was, after all, nearing fifty, but he felt equal to a man half his age. He certainly had no difficulty in meeting Jane's demands. He had kept his figure too — well-built but not an ounce of fat. He was careful about his appearance. He felt that he looked good, his dark hair greying only at the sides, and a short, crisp greyish moustache to add to his authority.

Jane slid gently away from him. 'Not in the office, darling,' she murmured.

'Of course not.' He pretended to be formal. 'Seriously, though,' he added, 'I don't think there's a soul who knows about us. We have both been remarkably discreet. I mean everyone knows about Joe and the woman he keeps at Pimlico, and old Arthur even has it off with his au pair. But have you ever heard a word of gossip about Stanley Hailston, or Jane Bacton?'

'It's your old training,' she said. 'Subterfuge, clandestine operations — up your street.'

'Up yours, too, my sweet.'

Jane chuckled. It was a deep, sexual sound.

Suddenly matter-of-fact, he said, 'Now, what is there?'

'Your constituency chairman, Sir Courtney Sloane, wants to bring a small delegation to see you.'

'What in heaven's name for?'

'There are two planning applications for the development of new villages in an area that hasn't had a new building for the past two hundred years — '

'I know. Esme told me. She does a good job in the constituency. They're all very cross.'

'Sir Courtney wants you to take it up with the Secretary of State for the Environment.'

'There's bound to be a public inquiry anyway. Better to let the thing run its course, and I'll nobble the Minister before the inspector reports.'

'There might not be a public inquiry. It might be fixed.' She looked seductively knowing.

'Oh, there are enough cross people to ensure an inquiry.'

Jane tilted her shoulders. 'That's why you'd better see them. Perhaps you won't want an inquiry yourself,' she added mysteriously.

'Well, fix it, will you? Sir Courtney is a personal friend of the PM.'

Jane looked surprised. 'Is he now? There's not much else — usual constituency letters, which I can deal with. Three more invitations to speak. I'll see if you can fit them in. There's a limit to how much you can expect Esme to do to keep them sweet.'

'You think I've been neglecting the grass roots? Gets a little sour with too much chewing.'

'Well, you have shuffled a lot off on to your wife, haven't you?'

'That's what political wives are for. Let it be a warning to you.'

'I told you there were compensations.'

'Yes, well, I've had a lot of other things on my mind.'

'Like ambition.'

He smiled. 'The pops are full of an impending Cabinet reshuffle.'

'You've seen the *Financial Times*?'

Hailston nodded. 'Tucked away, too, for their political man. And no one else has suggested it.'

'Well, is he right?'

'Hailston for Secretary of State? Would be quite a jump. But it *is* being talked about. I'm surprised none of the other boys have picked it up.'

'They will. Where one goes, the pack follows.'

'Yes. I don't want the band wagon to roll too publicly. Prime Ministers don't like having their minds made up for them.'

'Who are the other candidates?'

'Oh, you know that as well as I do. The PM can simply shuffle round a few top names. There are half-a-dozen who might fill the job. But if the idea is to bring in new blood, then I've as good a chance as anyone — perhaps a little better, because it opens up the ranks below.'

'The PM might even leave the Secretary of State where he is.'

'What, after that cock-up over the deal with Boeing? The party wouldn't wear it. They've had enough of him. Even Prime Ministers have to listen to their parties — eventually.'

'Would I make any difference?'

'You mean if the Chief Whip knew about . . . ' He hesitated before adding, 'our relationship? Yes, that could make a difference. Even these days I think a Prime Minister would prefer his Secretary of State for Defence to be a happily married family man.'

'Well, fortunately neither the Chief Whip nor anyone else knows. And you *are* a happily married man, darling. I think Esme's wonderful.'

'So do I for that matter. What have you got for me to sign?'

She handed him a bunch of letters, neatly interleaved in a holed blotter. Hailston settled behind his conventional oak desk, and gave the letters the merest glance as he appended his signature and turned over the pages. He pulled the diary towards him. 'Is there anything here I don't know about?'

'No.' She paused. 'We could have an early evening, darling. There's no division.'

'I had already planned it,' he smiled.

'Oh, there's one thing, of course — ten o'clock tomorrow. Doctor Willoughby. You won't forget, will you?'

'No, of course not.' Hailston was almost brusque. This was the one thing he had never fully come to terms with — his insulin-dependent diabetes. There had naturally been no sign of it during his SAS days; it had only begun to develop during those few years he was managing director of a security firm, before he had entered politics. Willoughby, a diabetic specialist, had explained to him that it was unusual to find this form of diabetes developing in a man after his twenties. To have an unusual condition only made Hailston resent it the more. It was a threat to his physical fitness. He tried to ignore it while, at the same time, being careful with his injections. Complete punctiliousness was sometimes difficult with the kind of life he led. But Willoughby had warned him about the importance of his routine. Tomorrow was merely a periodic check-up. He saw that Jane, looking up over her brows, was watching him.

'You hate it, don't you?'

'I don't intend to be affected by it,' he grumbled.

'Don't worry, darling, you're not. But . . . er, just keep your appointment.'

He was about to snap back when the telephone rang. Jane answered it, turned to him, and said, 'Foreign Office — a Mr Rackham.'

He picked up the receiver on his desk. 'Hailston,' he said.

'David Rackham here. It's about your daughter, Carolyn, Mr Hailston. She's in Bonn — '

'Bonn?' Hailston interrupted. 'She's in Prague.'

'She was in Prague, Mr Hailston. She's now at our Embassy

in Bonn, and she's returning tomorrow morning, flight BA 743, arriving Heathrow at eleven forty-five.'

Before Hailston could interrupt brusquely to know what all this was about, Rackham went on smoothly, 'I'm afraid she got herself arrested at a Charter 77 meeting in Prague, was detained by the authorities, and we were not informed. She was released and taken to the West German border, after she had signed her confession.' Sensing the interruption, Rackham added quickly, 'That, of course, will have been written for her. It would have been the condition for her release. It was sensible of her to sign it, otherwise they would have held her indefinitely.'

'They couldn't do that.'

'Not under international law perhaps. But they could do it, Mr Hailston — and they would.'

'But what was our Embassy doing?'

'Nothing. They didn't know. The Czechs had no intention of telling them. She's lucky to have been released so quickly.'

Hailston expelled a small gale of indignant air.

'Oh, of course,' Rackham added hastily, 'we have formally protested to the Czech government.'

'What the hell was she doing at a meeting of dissidents?'

'According to her "confession",' Rackham said amusedly, 'she was with her friend Josef Foerster, and conspired with him to abuse the laws of the Socialist Republic of Czechoslovakia by attending a meeting of a proscribed organization.'

'You've seen her statement?'

'I've seen what the Czechs have released. I suspect it's rather more than what she put her name to. The BBC, monitoring Czech radio, say that they are running a big news story that she was in Prague to spy for the British government.'

'Blast!'

To Hailston's annoyance, Rackham almost chuckled. 'Oh, the PM understands the form all right.'

Hailston hoped that meant that the whole affair would have no effect on his own prospects of ministerial promotion.

'Who the hell's Josef Foerster?' he asked.

Rackham paused. 'Her friend.'

'Do we know anything, other than what's in the statement?'

'Not really. She *was* at a Chartist group meeting with Foerster, but she didn't realize the significance of it. That much she has told to our chaps in Bonn. I take it, Mr Hailston, you will be meeting her flight tomorrow?'

'Well, more likely my wife.'

'Ah yes, of course. We shall want to debrief your daughter properly. I think I'd like to see her myself.'

'Certainly.'

'Don't worry about it, Mr Hailston. She's safe now. But tomorrow's papers — especially the pops — will have stories about Minister's daughter spying for Britain, say Czechs.'

'Yes, thanks for warning me.' Hailston put down the receiver. He turned to Jane, his blue eyes cold, his face stern. 'Carolyn's been kicked out by the Czechs. Confessed to spying. At least that's what they say.'

Jane looked surprised. 'That's . . . that's ridiculous.'

Hailston's fingers were drumming on the top of his desk. 'Ridiculous? It's bloody inconvenient.'

'Oh, that won't make any difference. It mustn't. The PM will know it's all nonsense. Anyway, if she was spying, it was for Britain.'

Hailston was thinking. 'It's the publicity. Press will want to interview her — that kind of thing.'

'All right, it's one story, isn't it? "No, the only spying I did was on old masters." Twenty-four hours and it will be forgotten.'

'I hope so. It buggers up our evening. I'll have to go home. Esme will have to meet her at Heathrow tomorrow.'

Hailston was cross. He had been looking forward to Jane. He glanced at the Commons order paper. There was nothing there to concern him; he had no reason to go into the chamber at all. He got up, locked the door, and drew her to him, kissing her passionately, urgently.

She disentangled herself. 'Not here, Stanley,' she smiled. 'You've got to go home to Esme.'

'Not there either,' he muttered.

The house in Chester Square had the clean, stuccoed dignity of Belgravia, relieved only by brilliant streaks of window boxes. These were Esme's innovation, and she was conscientious in keeping them trim and well-planted. The same sense of order and good taste was to be found in the large high-ceilinged rooms. Many of the antiques had been inherited from her family. The rest had been bought with her money, as indeed had the lease of the house itself. Hailston paid for its upkeep, and for Mrs Drury who cooked and housekept for them and occupied the basement flat.

'Oh good, you're early,' said Esme, meeting him in the hall. 'No division?'

'No.' He kissed her conventionally on the cheek.

She was a handsome rather than a pretty woman, with Pre-Raphaelite red hair and blue eyes — presumably the source of Carolyn's lighter colouring — and she had a style, an elegance. She dressed classically. Hailston admitted that she was a good politician's wife. He couldn't do without her.

As he moved into the drawing room, she was already at a side table, pouring him a weak scotch. She had also noted his grim seriousness.

'What's happened?' she asked perceptively, as she handed him the drink.

He peered for a moment at the amber liquid, and then muttered brusquely, 'Carolyn's been chucked out of Czechoslovakia. They say she was spying.'

Esme showed no surprise. She said only, 'Where is she?'

'At our Embassy in Bonn. Has she ever mentioned a fellow called Josef Foerster?'

'In her letters? No.'

'She was with him at the time. Could you meet her, darling — at Heathrow tomorrow? Eleven forty-five, flight BA 743.'

Esme gave him a half-smile. Her lips and jaw had a sculpted line. 'Of course,' she said. 'So what was she really up to?'

'Being damned stupid. Went to a Charter 77 meeting with the Foerster fellow. They got her to sign a confession, of course. Otherwise she'd still be there.' Hailston took a swig of his whisky.

Esme sighed. She said prosaically, 'I expect there's some perfectly reasonable explanation for it all.'

'That scarcely matters. It's just not helpful at this time, that's all.'

'Darling, if there's really a chance of you becoming Secretary of State for Defence, Carolyn's adventures in Prague are not going to make the slightest difference. Unless — '

'Unless what?'

'Well, they could even be helpful, Stanley. I mean, she's the victim. Won't do you any harm.'

He considered the remains of his scotch and grunted.

'Do you really want the job?' she asked.

Hailston looked surprised, pulled at the short hairs of his moustache. 'Of course. You must know that.'

'I suppose so. You could do it. You'd be good at it.'

'I know. That's why I want it.'

Esme smiled, and poured herself a dry Martini. She was proud of her husband. He was in politics because he knew about defence, had ideas. From the moment his party was elected, he said he was going to be a minister, and not in any old department. It was going to be Defence, or nothing. When the Prime Minister offered him a junior post in the Home Department he turned it down, and argued his corner. The Prime Minister put him into Defence. Since then he had worked tirelessly and determinedly, even at the expense of his constituency. That was where she came in. She had taken on a great deal of the constituency burden, stood in for him at fetes and meetings and, in fact, had become so popular herself that the chairman had once confided to her, 'You know, if anything ever happened to Stanley — God forbid — the local party would want you to succeed him.'

'What are you thinking about?' Hailston muttered.

Esme twisted the olive in her glass and looked up. She extemporized felicitously: 'I was thinking that, if you become Defence Secretary, then you won't be content until you are Prime Minister.'

'That's right. You'd make a good Prime Minister's wife.'

4

The day after Carolyn Hailston's return David Rackham called at Chester Square to see her. It had been agreed that the debriefing should be left to him. He was greeted by Esme Hailston saying, 'Stanley said you would be coming.' She led him into the drawing room, said that she would ask Carolyn to join him, and she would bring them some coffee.

Left to himself, Rackham inspected the selection of eighteenth-century drawings and watercolours — Michael Angelo Rooker, Thomas Malton, Thomas and Paul Sandby, Alexander Cozens and Rowlandson — and immediately assumed they reflected Mrs Hailston's taste. They were her style rather than Hailston's, not that Rackham had yet met the minister personally. But these were not the collection of a man of action, and Rackham saw Hailston as essentially an action man.

When Mrs Hailston returned with a tray bearing a silver Georgian coffee pot with modern Wedgwood coffee cups, she was accompanied by Carolyn.

'I take it,' she said, pouring the coffee at the same time, 'that you would prefer to see Carolyn alone?'

Rackham gave her a freckly smile. 'If you don't mind.'

Esme Hailston left, and Rackham found himself standing opposite a young woman who was just about his own height. He approved of what he saw. A slim, nicely shaped figure, slender legs, reddish-blonde hair, bright blue eyes, and a nose that had a slightly humorous tilt. She had her mother's erect carriage, but not quite the same degree of confidence. He grinned, looked her straight in the eyes, and decided that perhaps she could be ingenuous. She presumably had been in Prague. He handed her the plate of biscuits. She shook her head. He took one, looked about him, and said brightly, 'Well, shall we sit down?'

'Yes, of course.' As she settled into the easy chair with its Sanderson-print covers, she asked, 'And who exactly are you, Mr Rackham?'

He looked up over his coffee cup. 'You're a little wary after your experiences. I can understand that. Well, it may not be strictly true, but think of me as someone from the Foreign Office.'

'You're not a policeman then?'

'No.' He thought she looked sceptical. 'So you're studying art restoration?'

'Yes, with a relative of Mummy's. He runs a gallery — the Granville — and is a restorer.'

'What's Prague got to do with it?'

She pursed her lips. 'I had the chance to go there. They've some fine collections, and a Doctor Vladislav, who is a remarkable restorer.'

'And the Granville specializes in eighteenth-century work?'

'How'd you know?'

Rackham twitched his lips knowingly and glanced round the room.

Carolyn permitted a chuckle. 'Mummy loves them.'

'With good reason.'

'Yes, she has excellent taste.'

Rackham nodded. 'Now let's begin at the beginning.'

Slowly he took her through her Prague experience, and then her 'confession', and although he questioned her in unremitting detail, he somehow managed to convey a slightly insouciant air, as though it really was of no great importance.

At the end, she asked, wide-eyed, 'Have I really done anything very wrong?'

'Well, you did know what you were doing when you went to the Chartist meeting. That was perhaps unwise.' He saw her looking at him anxiously, as she nodded her agreement. 'But no damage has been done — at least to you.' He heard her sharp intake of breath, and knew that she was thinking of Josef. 'And,' he continued, 'you hadn't any alternative but to sign the confession. That was their condition for your release. I suppose each page was complete in itself, and they weren't numbered, were they?'

'That's right.'

'It's a pretty common trick. They insert pages of their own, making you say all sorts of things. Czech radio and television have been having a marvellous time with stories about the young British blonde spy.'

'The Press have been ringing up endlessly. I'm not talking to them.'

'Well, I should — just the straightforward story: you studying art, innocently went to a meeting with a friend, found yourself arrested and accused of spying, had to sign a confession to get out. But — ' he laughed, 'don't ham it up, will you?'

She looked serious. 'No,' was all she said. Then, as she saw him looking at her, she asked, 'What will happen to Josef?'

Rackham shrugged. 'Perhaps a term in jail. Perhaps nothing. You never can tell.'

Carolyn looked thoughtful. Rackham was watching her intently. He wasn't only admiring her, although he was certainly doing that. He was wondering what she had deliberately decided not to tell him. Ultimately he got to his feet, shook her hand and held it a little longer than necessary as he looked directly into her blue eyes.

'I'm surprised,' he said, 'that they didn't want something more than that statement.'

After a couple of days Carolyn decided to return to the flat she shared with Toni Bright. They each had a bed-sitter, and there was another spacious room which they could use jointly as a sitting room or dining room. The kitchen and bathroom were small but adequate. The arrangement worked well; so did their relationship.

Toni was a couple of years or so older than Carolyn and, at barely five feet five, somewhat shorter, but with a head-turning figure and a vivacious manner that made her instantly likeable. She was dark with flashing brown eyes and the kind of skin that detected the remotest sunlight like a radar screen, and instantly tanned. She ate the right health-giving foods, did her aerobics every day, and brimmed with health and vitality.

She worked as a secretary at the House of Commons, looking after two backbench MPs, and had been introduced as a potential flat-mate by Jane Bacton. Occasionally, she had accompanied Carolyn to Sussex for a weekend in the country. Otherwise, they mostly led separate lives, their orbits coinciding from time to time in a way that gave pleasure to them both. Toni spent far more time out of the flat, changing her personality for the evenings. The classic suit or dress was discarded for more modern casual clothes, and the dark hair that, for the House of Commons, was either neatly swept back or up, was teased out into a modest Kate Bush style.

There had only been one occasion of awkwardness or difficulty between them, and that had, inevitably, been Carolyn's fault. Afterwards, Toni had been puzzled, inquiring, thoughtfully trying to understand.

It had been a Friday evening about three months ago. Carolyn had intended going to Sussex for the weekend, and had changed her mind at the last moment when she discovered that, politically speaking, it was going to be an unusually quiet weekend, and her father would be spending most of the time at home relaxing. So she had decided to wait until Saturday afternoon before making the trip. She had spent rather longer working at the art gallery on the Friday, had a quick meal, and returned to the flat about nine o'clock.

She had rushed in, calling 'Toni! Toni!' meaning to add, 'I'm not going to Sussex until tomorrow.' But she had stopped suddenly in the open doorway of the sitting room. There was Toni and a man standing in the middle of the room. They had obviously been clasped in each other's arms, and they broke apart at the sound of her entry. They were both naked.

For a moment no one spoke. Then Toni burbled into a giggle that quickly developed into a full laugh. Somehow she had managed to say, 'This is Harry. Harry, this is my flat-mate, Carolyn.'

Carolyn had been momentarily transfixed. She just stared — at Toni, at Harry. The man had looked embarrassed, his member hard and erect. At first Carolyn had been unable to turn her eyes away from it. Then suddenly the tension broke. She half gasped, half screamed. Her hands flew to her face, stifling the sound. Then she turned and ran from the room to her own bed-sitter. She slammed the door, turned the key and threw herself on the bed.

She lay there, breathing heavily, struggling to make sense of herself. It was like opening a wound, feeling the sudden pain again. She supposed Toni had been right. The situation was funny. But she couldn't see that. No matter how hard she tried, she couldn't see it like that. But the more she tried to think and to make sense of it, the less she was able to. Thought got submerged in the sensation of horror and pain.

At last, when she had stilled herself, and was just lying there, no longer trying to think, she heard them — the distant sounds of their love making . . . the short cries and gasps, the long, relaxed moans, and words . . . words she tried to shut out of her mind.

Ultimately she must have fallen asleep. She was awakened by a soft tapping at her door, and Toni's voice, in a loud whisper, calling, 'Carolyn . . . can I come in?'

She got up and opened the door. Toni's dark hair was dishevelled, but her eyes were glowing, and she bloomed with happiness.

For a moment she stood there, looking at Carolyn for an explanation. Failing to find one, she took her by the shoulders and held her gently.

'Are you all right?' she asked.

Carolyn nodded. Then she said, 'I'm sorry, Toni.'

'Oh dear, I thought he looked so funny,' said Toni, her eyes mischievous, 'standing there with his thing sticking up.' Carolyn didn't know what to say. She tried to smile. She supposed it was funny really.

'Don't you . . . ?' Toni hesitated. 'Like men, sex?' she asked.

'I . . . I don't know. Sorry, Toni, I suppose I behaved stupidly.'

'It's all right by me.' She waited, but as Carolyn made no further response, she asked, 'Do you want to talk? You don't have to. Only if it helps.'

Carolyn shook her head. 'I can't,' she said.

Toni didn't try to intrude any more. She merely sat with Carolyn on the edge of the divan bed, holding her hands, trying silently to convey some sympathy and understanding. Ultimately, her own enthusiasm got the better of her, and she hoped it might jolly Carolyn back to her normal self.

'Sex is good, you know,' Toni said. 'D'you know, once I was at a party, and we were all asked to write down our most exciting moment, and then the papers were handed in and read out. You should have heard some of the things. A man had fallen half way down a rock face and survived. A girl said it had been the first time she had ski'd downhill alone; another said being driven round Brands Hatch at over a hundred and twenty miles an hour. But I wrote down just two words: having sex.' She broke into a laugh at the recollection, and was rewarded by seeing Carolyn smile. 'But it's true,' she continued. 'I can't think of any sensation more exciting or more exquisite.'

Carolyn was still smiling, but she felt awkward, discomforted, and it showed.

'Have I upset you?'

'No,' Carolyn muttered. 'I . . . I just don't know, that's all.'

'Well, there always has to be a first time — sometimes it's marvellous, sometimes it isn't.'

'I suppose so.'

'You all right?'

'Yes . . . yes, I'm all right now. I don't know what it was. I suppose I was being silly.'

'That's fine, honey. It must have been a bit of a shock. We all react differently, don't we? But, if you want to talk . . . '

'No.' Carolyn patted her friend's hand. 'Thanks,' she said.

But a lot had happened in the three months since that scene. There had been Prague; there had been Josef; there had been the magical escape from her past, and at last she had known how exquisite the sensation could be. But it had been more than that.

She had never seen Harry again, and Toni had never referred to him. Carolyn wondered how she would react when she returned this time if she should find him standing naked in the middle of the floor with Toni. She smiled at the thought, and felt that, perhaps at last, she might be able to share Toni's laughter. But not her lover. There could only be Josef.

As it happened there was only Toni in the flat when she arrived, and she threw her arms wide and shouted exuberantly, 'Welcome! Welcome home, baby! I'll open the champagne. At least I would if we had some. What have we got?' She rushed to the kitchen and returned with a nondescript bottle of white wine. The business of opening it and pouring out a couple of glasses seemed to occupy no more than a few enthusiastic seconds.

'To Carolynofski, the beautiful spy,' Toni toasted. 'Come on, you've got to tell me all about it. I'm going to my karate class tonight. Why didn't you tell me you were coming home? I wouldn't have gone. But there are tests. I've got to be there. Now what were you up to in Prague? I've read the papers, but — '

Carolyn laughed at her friend's torrential excitement.

'I was frightened.' She was suddenly serious. 'I thought I might never get out. I was ready to sign whatever they put in front of me, except . . . '

She broke off, the shine in her eyes changing to sadness.

'Come on, except what? Don't hold out on me.'

'They said it would help Josef.'

'You're telling me the end before the beginning. But I scent romance — yes?'

Carolyn nodded.

'But look,' Toni continued, 'start at the beginning, will you? I want to hear it all.' She slurped at the white wine, made a grimace. 'Oh well, it's better than nothing.'

Carolyn put the events of Prague into some sort of order, and her friend listened, brown eyes brilliant with rapt attention.

At the end of it all, Toni's verdict was: 'You're quite a girl.'

Carolyn smiled. 'Do you have to sound so surprised?'

Toni pealed into laughter. 'But this Josef guy — it's serious. They're a bunch of brutes, aren't they?'

'I try not to think of it too much.'

Toni, with undisguised admiration, said there were simply hundreds of questions she still wanted to ask, but she just had to go to her class. She bustled round the flat, calling remarks over her shoulder, as she got ready. 'Perhaps,' she said, 'you ought to join my karate class too.'

Carolyn had been back a week when she received the invitation to a reception at the Czechoslovak Embassy. That week had also seen the end of newspaper stories about the art-student daughter of a British Minister accused of spying in Prague. The Press, on the whole, had taken her side in the affair, and stressed her denials and the protests made by the Foreign Office to the Czech government. She had even returned to her work at the Granville Gallery, only to be told by her relative to take a fortnight off; she deserved a rest.

The sight of the neatly printed invitation revived her thoughts of Josef. She couldn't drive from her mind the picture of him crouched, unaware, in the corner of that cold, dank cell. Was he still there? Had he been charged, brought to trial? She thought of their walks together in Prague, he tall and confident beside her and proudly pointing out the details that tourists missed. She thought of them together in her room at the Zlata-Husa . . . his understanding, his kindness. Her escape from the complicated tangle of inhibitions, of fear, of misunderstandings, of pain and hurt and shame. How they had shackled her — with a familiarity that made her almost unaware of their intensity. And Josef had perceived what was at the root of it all. Thinking of him, she longed for him.

At least if she went to the reception she might be able to learn something about him. Her Czech interrogator had said that Josef could be treated quite well if she would agree to help them. She might even be able to see him. Carolyn visualized the fresh, scrubbed appearance of the benevolent-looking figure that had sat at the opposite side of the small table in the interrogation room. Could she trust him? She had no alternative. And if she didn't go . . . ? Carolyn dismissed the thought. There wasn't a choice.

Stanley Hailston did not see the point of receiving a deputation from his constituency at the House of Commons, when he could meet them, at greater convenience both to himself and to them, in the constituency itself. But as his chairman, Sir Courtney Sloane, sagely explained, 'They like to come to see you at the seat of power. A visit to the House is something special for them, Stanley.'

So it might be, but it was a damned nuisance to Hailston, having to entertain the six of them, seven with Sir Courtney. Still, as Esme constantly pointed out to him, they represented a large majority, and it would be very much worse if he were holding a marginal seat.

Sir Courtney was a distinguished-looking man — tall, slim, white hair close-cut and well-brushed, a sweeping white moustache sleekly trimmed, twinkling blue eyes, an outdoor complexion, and he still had the carriage of a guardsman. He managed his party committee, indeed the whole constituency party, with finesse, and Hailston accordingly almost always followed his advice. Sir Courtney was ten years older. But for that, Hailston often reflected that Esme would have made an admirable wife for Sir Courtney, instead of the curious dumpy little woman who had no interest in politics at all, rolled around in her garden like a teased-out ball of string, and looked disconcertingly surprised when she was called Lady Sloane. Hailston congratulated himself on his own good fortune.

So the small deputation had tea on the terrace and then crowded into his inadequate, oak-panelled room, and he listened attentively to their submissions. Village Life Construction, he was informed, was a very powerful consortium; they employed architects of distinction and they had original ideas. The whole concept was new, although it clearly owed something to village holiday developments in Spain and Portugal. So they were not dealing with a gimcrack organization, but a powerful group that would skilfully use all the resources of publicity. Superficially, the project undoubtedly had a certain appeal, but the damage it would do to unspoilt countryside was inestimable. So they went on — setting out the arguments against the development, and supporting them with well-marshalled facts drawn from history, tradition, local culture, wildlife, and farming. They needed to know that their MP was on their side, and would fight this threat until victory was theirs.

Hailston listened carefully, made sympathetic noises, and then, without committing himself, said he would be making a speech on the subject in the constituency in the near future.

When they left, Sir Courtney made an excuse to stay behind to discuss a private matter with the Minister.

'Stanley,' he said, his eyes glinting with amusement, 'you're not going to be able to ride this one for long. You're going to have to come down on one side or the other within a fortnight.'

Hailston drummed on the table impatiently. 'I know. But I think I should hear the other side's case. I represent the constituency, not just the party.'

'Oh, admirable, Stanley, admirable, but not feasible in this case.'

'The trouble is,' Hailston muttered, 'it would provide employment. It's damned hard to oppose projects which give people work.'

'Not much employment for local people though,' Sir Courtney interposed.

'So your advice is that we have to fight it. On the side of the greens, eh?'

Sir Courtney smiled and nodded. 'That's about it.'

Hailston wished he did not have to bother with these constituency affairs when there were important issues of national defence to occupy his mind. He felt he was meant for the wider world of government policy. Esme would be far better with these local matters; sometimes he even thought she would make a better local MP, but — oh well, it was the cross he had to bear if he was to fulfil his political ambitions.

'I'll be in touch in a day or two,' Hailston said, as he walked with his chairman along the statue-lined St Stephen's Chapel towards the entrance where the constituency delegation were patiently waiting. After their warm handshaking and cheerful smiles, he waved them goodbye, and then returned to his room to consider more important matters.

Kensington Palace Gardens in London is one of those exclusive roads lined with plane trees and barred from general access by a yellow-and-black barrier arm, operated by a man wearing a dark green tail coat and top hat. While thus checking on motor traffic, he allows free access to pedestrians using the footpaths.

The Czechoslovak Embassy is number 25, and it is on the right-hand side immediately as you enter Kensington Palace Gardens from Notting Hill Gate. It is quite unlike any other building in that distinguished road, and is a brutal contrast with its immediate neighbour — the Saudi Arabian Embassy which, with its magnolia stucco, chimneys and top balustrade graced with small onion domes, has the dignity and elegance of the wealthy Middle East. The Czechs, however, have erected a bunker — an ugly block of concrete, relieved only by the large and diagonally recessed picture windows. The concrete tentacles stretch round and out of the road to occupy a whole block facing Notting Hill Gate.

So Carolyn was surprised by the modern sumptuousness of the large room in which the reception was held. She wore a suit of blue crepe de Chine with scooped neckline, and a pencil-slim skirt, and was gratified to see that other women guests were also informally dressed. The men all wore lounge suits. She wondered who they were. Probably journalists, some of them. She was offered a choice of fruit juice, gin and tonic, scotch, red or white wine, or a Czech sparkling wine. She chose the latter, and stood by the drapes of one of the picture windows, wondering who was going to talk to her and what would happen next.

She had not long to wait. She was soon approached by a willowy, dark-haired, suave man, a little taller than herself, and quite astonishingly handsome.

'You must be Miss Hailston,' he said. 'Welcome to the Czechoslovak Embassy. I do hope you will enjoy the evening. And I'll introduce you to some other guests.'

His English was faultless, and coloured only by what Carolyn had to admit was an intriguing accent. The man's eyes were deep, dark and liquid, and frankly seductive.

'Oh,' he said suddenly, 'how remiss of me. I haven't introduced myself. Suppose you just call me *Eevan*. It is spelt with an I. You like the wine? Perhaps you had some in Prague. It is champagne method.'

'Yes,' she said truthfully but a little coolly, 'it is quite nice.'

Ivan smiled. 'I can't say how sorry I am you had to leave Prague, Miss Hailston. What a pity I was not there.'

Carolyn raised an eyebrow.

'Well,' he continued, smiling, 'I am sure it was all a silly misunderstanding. The STB, you know, they take their work so seriously.'

'Is that what you call it?' she said sharply. 'Brutally would probably be more accurate.'

'Oh come.' His charm was unabashed. 'I hope you were treated kindly.'

'I wasn't ill-treated. But kindly I think would be an exaggeration.'

'Then I can only apologize most sincerely. You know, it is different there, conventions are different — you understand?'

'I know that if a person in this country was held in the way I was held in Prague there would be questions in the House of Commons.'

'Ah.' He gestured broadly with his well-manicured hands, as though to imply envy of the British traditions, as he added only, 'It is so different.'

He took her elbow and smilingly began to move her towards a small group of other guests, but Carolyn held back.

'What about Josef Foerster?' she asked. 'What has happened to him?'

'I'm sure you have no need to worry.'

'I have — that's the point. I saw him. Your people had beaten him up. He was in a cell.'

'Oh.' He shook his head, as if in dismay. 'They act too hasty — you understand? We made you a promise. We keep our promises. For the moment he is all right. Do not worry.'

'Shall I ever see him again?'

'Why not?' He drew her aside. 'Miss Hailston, suppose we meet for lunch? I might have some news for you about Josef.

And I think we can help each other. I do understand how you feel.'

He looked at her so plausibly. Carolyn hesitated briefly, but she was only concerned with finding out about Josef.

She nodded. 'All right.'

'Tomorrow? Why wait longer? Do you know Traceys in Victoria? Shall we say twelve forty-five?'

'Yes, OK,' she said.

'Ah, I'm sure we can help each other, Miss Hailston. Now let me introduce you to . . . '

He led her towards the centre of the room, where two women and two men were chattering loudly. Carolyn hadn't the least idea what to say.

While Carolyn was experiencing the hospitality of the Czechoslovak Embassy, her father was attending an unusual meeting of a small group of his party's backbench MPs. It was not being held, as might have been expected, in one of the rooms in the Grand Committee corridor, but on the interview floor in the basement, in one of the smaller rooms invariably used by MPs either for meeting with constituency groups, or to brief Press correspondents on some personal campaign. It had been called by Julian Smithers, the chairman of the party's backbench Defence Committee, but there were only two or three other members from that committee present. The remaining six or seven were chairmen of other backbench committees, and MPs known to have influence with their colleagues.

Smithers, who had had a military career himself, and was never one for mincing his words, said at the outset that the reason he had chosen the interview floor was because he did not want to draw attention to their meeting. Moreover, he would not be there had he not already sounded out the opinion of those present, and others in the party. He then turned to Hailston and thanked him for coming.

'I won't beat about the bush,' he said. 'There's a growing feeling in the party, Stanley, that you should be the next Secretary of State for Defence. Now, I think I can carry our committee, and others here think they can carry theirs. Oh, I know it's not in our gift. It's the Prime Minister's decision, and Prime Ministers make up their own minds. But some of us carry weight. And it doesn't do the PM any harm to know the kind of person who would have the confidence of the party. I mean this is going to be a damned difficult job in the years ahead, and it's important that the party has the best man for the job.'

He glanced round the room, as colleagues nodded and murmured their assent.

'Well, Stanley,' he continued, 'we simply want to know if you want the job. It's no good our getting a campaign under way if you're not interested. I know a minister doesn't usually jump from your job straight to Secretary of State. It's more likely a shuffle from another department. But it has happened, and it's happened more than once. No reason why it shouldn't happen again.'

Hailston drew himself up with something of his old bearing. He knew what they expected, and he wasn't going to disappoint them.

'Thank you, Julian,' he said and nodded his appreciation to the others, 'it's good of you to invite me here. The answer to your question is "yes". I want the job because I see the immediate years ahead as calling for some of the most difficult decisions a government has ever had to take in the defence field. That will demand not only a comprehensive knowledge, but an unwavering sense of purpose, and a determination to take the right decision. I believe I can do that.'

There was a mumbling of 'hear hears', and Smithers said, 'Good. Thought so. Now there's been the odd story, but we don't want the Press to get the idea that we're running a campaign. That would kill your chances, Stanley. So, if any of the lobby boys canvass our opinion, it would be as well to play down Stanley. He's only one of a number — no better chance than anybody else. We can't have the Prime Minister feeling pressurized. But one or two of us — a quiet word with the Chief Whip . . . you know the kind of thing.'

There was general assent to tactics, and then a number of them questioned Hailston about his attitude to current defence issues. He answered crisply and authoritatively, and was gratified to see that they were impressed.

When he returned home to Chester Square that night he proudly told Esme about the meeting and the enthusiasm of his backbench colleagues.

'I'm delighted for you, darling,' she said. 'But don't count too much on it. Prime Ministers are not swayed by committee opinions. They have their own reasons for making Cabinet appointments.'

Hailston stroked his short moustache with the merest suggestion of impatience. 'I know, I know,' he said. 'But on controversial defence issues it helps the PM to know that the Secretary of State can rely on united backbenches.'

Esme saw his confidence. She felt proud of him, but knew that if he was passed over he would be furious. She would be much better at handling the situation.

He saw her small smile of understanding. 'Smithers has had it from the PM's Principal Private Secretary,' he continued. 'I'm at the top of the list.'

Esme took him by the shoulders, looked at him, and kissed him on the cheek. 'Congratulations, darling. I just don't believe in counting chickens, that's all. Better if you don't too.'

'I have the feeling nothing is going to stop me.'

'You've thought about the constituency?'

'For God's sake, Esme, you don't put your constituency before a job in the Cabinet. They should be proud of their Member.'

Esme's smile was tolerant. She admired his ambition, his enthusiasm, but she realized, probably better than he, that it would result in a great deal more work for her in Sussex.

'No, of course a Cabinet post comes first,' she said. 'But it will mean that you will have even less time for constituency matters, and there are some in the party down there who feel they don't see enough of you.'

'They see plenty of *you*.'

'Not the same thing, darling. You're the MP.'

'Damn it, they'll have a voice in the Cabinet now. They should be grateful.'

'Oh darling, you're incorrigible. Sounds good. But it won't make the slightest bit of difference on any constituency issue, and you know it.'

'Who's the politician — you or me?'

'Oh you. I just carry out instructions. But there are things boiling up in Sussex, you know. There are those village developments, oil exploration applications. You're going to have to take a view.'

'And I shall, but there are more important things at the moment.'

'Like going to bed,' she murmured. 'You look as though you've had a hard day. I'm tired too.'

Esme thought, as they undressed, that she could still admire his body — he was in good shape — but she didn't feel desire any more. Had not done for years. It had really begun to fade after Carolyn's birth. It had been a difficult pregnancy and an even more difficult birth. Painful, dangerous. And afterwards, that was the end. She couldn't have any more children. At the time Stanley had not seemed greatly affected; he had been understanding. After all, it wasn't going to affect their sex life. For a few years it didn't, although she had to admit that she had shown rather less enthusiasm. Then gradually it had begun to fade, and when Stanley went into politics, all his energy seemed to be concentrated upon his new career. Later, when he had tried to return to her, she wasn't really there. For a while, they had pretended, and then Stanley had seemed to realize that it wasn't any good. For her part, she had thrown herself into his new career as well. They were seen as an ideal political couple, one supporting the other — always together in the constituency, canvassing together, at meetings together. It was a good political marriage.

As she slipped out of her clothes, and caught sight of herself in the mirror, she saw that she still had a good figure. Her posture was good; she was trim. Stanley did not seem to notice. It was too long ago. There had been new conventions. In a way, she thought, it was strange that she didn't mind. But why should she? It was no longer necessary. Almost without knowing it she had found satisfaction in being his political wife. And it was satisfying. She enjoyed the work in the constituency . . . the meetings, the coffee mornings, the fetes, the sales of work. She had become part of Stanley's career, and she had his total confidence. She knew, too, that he was grateful. They were a happy couple, each finding fulfilment in his political ambition. In its way, she conceded as she climbed into bed, it was all very satisfactory.

For about an hour Stanley sat up against the pillows, his red box on a nearby chair, as he went through the variety of papers that it contained. She never asked what they were; that would be improper. For the same reason, Stanley never told her, although he frequently discussed with her his ministerial responsibilities and broad principles of policy. He valued her opinion, and she enjoyed giving it.

He was lit by a single light on his side of the bed. She lay in a shaded penumbra beyond it. She could have gone to sleep. He was not disturbing her. But she never did. Tonight she wondered, as she had occasionally wondered before, if he had given up sex. He was a healthy man — well, apart from his diabetes, and that didn't seem to trouble him. Had he really submerged himself so completely in his career to find it unnecessary? Or . . . ? She sometimes wondered if he had transferred that side of his life to Jane Bacton. She was very attractive. Esme watched him as he scribbled a note in the margin of the paper he was reading, and she wondered again. Not that it mattered. Supposing it were true, it had never impinged upon their home life, or their political life together. And it wouldn't. She was sure of that. Stanley had got too much to lose. It wasn't merely this home in Chester Square, the house in Sussex, the comfortable familiarity of all their belongings. It was the way she had become necessary to him, indispensable to his career and his ambition. Maybe habit had a lot to do with it, but that wasn't to be despised. No, she was not threatened; nor was their life together.

Stanley slammed shut the lid of his red box. 'Well, that's that,' he said. 'Goodnight, darling.' He kissed her, and they each sidled to their sides of the bed, and fell asleep.

5

Traceys is one of those small restaurants with a reputation for good food which is more than adequately reflected in their prices. It is situated in one of a number of narrow lanes or pedestrian ways that link main streets or squares in Victoria. Its glass doorway is flanked by two bay trees in green tubs.

Carolyn knew the restaurant because of its proximity to her parents' home in Chester Square, and she arrived punctually at twelve forty-five. As she entered she saw that the Czech she knew only as Ivan was already seated at a table in the far corner of the room, conveniently isolated from its neighbours. He rose smoothly to his feet the moment he saw her and bowed graciously as she approached.

'Inherited from your father's military training, no doubt,' he murmured with a purring smile.

Carolyn looked puzzled.

His smile broadened. 'Your punctuality,' he explained. 'It's what you call "on the dot", h'mm?'

Carolyn managed a smile. She was unsure how to respond. A waiter hovered as she sat down, but she declined Ivan's invitation to have an aperitif. She looked at him, met the warm glowing depth of his dark eyes with the bright questioning blue of her own. She was the first to look away, still unsure of herself. The man had an excess of charm, a suavity that would normally be reassuring. For her, however, it was a little disconcerting. She did not know what to expect. Her anxiety was for Josef.

The room was full of green plush, the walls even had some original oil paintings. Her host's urbanity fitted well with an atmosphere of opulence. He insisted quietly that they order immediately. She settled for melon, followed by Dover sole. He joined her in the sole, but chose smoked salmon to begin with. He ordered a premier cru Montagny and, as he tasted it, he murmured, 'I must admit better than we can grow.'

From the behaviour of the waiter she had the impression that Ivan was a regular customer. She was tempted to suggest that they did not need such good wine to go with their endless dumplings, but kept the thought to herself. She had got out of Czechoslovakia, but she had not escaped from them. She faced his smile, wondering what to say to him.

'You've been in England a long time?' she suggested.

'I am glad to say — yes. I am very fond of your country. We have a lot in common.'

'Have or had?' Thinking of Josef, she had uttered the words before she knew what she was saying.

He gestured with his open hands, and even his eyebrows seemed to smile. Carolyn remembered that Josef had told her that their famous monarch, Charles IV, had a daughter named Anne, who had come to England to be the first wife of Richard II, and that, largely through this union, the religious reforms of John Wycliffe had spread to Czechoslovakia. But that was a long time ago — in the fourteenth century. The only other thing in common, in more recent times, had been democracy, which we had betrayed and Ivan's lot had later overthrown. She saw no future in that strand of conversation.

'You are looking very serious,' he said, the colouring of his accent almost putting a question mark at the end.

Her reply was prevented by the waiter arriving with her melon. She watched Ivan fuss elegantly with the paprika and lemon on his smoked salmon, and then look up with a quizzical smile as the waiter left them.

'Last night you said you might have some news for me about Josef.'

'You are very fond of him?'

She ignored the question. 'Have you?' she asked.

He swilled the crisp white wine in his mouth and nodded.

'He has inquired about you. We were able to tell him that you were safely at home, and he was very pleased. He . . . ' Ivan paused deliberately, patted his mouth with his white napkin. 'He sent his love to you.'

'But how is he?' Carolyn persisted.

'He is well. He is all right. I told you, you have no need to worry.'

'Is he still in prison?'

'Of course, but — '

'Still in that awful cell?'

'His conditions are now comfortable, not at all unpleasant. But he has to be tried.'

'So, you're not going to release him?'

'He has committed a serious offence.'

'And you have already decided he is guilty.'

Ivan again gave a little dab at his lips with his napkin, and then took another sip of wine. 'Well,' he said, 'Josef was arrested at an illegal meeting.'

Carolyn had finished her melon, she tidied her fork and spoon, sighed with impatience. As she was about to speak, he lifted his hand, and she saw the waiter approaching. She waited until he had removed their plates, and then she said, 'Yes, you mean to keep him in prison.'

'Carolyn.' His voice was soft, ingratiating. 'You don't mind that I call you Carolyn?'

She didn't reply, merely shook her head, which could have meant 'no', or could have been an indication of despair.

Ivan continued expansively, 'We might release him from prison. Without a trial. Say a mistake was made.' He looked directly at her. 'Would that make you happy?'

'If I could be sure it was true, yes.'

'It could be — with your help.'

'My help? What do you mean?'

The waiter brought their main courses. Ivan waved aside her question. 'Let us enjoy the food, the wine, h'mm? Then perhaps we can talk some more.'

As she pared the white flesh of the sole from its bone, Carolyn saw him watching her, but she was sure he was not simply assessing her. He was too sophisticated not to have done that long ago — probably in just a few seconds last night. Was his expression ironic? If so, that made her uneasy.

He asked her if she had been to any concerts when she was in Prague, and she replied that she had seen a performance of *The Bartered Bride*, and had heard a programme of Suk, Smetana and Janáček by the Czech Philharmonic, both of them in the National Theatre which, she smiled, was just dripping with red plush and gold leaf. Ivan nodded approvingly, and told her that his government was very properly spending a lot of money on restoration. But all she wanted to know was what it was that she could do to help Josef. She loved him so much. She would do anything, she knew that. But again Ivan dismissed her questions until their coffee had been brought. Then he took the solitary golden-yellow rose from the small cut-glass vase in the centre of the table, and handed it to her.

'We have a saying in Czechoslovakia — '

'I know,' she said, ' "Patience brings roses".'

He raised a dark eyebrow, and then gave her a long, understanding look. 'You really want to help Josef?'

'Of course.'

'I give you a promise, Carolyn. We will release your Josef if you can help us in the way we want. It might even be possible for the two of you to be together again.'

'What do you want me to do?'

Ivan smiled. He looked round, then leant across the table earnestly. 'Provide us with certain information,' he said.

'I don't think I know anything that would interest you.'

'No, that may be so. But your father does. Or at least he would have access to it.'

Carolyn did not know what to say. She might have realized it would be something like this. She was naive not to have known it. Then she found herself asking, 'What information?'

'There are a number of British firms who have received contracts under the American SDI, Strategic Defence Initiative.'

'Star Wars,' she muttered.

He smiled, and nodded. 'We should like to know the names of those firms. Moreover, your father's ministry has recently received a report from a research unit at the Heriot-Watt University in Edinburgh about the latest designs in optically controlled computers. We would like a copy of that report.'

Carolyn stared at him in astonishment. His sheer audacity, and yet the persuasive urbanity of the man.

'But that would be spying,' she protested.

'Co-operation I would call it. Of course, you don't have to co-operate, Carolyn. Depends how much you want to help Josef, doesn't it? If you really want to get him released . . . '

She felt inadequate to the situation. Her mother, now, would know how to deal with it. But then there was probably nothing *she* wouldn't do for her husband either. Carolyn briefly shuddered at the thought.

'In any event,' she said, 'how do I know that you would release him?'

'You have to trust me. I give you my word.'

'But I would never be able to get that kind of information from my father. He just wouldn't give it to me. Do you think he cares about Josef?'

Ivan shrugged. 'What matters,' he said, 'is how much *you* care. If you want him released, if you want to see him again, then you will help.' He drained off his coffee, and before she could reply called the waiter over to replenish their cups. Then when they were alone again, he did no more than raise his eyebrows.

'I . . . I couldn't,' she said.

'Then Josef — ' He said no more but gestured hopelessly with his hands.

'I couldn't,' Carolyn repeated. 'My father and I don't have that kind of relationship. We are not that close.'

Ivan smoothed his chin. The dark, liquid eyes stared back at her knowingly. He murmured softly, 'But you were once.'

Carolyn was startled. He couldn't possibly mean . . . ? He couldn't know.

'What do you mean?' she asked apprehensively.

He smiled, glanced around to assure himself that they were not overheard, and then leant forward confidentially.

'Oh come,' he said, 'we don't want to talk about that, do we? Shall I just say that we have information that should make it easier for you to get those details from your father. It is information which he would not want made public. Put simply, it would ruin him. That ought to make it easier for you, no?'

She stared at him in disbelief. He might just be bluffing. She tried, tentatively: 'I don't see what information you can possibly have. My father has had an honourable career in the Army, in business, and now in politics.'

Ivan eyed her tolerantly. 'I think,' he said softly, 'we both know what I am talking about. What — ten, eleven years ago? You were about thirteen — yes?'

'You bastards.'

'I thought you wanted to help Josef?'

'You've tortured him. He's the only person who knows. He would never have told you. What have you done to him?'

Ivan was unperturbed. He shrugged. 'I have told you, he is all right . . . he is well. He sends you his love.'

Carolyn strove to control herself. Her facial muscles tightened. She mustn't let him see her distress; only her anger.

'If you've hurt him, I — '

Ivan smiled. 'Come, my dear, let us be realistic. Josef is in

Czechoslovakia. You are here. If you want to get him out, you can. If you don't — well . . . you know, h'mm?'

Carolyn's hands gripped the sides of the table where the cloth draped in folds. She saw her knuckles moon-white. She had seen them like that before — when she had gripped the table in the interrogation room in the STB headquarters in Prague. Only now it was more anger than fear. But she felt trapped, just as she had done then.

Determined to maintain her control, she said quietly, 'Yes, I know.'

'I am only trying to help you,' he said. 'If you can get what we want without making use of . . . ' He paused and added even more quietly, 'Well, the knowledge we have — that is good. But Mr Hailston does not strike us as the kind of man who will part with information very easily. When he learns that we know about his discreditable behaviour with his own daughter — that should help, yes? I am making it easier for you, that's all.'

Carolyn wanted to smack his smiling, handsome face. But a lot of good that would do for her, and even less for Josef. If she was going to be of any use to him, she had no alternative. God, what had they done to him? He had sworn that it was something that would always be known only to them. He would never have betrayed that. So how had they forced it out of him? She shivered at the thought, and in her mind was only the sight of him crouched like an animal in the corner of a cell.

She withdrew her hands into her lap and, without raising her eyes, whispered, 'What do you want me to do?'

'The list of firms' names to start with. That should not be too difficult. Say, in a week's time?'

Carolyn sighed. She was thinking only of Josef . . . what he must have suffered. 'I'll try,' she said. 'Do I bring them here?'

'No, I think perhaps if we meet in the open. Do you know Coldfall Wood?'

Carolyn shook her head.

Ivan reached down the side of the table to his brown leather document case. He took out a street atlas of London and opened it at page 24. 'You see, it is very small. There is open ground to the north of it, and you can enter that from Coppetts Road, and then walk down here' — he indicated with his finger — 'to the wood. There is a seat on the edge. I shall be waiting there. Say, this day next week, at twelve noon.'

'All right,' she said, suddenly determined.

'If you do this for us,' he said, 'I will get Josef to London for you. What about that?'

Carolyn had come to a decision, and she preferred not to think about it any more. It was the image of Josef that she could not shake from her mind. All she did was nod her head.

'Oh, there's one other thing,' he said, putting out his hand to restrain her from leaving the table. 'It is important for us that your father remains at the Ministry of Defence. That is obvious — yes? A vital source of information. You might be able to encourage him to take a certain decision which might ensure his promotion in the Ministry.'

Carolyn struggled to concentrate on what he was saying. He saw her puzzlement, patted her hand, and smiled.

'Decision? What kind of decision?' she asked.

'There is a proposal to build two new villages — very unusual modern development, I believe — in the heart of the countryside in your father's constituency. There will be a lot of local objections, I am sure. Your father might well take the side of the objectors. That would be a mistake.'

Carolyn gasped — half a gasp, half a laugh. 'Why? I don't understand.'

'The company behind these imaginative proposals,' Ivan said authoritatively, 'is Village Life Construction. Now one of the directors of this company is the brother-in-law of the Prime Minister. It seems to us,' he continued, 'that if your father were the cause of this village scheme — which will provide new employment, of course — if he were the cause of it being rejected, that would not please the Prime Minister. Then he would be unlikely to become Secretary of State for Defence, which is what he wants. What we want, too — yes?'

In spite of her mood even Carolyn could not restrain a chuckle. 'British politics don't work that way,' she said. 'Even I know that.'

Ivan gestured with his hands. 'Maybe, maybe not.' He looked at her, as though tolerant of her foolishness. 'He wants to be Defence Secretary, yes?'

'I suppose so.'

'Well, then, it is better he does not disappoint the Prime Minister — that is obvious. It is obvious to us. He would do well to back the village project.'

Carolyn sighed. She got up to leave. This time he made no attempt to stop her, merely confirming, 'A week today.'

She nodded, and walked briskly to the door. She stood for a moment on the other side, between the bay trees, and breathed deeply. She glanced at her watch. It was half-past two.

As she stepped out towards Victoria, she suddenly had the impression that she was being followed. She paused before crossing Buckingham Palace Road and looked sharply behind her. But how could she tell among all those people? It was just an irrational thought. She waited for the lights to change, and then hurried across the road to catch a Circle Line train to Notting Hill Gate.

Carolyn studied her fellow passengers and decided that none of them looked in the least interested in her, apart from a young man who was already in the car when she entered, and whose repeated glances in her direction had more to do with lust than anything else. So it had just been imagination. That wasn't surprising. Her mind was in a turmoil, as she wondered how she was going to approach her father. But it had to be done. She had made that decision in Traceys, and there could be no going back. She was so preoccupied that she nearly missed her stop, having to jump up at the last moment and slip through the doors immediately before they slid shut.

She walked back along the Bayswater Road, and then turned left into the narrow street that led to her flat. As she stepped into the entrance, she heard someone cry, 'Hi there!'

Carolyn looked round into the smiling, freckled face of David Rackham.

'Have you been following me?'

'What an outrageous suggestion.'

His eyes twinkled mischievously.

'No, I'm serious. Have you?'

'I'm serious, too,' he said. 'I haven't. Why?'

'I just had the impression that someone was, while I was waiting to cross Buckingham Palace Road, that's all.'

Rackham eyed her up and down, not disguising his admiration. 'Well, I can understand anyone with good taste following you,' he quipped.

There were circumstances in which Carolyn might have found his manner irritating, but at present she felt so mixed-up and exhausted that his good humour was almost a relief.

'Is it a coincidence that you are here then?' she asked.

'No. I've come to have a chat. May I?'

'Come in.'

He followed her up one flight of stairs. She led him into the room that served as their joint sitting room and dining room. There was a table and four chairs, a divan-type put-u-up with a scatter of bright cushions, and two deep easy chairs with floral-print covers, which he suspected had been discarded from Carolyn's family home. There were two or three original oil paintings, which looked like the work of student artists, and a bookcase, the lower shelf of which was piled with art books. He approved of what he saw — a room that was lived in without being too untidy.

'Coffee?' she inquired. 'Not instant stuff.'

'Thanks.'

While she busied herself in the kitchen, he inspected the other books. Most were also related to art, and there were some dealing specifically with restoration. He sprawled on the divan and waited.

She returned carrying two pottery mugs of hot coffee, handed him one, and lowered herself into one of the armchairs. She felt at ease with Rackham. For some reason, he gave her confidence.

'So,' she said, 'chat. What about?'

'Ah — but first' — he sipped the hot liquid — 'this is good,' he said. 'Do you use gas or electricity here?'

'Electricity. Why?'

'Have you had a visit from an electrician, or from a plumber to see about your taps? Or what about a telephone engineer, because your phone's been out of order?'

'It hasn't. No one has called — why?'

'Good,' he replied, not answering her question. 'Have you heard from Josef?'

She hesitated. 'No.'

'Were you going to add something?'

She paused again, knowing that she was giving herself away. She saw the sceptical look in his hazel-green eyes, as she muttered, 'No, I don't think so.'

Rackham took a long draught of his coffee. Then he said, almost teasingly, 'I thought you were going to tell me why you went to a drinks party at the Czech Embassy last night.'

This time she was unable to hide her surprised expression. 'How did you know?' she asked.

Rackham wagged a finger. 'That's a question you don't ask. But I'll tell you. You were seen.'

'So I *am* being followed?'

He shrugged. 'As a matter of fact, no. But I think perhaps we had better keep an eye on you.'

'We? Should I be grateful?'

'How about answering my question? What were you doing there?'

'I was invited.'

'Of course you were invited. But — '

'I hoped I might find out something about Josef.'

'And did you?'

'They said he was all right.'

'Naturally.' He leant over and put his empty mug on a nearby occasional table, alongside a pile of magazines and books. He got up, strolled casually across the room, and then turned suddenly, facing her. 'So what are they asking you to do?'

'Nothing.' She uttered the word as quickly as she could. Something made her unhappy about lying to Rackham, but she did not see that she had any option.

'They were just being kind to you — making up for arresting you in Prague?'

'I . . . I suppose so.'

Rackham went over to the window, and looked down into the courtyard at a few grubby trees.

'That's not very convincing.' It was almost as though he were talking to himself. Then he turned round and came to stand in front of her, so that she found it impossible not to look at him. 'A confession that they got a lot of publicity out of — Minister's daughter spying for Czechoslovakia — that's a good enough reward for releasing you. But then to have you at an Embassy reception just to say sorry, I don't believe it.'

Had he not been standing immediately in front of her, Carolyn would have got up. She felt the need to move. But there he was, and he didn't believe her.

'What do you expect they want then?' she asked uncertainly.

'Well, I don't think it's your expert knowledge on restoring old masters. You're still learning, aren't you?'

He sounded so off-hand that Carolyn nearly laughed. She liked Rackham, but . . . she wondered how much she dare tell him, and then instantly rejected any thought of it.

'I had some sparkling wine — champagne method I was informed. Are you suggesting that everybody at that reception was there because the Czechs wanted something from them?'

'Very nearly, yes. There are even MPs who have regular contacts with that Embassy. Indeed, there were at least two of them at the reception.'

He returned to the divan and sat on the edge of it, leaning forward.

'You seem so well-informed,' she said, smiling, 'that I'm sure there is nothing I can tell you that you don't know.'

'Flattering, but not true.'

'More coffee?'

'No thanks. Now tell me, how are they blackmailing you?'

She looked up at him, then instantly lowered her eyes. 'They're not,' she lied.

'Don't make it harder for me later, Carolyn . . . please.'

She thought he sounded mocking, and was still wondering how to respond when he spoke again.

'If they're not blackmailing you yet, they soon will be. When do they want to see you again?'

'They . . . ' She hesitated. 'They don't,' she said, 'at least as far as I know.'

Rackham got up and moved towards the door. 'Thanks for the coffee,' he said.

As she got up and came towards him to let him out, he took both her hands, and looked into her eyes. 'Why don't you think things over?' he said. 'I'll be in touch.' Then with a tiny quizzical twist of his lips, he added, 'Czech-mate?'

6

Where the river Thames snakes under Putney Bridge there are a number of narrow streets between the Embankment and Lower Richmond Road packed with small terraced houses. Once they were workmen's dwellings; today, restored and modernized, they have become fashionable small homes and useful for anyone needing a *pied-a-terre* in London. Jane Bacton had managed to buy one of them five or six years ago before prices had become unreasonably high. She had furnished it comfortably and tastefully, and now cherished it for its convenience. So did Stanley Hemingford Hailston MP.

On this particular Thursday evening, he and Jane had settled for a quick and early meal at a nearby bistro, and then returned to her home with an additional bottle of wine, which they took to bed with them. They stood naked, facing one another, each holding a glass of red wine. He trickled a little of it over her pert breasts and caught it in his mouth as it dripped from her nipples. They kissed, exchanged mouthfuls of wine, and then made love slowly and extravagantly.

She was so much better in bed than Esme had ever been. He didn't quite know what he would do if Esme ever showed any interest again. It would be boring after Jane.

Her eyes were half-closed. He ran his hand through the red-blonde of her hair and saw her lazy smile of satisfaction. He supported himself on his elbow and looked at her. She was lovely. Again he reflected on his good fortune, without asking himself if he was in love with her. She was necessary to him.

He urged himself into a half-sitting position against the headboard of the bed. 'You know,' he said, 'if I do become Secretary of State, then — well, once I'm established in the Cabinet, it might be possible for us to . . . make all this legitimate.'

She turned to look at him, her lips parted, her grey eyes sceptical. 'A divorce?' she said incredulously.

'Well, why not?'

Now she sat up completely, half-turned to him and chuckled.

'Oh, darling, that's not like you. You're professional, efficient, a realist. And that was very unrealistic. On what grounds? Besides, you need Esme.'

Too bloody right he did. He knew it.

'I need you too,' he muttered truthfully.

'OK, you've got me. I'm not complaining.'

'But the secrecy — '

'Second nature to you, darling. Let's enjoy it.' She ran her hand over his chest, down over his flat stomach to his thigh. His body was hard with muscle; there was no fat. Her fingers drew invisible lines over the inside of his thighs and back over his stomach.

He could feel himself becoming aroused again. He lay there enjoying the patterning of her fingers, but when he felt her lips puckering on the flesh of his chest, he could bear it no longer, and turned urgently towards her.

'See,' she said afterwards, 'you're my Secret of State. Let's keep it that way. You might not even get the job, darling. In which case,' she laughed, 'you'll have more time to minister to me.'

'I want the job,' he said. 'And I want you too.'

'Well, at any rate, Carolyn's Prague escapade doesn't seem to have made any difference, does it? I told you it wouldn't. If anything the reaction has been sympathetic.'

Hailston nodded, as he slung himself off the bed, and began slowly and methodically to dress. 'A chap from the FO — David Rackham — has been debriefing her, I gather.'

He was silent for a bit, took trouble with his collar and tie, straightening the knot carefully before the mirror. Then he said, 'You know, the PM is taking a bit of a time over this reshuffle. I'd expected it by now.'

'Prime Ministers don't like to seem to be reacting to Press speculation.'

'I suppose not. I just thought I might have had some official hint.'

Jane smiled mysteriously. 'Have you thought about Village Life Construction?'

'Yes. I'm going to fight them.' He looked determined. 'That means I shall win,' he added.

'What does Esme think?'

'She agrees. It would set a precedent for other developments all over the country. Nothing would be safe.'

She slipped off the bed and slithered into a brightly patterned kimono. Hailston couldn't take his gaze from her.

'A slight exaggeration, darling?'

Hailston shook his head. 'I don't think so. Once you have plonked one of these village developments in the middle of un-spoilt countryside in Sussex, why not do it in Northumberland?'

'Have you studied the brief Village Life have sent you?'

'Yes — bloody plausible. I don't like it. But, more important, I know my constituents won't like it. Esme tells me they won't like it, so does Sir Courtney.'

She sat on the bed, swinging one leg provocatively over the other. 'You ought to see them, oughtn't you?'

'They haven't asked for a meeting.'

'They're bound to.'

'Well, when they do, I'll see them. But I'm not likely to change my mind.'

She looked up seductively over her skilfully defined eyebrows, smiling faintly, and Hailston began to feel that, if he stayed much longer, he would want her again.

'A bit stubborn?' she teased.

'You know me.'

'H'mm. What do you want most? After me, I mean,' she smiled.

'Secretary of State — you know that.'

'You know who the MD of Village Life is, don't you?'

'Tell me.'

'The Prime Minister's brother-in-law.'

Hailston stroked his moustache, considering.

'The development,' Jane continued, 'would provide a lot of jobs. That should recommend it to the Prime Minister.'

'You got shares or something?'

Jane laughed. 'No. I'm giving the facts, love.'

Hailston considered again. 'I've got more faith in Sir Courtney and Esme.'

'Well, think about it. More employment. And the scheme's being promoted by a relative, even if only by marriage. That might be enough to tip the balance. And if the Prime Minister should decide to back it, that might influence the PM's thinking on your appointment.'

'Are you telling me I wouldn't be made Secretary of State if I opposed this project?'

'Even Prime Ministers are human — so they tell me.'

'Well,' Hailston exploded, 'if I believed it was a choice between Courtney's influence with the PM — he's an old friend, you know — and the brother-in-law — '

'And more employment,' Jane chipped in.

'I still think Courtney would swing it.'

Jane shrugged. 'Think about it,' she said, as she got up, came to him, and stroked her hands down the lapels of his jacket. Then she kissed him fully on the lips.

The silk partly fell away from her body, and Hailston wished that he was staying. But he heard the taxi before she did. He had never lost his old SAS alertness. He had learned that in the jungles of Borneo. The faintest sound — the skitter of a leaf to the ground, the brushing of a moving tendril — could determine death or survival. He had automatically noted the sound of the taxi long before it had idled to a stop precisely at half-past nine.

For a moment they clung to each other behind the front door. Then Jane left him to open it alone, calling to him just before he did so: 'Don't forget your injection.'

She was always reminding him. It was as well that she did, because he sometimes found the pressure of his job forcing the immediacy of it from his mind.

There was a three-line Whip tonight which required his vote at the Commons at ten o'clock. After that he would go home to Chester Square. Then he and Esme were going down to Sussex on Friday, just as soon as he could escape from the Ministry.

The traffic was heavy, and by the time he strode, erect and purposeful, through the Members' entrance, bells were ringing and policemen throughout the Palace of Westminster were shouting, from one to another, 'DIVISION!' Each syllable was given a long emphasis.

It was the second reading of a Bill in which he had not the slightest departmental interest and about which he knew even less. The three heavy lines on the piece of paper known as the Government Whip, however, meant that his vote was regarded as essential for the government's majority. He made his way into the Aye lobby — a long and wide book-lined corridor to the right of the Speaker's chair. Soon it was crowded with ministerial and backbench colleagues, who had come from the chamber or hurried from all parts of the Palace and beyond. He made himself friendly, exchanging political small talk with anyone who was so inclined. After the doors had been locked, and he had called out his name, filed past the two clerks sitting at their high oak desks, and shuffled through the narrow door where a Whip from each party loudly checked the number of votes, he returned to his own room and sat there for a few minutes, quietly.

Hailston felt confident. Things were going well. He was due for promotion, of that he was certain. Even some of the hostile

Press had conceded that he was one of the most able of the lower-ranking ministers in the government. He was going to achieve his ambition. He felt sure of it.

He had to wait only a couple of minutes beneath the great canopy of the Members' entrance before a taxi swung round New Palace Yard to take him back to Chester Square. He was really quite looking forward to seeing Esme.

Mrs Drury opened the door for him just as he was fiddling with his key.

'Sure, I thought I heard you, sir,' she said. 'Miss Carolyn's in the drawing room. She came about half-an-hour ago. And Mrs Hailston has gone down to Sussex.'

Hailston thanked her and assured her that there was nothing further he wanted that night, and then made his way briskly to the drawing room. Carolyn was looking at television. She promptly got up and switched it off.

'That's all right,' said Hailston. 'Don't let me stop you.'

'I don't really want it. I was just waiting for you.'

'I was expecting your mother to be here.'

To his daughter Hailston always called Esme 'your mother'. He couldn't bring himself to use anything so sloppy as 'Mummy', and somehow he had come to think of Carolyn as Esme's daughter. Since she had grown up it had been impossible for him to be close to her. He had always felt a barrier there. At first he had thought it was created from his own guilt, but it wasn't only that.

'She had intended to be,' Carolyn said, 'but Sir Courtney rang, and Mummy said there was an awful lot to do tomorrow, especially as you couldn't be sure what time you'd be free. So she decided to go down there tonight. She tried to get hold of you, but couldn't get a reply anywhere.'

'I did go out for a meal with a colleague,' he muttered. 'Otherwise, I've been at the House.'

'Do you want a scotch?' she asked. 'You usually have one when you come in, don't you?'

'Sometimes. But, no thank you.'

Carolyn shrugged. 'I think I'll have a gin. Do you mind?'

'Not at all. Help yourself.'

She did, putting in liberal quantities of ice and tonic.

'So there's something you want to see me about?' Hailston automatically squared back his shoulders.

Carolyn was standing about four feet from him, and she looked steadily at him as she sought within herself to feel something of her mother's poise and control. She felt nothing for him, nothing at all. And she had her own life. She chinked the ice in her glass. She, too, squared back her shoulders.

'I told you about Josef,' she began.

'The fellow in Prague?'

'Yes. They've still got him. He's still in prison.'

'I expect he is. They don't like dissidents.' Hailston felt his time was being wasted.

'And they've tortured him.'

'That wouldn't surprise me either. What do you want, Carolyn — sympathy? He can't mean that much to you. He's one of hundreds. Of course they've tortured him.'

He turned away and stood with his back to the Adam-style fireplace. 'There's nothing I can do. There's nothing the Foreign Office can do. It's got nothing to do with us. He's a Czech.'

Carolyn felt her anger rising. She took a gulp at her drink, and controlled herself.

'I can get him out of prison,' she said.

'Don't be absurd.'

'I've seen them.'

'Seen who? The Czechs?'

'Yes.'

'You damned fool. You ought to have more sense than that — especially after what happened in Prague.'

She looked at him resolutely over her brows, determined not to give way. She said firmly, 'They will release him in exchange for some information.'

Hailston snorted with contempt. 'And you believe it?'

'I haven't any alternative. I want him freed.' She sipped at her gin, paced the carpet. 'I'm in love with him.'

'Don't be ridiculous. You hardly know him. And all he succeeded in doing was getting you bloody well arrested. The whole thing might have blown up into something that could have — well, ruined my chances.'

'Your chances! What about his life, his freedom?'

Hailston looked at her as he might have looked at an anti-NATO protester. It was useless pretending that he had any filial feeling for her. He couldn't avoid showing his scorn.

'I don't care about it, Carolyn.'

Now she was angry. She bit her bottom lip, controlling herself. She said as quietly but as determinedly as she could, 'But I do care. I care very much. And if there is anything I can do to get him out, I shall do it.'

'By all means go and parade with a banner outside the Czech Embassy. You're bound to find some other cranks who'll join you. Why bother me?'

She thought of her mother's quiet, elegant style, and tried to emulate it. 'Because,' she said calmly, 'you have the information I need. Or you can get it.'

Hailston flicked at his crisp moustache with the side of his forefinger, and stared at her in disbelief. Carolyn watched him silently. He thrust his hands defiantly on his hips.

'Have I got this right? You've seen the bloody Czechs, they've asked you to get some information from me and, in exchange, they'll release this fellow Josef Foerster?'

Carolyn nodded. To give herself confidence she sat on the broad arm of one of the Sanderson-covered chairs, with one shapely leg swung over the other. She swilled the remains of her gin and tonic in the bottom of the glass.

'That's more or less right,' she said.

'I'm damned.' Hailston was incredulous. 'You seriously think — ?' He shook his head in astonishment. 'They're asking me to spy for them, and blackmailing you to get me to do it? You don't think I'd — ?'

'I love him,' she said firmly. 'I've told you — I'll do anything. If you had seen the way they treated him — '

'But I didn't. And I couldn't bloody care.'

'I do care,' she repeated. 'You don't understand. I've told you, there's nothing I won't do.'

'Don't be such a fool. You could ruin all of us with this damn nonsense. The fact is, you'll do nothing . . . do you understand? The whole thing is preposterous.'

He looked at her with a mixture of scorn and dislike. Her own eyes were bright with anger, but she was determined to remain cool, purposeful.

'I'll tell you what it is they want,' she said.

As though ignoring her, he turned away crossly from the fireplace and went and stood by the long folds of the velvet curtains drawn across the windows. She remained seated on the arm of the chair. She felt more confident that way. There was only the remains of the ice in her glass. She chinked it noisily before putting the glass aside.

'You're wasting my time, Carolyn. And your own.'

'They want a list of those firms who have been contracted to do special defence work under the American SDI programme.'

Hailston snorted again contemptuously. 'Some of that's public knowledge.'

'Not the important contracts. Those are the names they want.'

'I'm sure they do. On behalf of their Soviet masters. You don't honestly think that I — ?' He broke off, speechless with indignation.

Swinging her crossed leg as casually as she could, Carolyn added, 'Apparently your Ministry has recently received a top secret report from the Heriot-Watt University about the latest research into optically controlled computers. They want a copy of that, too.'

'I . . . I can't believe I'm hearing this.' Hailston strode the length of the room, then stopped in front of her. He controlled his anger. 'Look,' he said, 'you'll have nothing to do with them. Keep away from them. Forget the whole thing. There's nothing they can do to you, or me. Finish.' He flung his hands apart as though he were cutting something off irrevocably.

Deliberately looking down into her lap, she said, 'There is something they can do. They can ruin you.'

'Huh,' he scoffed. 'You're being absurd.'

He stepped back as slowly she got to her feet. She stood facing him. 'There's one thing you haven't understood,' she said. 'My determination to do all I can to help Josef.' She paused. 'That's because I love him, and because I owe him so much.'

Hailston took a deep breath. He felt indignant, impatient, angry, but he maintained a taut control of himself, as he replied, 'More important, Carolyn, there's one thing that you too have not understood. This has nothing to do with me. I refuse to be concerned with your lovesick feelings for some bloody fool in a Czech jail, and I order you to have nothing further to do with this business. You will not see these Czechs again. That's an end of it.'

He was about to stride away, but she put out a hand to his arm to restrain him. He turned back in astonishment.

Carolyn reminded herself that she was going to stay cool. 'I'm sorry,' she said, 'I hoped you would help me without . . . ' Her voice trailed away. She looked up at him, saw something near hatred in the cold blue of his eyes. She continued reluctantly, 'Without me having to tell you.'

'Tell me — what?'

'*We're* being blackmailed,' she said quietly. 'They know . . . they know . . . about us.'

Hailston shifted uneasily. He saw that it had been painful for her. 'I'd hoped you'd forgotten,' he said awkwardly. 'It was a long time ago.'

'Eleven years,' she murmured, barely audible. Then looking directly at him again, she said fiercely, 'Forget? You thought I could forget? God!'

'You bloody told them,' he shouted, his shame finding refuge in sudden anger. 'You — '

Carolyn shook her head. 'No. It doesn't matter how they know. But they do. I told you they could ruin you.'

He looked at her coldly. 'So I provide you with the list of names, or they make public my . . . ' He searched for the word, and rejected 'indiscretion' for a heavily emphasized, 'tragic mistake?' He grunted derisively. 'Tell 'em to go to hell.'

She stood her ground, close to him, feeling the chill of his hostility.

'Tragic mistake — that's what you call it?' she said, quietly mocking.

Part of Hailston — the residual feeling of shame — wanted to explain, to insist that there were unusual circumstances, a kind of justification. But the experienced Hailston preferred to dismiss the past, to reject any significance that it could have had, and to disclaim any affection for her. So he ignored the remark. 'I said tell 'em to go to hell. How're they going to do it? Through *Private Eye*? No one would believe it. The whole story would be laughed out of court.' He looked at her scornfully. 'My God, you're naive, Carolyn, if you think rubbish like that can do me any damage.'

She stepped back from him. Then suddenly the anger snapped in her. 'You bastard. You bastard,' she shouted. 'Don't you know what you did to me? I was damaged. Soiled. My own father. Me, naive? Can't you even imagine what you did? I couldn't face a man — not like that. I was finished. Finished, before I'd known anything. You made it impossible for me . . . '

She could feel her nails biting into the palms of her hands, and tears trickling on to her cheeks. 'Impossible! Impossible!' she cried. 'Do you know what I did?' she continued, now quite distracted. 'D'you know? I even shaved myself. Yes, to keep myself like a little girl, unspoilt, unblemished . . . to keep me like I was before you did it to me.' She wiped away the tears with the back of her hand, sniffed, then reached for a handkerchief and wiped her face. She looked up at him, to meet the hatred of his cold blue eyes. She felt suddenly calm again. She turned away from him, took his former position by the fireplace.

Hailston growled, stroked his moustache irritably. 'All right, you've got that off your chest, have you?'

'Father,' she said, once more in control of herself, 'I think you should let me have that list of names. You've plenty of time to get them. I'm to hand them over at twelve noon, next Thursday — Coldfall Wood. You should be able to get them by then, shouldn't you?'

'You're mad. I've told you, they can go to hell. Nobody would believe whatever rubbish they put out.' He came and stood in front of her, his expression one of near contempt.

She said, almost in a whisper, 'I owe my escape from you to Josef. I'll do anything for him. Even if you were to brazen it all out, it would still be an unpleasant atmosphere, wouldn't it?'

'Nothing I couldn't deal with.'

'There's one person who would believe it — and that would finish you.'

'What do you mean?'

'Mummy. You need her. For her money, if nothing else.'

'That's the last thing your mother would believe. What? A bloody Communist conspiracy to do down a British politician? She wouldn't give it a thought.'

'She would believe it all right — if I told her.'

'You bitch. You bloody little bitch.'

She didn't have time to move before the flat of his hand swiped her stingingly across the cheek and sent her reeling towards the wall.

Hailston showed no sign of regretting his action. He stood glowering at her. Already he was beginning to calculate his chances of getting some names together. It would be the end if Esme knew. That possibility had always been an apprehensive shadow in the back of his mind. Nothing was going to prevent him being Secretary of State if that's what the Prime Minister wanted — certainly not a blackmailing little bitch of a daughter. He knew well enough that even an article in *Private Eye*, skating just the right side of the law but laced with innuendo, would be enough to put the PM off. No government wanted a scandal.

Carolyn recovered her balance and stepped further away from him. She did not feel afraid. She simply despised him.

'I think we have a deal,' she said.

He turned away and strode towards the door. 'I begin to understand why I've never really liked you,' he snapped.

'Except when I was a child,' she called, as he slammed the door.

7

Carolyn saw nothing of her father in the days that followed her visit to Chester Square, but on the succeeding Wednesday an envelope was delivered to her flat by hand. She slit it open. Inside was a list of company names and addresses, occupying two sheets of paper.

There was nothing on the envelope or on the paper to indicate where they had come from. Carolyn smiled to herself as she read them through. Except for the occasional well-known name they meant nothing to her. That only left a copy of the research report. If necessary she would have to see her father again. The prospect no longer daunted her.

More than once in the intervening days she had wondered to herself whether she would ever tell her mother. It would make her so desperately unhappy, shatter so many convictions. Yet, if it were a choice between leaving Josef in a Czechoslovak prison cell or the chance of him being released, she knew she would not hesitate. It looked as though she was not going to have to make that choice.

David Rackham had telephoned her and asked if there was anything she wanted to tell him, and she hoped that he had not noted her hesitation when she answered, 'No. I don't think so.' Then, deliberately to match his own light-hearted tone, she had added, 'Is there anything you want to tell me?'

'Yes,' said Rackham. 'I like red-heads, and I like blondes.

So someone who is a mixture of both must be extremely likeable. How about having lunch?'

'What, so you can persuade me to tell you something I haven't got to tell?'

'Sounds complicated. But, yes, if you like.'

Carolyn approved his facetious style. He was amusing, good company, but she suspected that his manner disguised a much shrewder temperament, and she was afraid of his skill in eliciting information that she saw no reason to disclose. So reluctantly she had told him that she would love to have lunch with him, but she hadn't got a free day at the moment. She would let him know when she had.

'That,' he said cheerily, 'is a brush off.'

'No, just a flick,' she said.

Then suddenly serious, he added, 'You're not being black-mailed, are you?'

'No.'

'I hope I'm not going to have to insist on seeing you.'

'Threatening?'

He laughed. 'A pity you haven't thought things over yet.'

Afterwards Carolyn wondered if Rackham knew more than he pretended. If that were so, ought she to confide in him? She didn't believe for a moment that he was really from the Foreign Office. He might, of course, merely be making excuses to see her. The thought amused her. She decided that, for the moment, she had to handle this thing herself. In any event, she couldn't imagine that Rackham would be very interested in getting Josef out of Czechoslovakia, especially on the terms offered. So when the envelope arrived with its list of names she felt, with quiet satisfaction, that she was making progress.

Rackham, for his part, was also facing the prospect of an unwelcome interruption. It began with a summons from the Director-General of the Secret Intelligence Service himself, Sir Dick Randle.

He was a tall, thin, ascetic-looking man with a wide forehead, receding hair, and a sharp triangle of a face. The rather bent, crane-like appearance was accentuated by his aquiline nose, which he had a habit of stroking with his forefinger when he was thinking. He was doing it, as he leant against the mantel-shelf, when Rackham went in. He came straight to the point.

'Beetle wants out,' he said.

'Do we want him?'

'You mean, like Čapek's character, he's collected his ball of dung, and there's no more to be had?' Sir Dick said wryly.

'Something like that. He could continue to be useful in Prague, but what can he give us if he defects?'

'I've considered that. Admittedly, nothing momentous, but a useful contribution to our general sum of knowledge.'

'So?'

Sir Dick stroked his nose. 'Since you're looking after this Hailston business, I thought you should get him out.'

'When?'

'Soon. He thinks they may be on to him. I expect you can manage a trip to Prague.'

'Have you ever tried eating their food?'

'Rackham, don't you ever take life seriously?'

Rackham grinned. 'Am I making my own arrangements?'

Sir Dick nodded loftily. 'Then you've only yourself to blame.'

'This talk in the Press about a Cabinet reshuffle — do we know when it's going to happen?'

Sir Dick shook his head, and a thin strand of hair fell over his brow. 'That is not our concern,' he said. 'We shouldn't let it interfere with our own timetable.'

Rackham sighed. 'Oh, "The persons I pity who know not the city, The beautiful city of Prague".'

A Thursday was really just about the most inconvenient day so far as Hailston was concerned, but this was an opportunity not to be missed. He was not yet sure how he would make use of the photograph, but he felt instinctively that it was going to be useful to have it. So he loaded his camera with a roll of twelve exposures of 35-millimetre film, and fitted his zoom lens. He had no idea where Coldfall Wood was and had to look it up in a London street map. He found it a little north-west of Muswell Hill Broadway. He drove there in his own car and, to ensure that Carolyn would not spot it, parked it in a side street about half a mile away. He deliberately arrived early, and approached Coldfall Wood from Creighton Avenue. The wood itself, he reckoned, was not much more than two hundred and fifty yards square. He was able to explore it thoroughly, and note how it led into open ground to the north. He presumed Carolyn and the Czech would both approach from that direction. He was able to position himself some distance from the seat, well hidden by trees. With his zoom lens focused on it, he would get a good half-length close-up.

As he crept through the trees and finally settled himself he felt, almost like a memory in the bloodstream, something of the zest and tension he had known those years ago, tracking with infinite care silently through the jungle of Borneo. This was what he was professionally good at. He waited, totally still and quiet.

The Czech arrived first, went straight to the seat and sat down. Hailston shot four frames, when he saw Carolyn arrive from the same direction. The Czech rose to greet her. He still had a perfect view of the man, and Carolyn was standing with her back three-quarters to him. Hailston checked that his focus was pin-sharp, and pressed the shutter four more times. He succumbed to an old feeling of satisfaction and personal pride.

He edged back silently, further into the wood. As he did so he saw his daughter move towards the seat. There was no need for him to wait any longer. He had got what he wanted.

He checked that his retreat could not be seen from where the pair of them sat, then walked swiftly and quietly back the way he had come. A spaniel dog came bounding towards him, followed by a woman, who said, 'I don't know where he gets his energy.' Hailston only nodded.

He stopped his car once on the return journey, leaving it briefly on a yellow line in the West End, while he took the film into a shop offering a twenty-four hour service.

He had missed his lunch, and that wouldn't do him any good. He reckoned he would have time for a snack in the Members' Cafeteria when he got to the House. By the time he was in the narrow lift that led up from the underground car park in New Palace Yard he was feeling slightly off-colour. He recognized the signs. Maintaining regular eating habits was not always easy with his kind of life. He made his way to the cafeteria as fast as he could.

Normally Carolyn's bright red Ford Fiesta spent the week in a lock-up garage near her flat, but this Thursday morning, she drove it through back streets across Paddington to Regent's Park, and then north to Highgate and Muswell Hill. She parked it some distance away in a side road off Colney Hatch Lane, and then made her approach to Coldfall Wood from the north, entering the open ground from Coppetts Road. It was a bright day, although the sun was weak, but birds were singing, and she felt a lightening of spirits as she stepped out across the rough grassland towards the wood. She was alone — no one else taking advantage of this small but surprising green oasis amid a semi-detached suburbia.

There was the wood. And there was the seat, and Ivan. She quickened her pace, approached him smiling. He rose to greet her.

'So you have come,' he said. 'How sensible. I think this is what you call an English day — yes?'

'It would be if the sun was a little more sure of itself.'

Ivan looked so effortlessly self-assured, aware of his own charm. He indicated the seat. They both sat down.

Carolyn eased away her shoulder-bag, unzipped it, and removed a white foolscap envelope. Ivan appeared to know that they were alone without looking round. 'It is very good here,' he said. 'Surprisingly few people use it . . . a few with their dogs. Not big enough, I suppose.'

She handed over the envelope.

'Ah, so Mr Hailston understood?'

'I hope that's what you want,' she said. 'The research report — I think that should follow later.'

'I hope so.'

He somehow had managed to inject those three words both with polite gratitude and implied threat.

He slit the envelope neatly and withdrew the two sheets of paper. He looked down the typewritten list of names and addresses, and his expression changed.

'These are no good,' he said brusquely. 'Does Hailston think we are fools?'

'What do you mean?'

'This is a list of well-known British companies. Two of them are engaged on SDI research. That has been announced publicly. The others are not.'

'But how do you know?'

He smiled tolerantly, without warmth. 'We do know, Carolyn.'

She sighed, despairingly.

Ivan turned to look at her. 'I hope you take me seriously,' he said. 'This kind of thing is not going to help Josef Foerster at all. Do you understand?'

Carolyn nodded. She felt angry and cheated. 'I didn't know,' she said. 'I didn't know.'

Smoothly, almost soothingly, but still without the suggestion of a smile, Ivan replied, 'I believe you, Carolyn. But your father must understand we shall not tolerate this kind of thing. If this happens again . . . ' He spread his hands. 'We shall make it public. And Josef . . . oh, poor Josef.'

Carolyn bit her lower lip. 'All right,' she said suddenly, 'all right, I'll make him give them to me.'

'And the report.'

'Yes, and the report.'

'Shall we have another little lunch at Traceys? Say next Wednesday?'

Very precisely, Ivan refolded the two sheets of paper, replaced them in the envelope and handed it to her. Then he got up and walked away.

For a few moments Carolyn remained motionless on the seat. In the quiet, she was conscious of the birdsong. Then she thought of Josef — saw him huddled in the corner of that Prague cell. A few seconds later, she got up, angry and determined.

Carolyn's rage had driven all thought of lunch from her mind. It had not even subsided when, less than an hour later, she ran up the white steps between the columns of the Ministry of Defence in Horseguards Avenue. At the reception desk they telephoned her father's office. A secretary informed her that Mr Hailston was not at the Ministry. He had gone down to the Commons. She turned on her heel, and hurried back to Whitehall to the nearest telephone kiosk.

She punched out the number of her father's room in the House of Commons. Jane Bacton answered. No, she was sorry, Mr Hailston wasn't there. She didn't know where he was. She expected him back in the Commons later in the afternoon.

'Are you sure he's not there?' Carolyn insisted.

There was a pause before Jane, astonished, said, 'Why, of course. I really don't know where he is.'

Carolyn hung up. Knots of staring tourists were clustered about the red-coated, bearskinned guardsmen on their sleek horses at the entrance to Horseguards. She pushed her way through them, crossed over the parade ground to St James's Park. She walked briskly along the paths, preoccupied, feeling the need to work off energy. Then she slumped into a deck chair, and thought. He had got to come up with the information. She didn't give a damn about his political ambition, but she did care about her mother. She didn't want to give her the suffering and anguish of knowing. But if there was no alternative, then her mother was going to have to know.

It was early afternoon when she walked across St Margaret's churchyard to the telephone box opposite the Houses of Parliament. Again she phoned her father's office, and again Jane said he still had not come in but, as he was not at the Ministry, she was sure he would be returning shortly.

Carolyn was still not sure whether she believed Jane Bacton. She crossed the road to St Stephen's entrance, and at the security booths, where her handbag was checked, she explained that she was meeting her father in the Central Lobby.

Carolyn took her place, like many a constituent, on one of the green-leather benches at one side of this richly decorated, octagonal space that served as a kind of crossroads in the Houses of Parliament — the Lords in one direction, the Commons in the other. Footsteps echoed on the ornately tiled floor, and seventy-five feet above her arched the embossed ceiling with its Venetian mosaics, emblems of England, Ireland and Scotland and, in the centre, the enormous brass chandelier. She felt that the whole scene, in its Gothic splendour, was meant to overawe, with its statues of Parliamentary figures and monarchs in niches; and, indeed, it was awesomely impressive.

After about fifteen minutes she approached one of the policemen standing by the high desk at the entrance to the corridor leading to the Members' Lobby. She asked to fill in a green card for Mr Hailston. The policeman looked at her intently for a moment.

'Aren't you Miss Hailston, Miss Carolyn Hailston?' he asked. 'Yes.'

'Thought I recognized you. Don't worry about the card. We'll see if we can find him for you. Have you checked his room?'

Carolyn confirmed that she had. The policeman summoned a colleague, who said he'd have a look in the likely places — the library, the tearoom, the Members' Lobby, and so on. Meanwhile Carolyn scribbled a terse note to her father explaining where she was waiting for him, and this was taken to the message board in the Members' Lobby. She resumed her seat, and about fifteen minutes later, the young policeman returned to say that he hadn't found Mr Hailston anywhere in the Palace. The senior officer asked if she would like to be taken to his room, but Carolyn declined. She didn't want to say what she had to say in front of Jane. There was nothing for it but to sit and wait.

In the next couple of hours she watched people coming and going across the patterned tiles — some of them turning into the carpeted corridor, past the John Piper painting of the bombed chamber, to the Strangers' Gallery; others filling in green cards in the hope of seeing their MPs and then, like her, sitting down to wait. Sometimes little groups collected, whispering to each other.

The longer she waited the more determined she became. Whether or not Ivan was to be trusted had become irrelevant. She had no choice; it was her only hope. The only thing she could possibly do that had the remotest chance of helping Josef. Her father was going to have no choice either.

At last he came, stepping briskly along the corridor from the Members' Lobby. He looked athletic, commanding and confident. He gave a little brush to his short moustache as he approached.

'What is it?' he asked peremptorily as she rose to meet him.

'You know damn well what it is.' She held out the white envelope.

'Keep your voice down,' he said. 'This place is like an echo chamber.'

For a brief moment she felt like shouting at the top of her voice, but she found herself saying quietly, 'Those names — they were phoney.'

'For God's sake, Carolyn, not here.' He took the envelope from her.

'Where then? There isn't much time. I shan't hesitate, you know.' Her voice rose. 'I shan't. I've told you.'

'All right, all right.' He spoke through his gritted teeth, as he watched her, his eyes cold with calculation. 'Your mother's at home. So your flat this evening?'

'Yes. Toni's out. She'll be late. But you'd better come. If you don't, I . . . well, you know.'

'I shall be there,' he said irritably. He turned about, as though he were on a parade ground and marched back to the Members' Lobby.

Carolyn spent the evening reading and listening to music — for sentimental reasons, Dvořák and Smetana. The two things both calmed her and reinforced her resolution. She would try to emulate her mother's dignity. She must not let him provoke her. She must keep control. After all, she held the cards. She didn't consider for one moment that what she was doing might be dangerous. There was an overriding imperative: a man in a small cell in central Prague.

It was about eight-thirty when she let her father in.

'I thought perhaps you'd be even later,' she said.

'I'm paired.' He stood by the dining table, resting on it, as though emphasizing that he did not intend to stay.

Carolyn reclined on the put-u-up, intent on appearing at ease.

'Now,' she said coolly, 'those names weren't the list at all.'

'Of course they weren't. I'm not giving information to those bloody Czechs for you, or anyone — least of all for you.'

'I don't see it as giving information to the Czechs,' she said with the same calm. 'I see it as helping to get a man I care deeply about out of jail.'

'I don't give a damn how you see it.'

There was no mistaking the cold hostility in his pale blue eyes.

'So when it becomes known that you raped your thirteen-year-old daughter, you think the Prime Minister will say, "Oh dear, how unfortunate," and make you Secretary of State for Defence?'

Hailston winced. The little bitch. She could destroy him. And she would, he could see she would. What was she saying?

'If you think I wouldn't dare tell Mummy,' Carolyn continued, leaning as casually as she could on her elbow, 'I would. At first, I thought I couldn't do that, for her sake. But I've thought about it,' she added, with something near to his own crisp determination, 'and I would do it. If you don't bring me those names — the right ones — I shall tell her everything. I shall. I don't care about your ambition, your career. It's nothing.'

Hailston had no doubt that she was speaking the truth. He could see in her a mixture of his own toughness and Esme's cool dignity. And this was the creature, his own daughter, who was going to destroy him just when he was likely to achieve his political ambition. The hell she was. He wasn't going to let her, or anyone, do that — not now. He felt the fury like an uncontrollable energy. Only his old training held it in check. There was no point in arguing with her. He could see that.

Turning his head away, he said, 'When do you want them?'

She answered immediately. 'Monday.' That gave her another day if he again proved difficult. 'And the report,' she added.

He glowered at her. 'I can't get that by then.'

'Then the names had better be right this time. They'll know if not. And if they're not, I'm going straight to explain everything to Mummy. I . . . I just don't care.'

He glared. 'My God,' he seethed. 'You're a nasty calculating little bitch.'

She made no reply, still sitting back at ease. He took a step or two towards her, and for a moment she felt a quick shaft of cold fear. Somehow she managed to hold his gaze.

'I don't have to stay here any longer,' he snarled, turned quickly on his heel and walked out.

* * *

Hailston thought Jane Bacton looked more disconcerted than surprised when she opened the front door to him.

'Oh, hello,' she said, 'was I expecting you?'

'I suppose not.'

'But what a nice surprise. I thought I'd lost you until Monday.'

Hailston strode past her in the narrow hall. She followed him into her small sitting room.

'What is it?' she asked.

'I had to be with you — that's all.'

'Something's the matter, isn't it?' She stood near him, looking into his eyes.

He cupped his hand at the back of her head, drew her near to him and kissed her fiercely. 'Not now,' he said.

Jane shook her red-blonde hair free, then held him close, feeling the hardness of his muscular body. 'I'm sure something or someone has upset you,' she murmured.

'No one's going to stop me now.'

She knew well enough what he was talking about. The strength of his ambition had always attracted her. 'And who is trying to?' she whispered.

He wanted her, wanted to submerge his anxieties in her body. He kissed her again, running his hands down her back. 'Carolyn,' he gritted through his teeth. 'She's a little bitch,' he muttered, kissing her again and pressing his body urgently against hers.

'I don't understand.'

'I can't tell you — not now. I will — eventually. Jane, I want you — God, I want you.'

Hailston took her quickly, almost roughly, on the floor where they had been standing. Then they dragged themselves on to the couch, and he let her soothe him with her hands. Sometime later she said quietly, 'That was all a bit desperate, darling.'

'I needed you,' was all he said. But he was not at all sure what he had achieved. Had he been trying to obliterate something, to wipe out a memory perhaps, or relive it as a kind of expurgation?

* * *

112

By the time Hailston let himself into the Chester Square house he was feeling much calmer, and the sight of Esme somehow reinforced his self-assurance. He could see her as the wife of the Secretary of State, even eventually of the Prime Minister.

As she stood at the sideboard, pouring his scotch, she glanced over her shoulder and said, 'Sir Courtney phoned.'

'Oh yes.' He noted, as she handed him his drink, her small secretive smile of pleasure.

'Yes,' she said, 'he's spent the evening with the PM.'

Hailston looked up, distinctly more interested. He had feared it might have been those damned projects by Village Life Construction, or perhaps the oil-drilling applications.

'Come on, old girl,' he said, 'out with it.'

'Well, he says he doesn't think the Prime Minister will reshuffle the Cabinet for at least another fortnight, but Sir Courtney got the impression that there was little doubt about your appointment. They are old friends, after all, and the PM even values Sir Courtney's advice.'

Beneath his crisp moustache Hailston's lips moved into a stern smile. He got up, raised his glass. 'Here's to it then,' he said. 'The Right Honourable Stanley Hemingford Hailston MP, Secretary of State for Defence. A couple of years, Esme, and then, Sir Stanley Hailston, h'mm?'

He gulped at the scotch, and Esme took his other hand and squeezed it. 'If you want it, I'm sure that's what it will be,' she said.

He nodded, his expression one of pleasurable anticipation. Then he turned away, as though thinking, but Esme had noticed that suddenly he had become more grimly serious. He stood with one elbow on the Adam-style fireplace, staring down at the brass dogs in the grate. He was thinking, thinking hard. Nothing now, nobody must stand in his way.

He finished his whisky, then had a few moments of inconsequential chat with Esme about their constituency engagements for the weekend. Ultimately he said, 'Look, don't wait up, darling. There's a bit of work I want to do, and then I'll be up as quickly as I can.'

She was immediately understanding. 'Oh, all right then. Don't be long. I'm sure you need the rest. We've got quite a weekend.'

'Yes, on second thoughts, you'd better go down first thing in the morning. I shan't be able to get away, certainly until the afternoon.'

Esme was not surprised. It was by no means an unusual occurrence. By now she was accustomed to the strange exigencies of his job. It would be worse when he became Secretary of State.

'All right,' she said. 'But don't overdo things.' Then she left him sitting thoughtfully in one of the floral print-covered chairs.

Hailston immediately poured himself another scotch. All of this could be so easily destroyed, the Cabinet job snatched from him. Bloody hell, it could. Bloody hell, it wasn't going to be.

He would have to provide the list of names — that was certain. There was no alternative. But that would be the one and only concession. Then the threat would have been removed. All right, there would be publicity again, but it would be linked to the previous story and, if anything, would only engender more sympathy for him.

There wasn't much time. That was the only problem. He downed the scotch, stroked his moustache reflectively, then buried his head in his hands, searching his mind.

Sergeant Bill Hunter — what had happened to him? He was a brave bugger, ruthless. Civilian life had not suited him all that well. He'd done a bit of mercenary work in Angola, been damned lucky to avoid the 'Colonel Callan' fiasco, but then Hunter had always had a way of slipping out of imminent danger. After that Hailston had taken him on for some of the riskier assignments of the security firm he had managed before going into politics. Since then they hadn't seen much of each other. Once at a reunion they had exchanged addresses and telephone numbers, but had done nothing about it, perhaps because both had recognized that, since their SAS days and their brief spell together afterwards, they had each gone their separate ways. Maybe Hunter had thought his old captain had become too respectable.

Hailston went into his study, found an old address book in his desk. He turned over the pages . . . G, H — there it was: Bill Hunter, with an address in Wembley and a telephone number.

Hailston immediately picked up the telephone and punched out the number. No, Hunter wasn't there, but he had left an address in Camden Town for forwarding mail. Hailston then tried directory enquiries with the name and the new address. This time he was luckier, and was about to call the number when he had second thoughts. No point in taking an unnecessary risk.

He let himself out of the front door quietly, being careful to ease the latch back in position. Then he made for the nearest telephone box, and a minute later heard the former SAS sergeant's voice at the end of the line.

Hunter was enthusiastic with his greeting, and then asked, 'It's not the old business, sir? Thought you were settled in politics — in government, aren't yer?'

'That's right, I am.' Hailston's answer was abrupt. 'But it's the old business I want to talk to you about — after a fashion.'

'I'm all ears, sir. Life's been a bit dull lately.'

'Would you still take a mercenary job?'

Hunter didn't even need to think. His reply was immediate: 'If it paid enough. Is that what you're offering? Is it some undercover job for the bloody government?'

'No. And I'm not recruiting mercenaries, Bill. I just wanted to know if you liked the same kind of . . . ' He paused, and then added, 'activity?'

'Yeah.'

'Name a restaurant near you.'

'Know Oslo Court? It's on the ground floor of a block of flats in Prince Albert Road.'

'I'll see you there one o'clock tomorrow, Friday — OK?'

'Yeah. See you, sir.'

Hailston replaced the receiver, and paused for a moment. The old adrenalin was working. It was like being in charge of an operation. Decisions were taken, then you were committed. He was committed now, and he enjoyed every decisive step.

Esme would have needed unusually sharp ears to hear Hailston entering the front door. He moved with the same silent expertise to her own bureau, unlocked it, and searched through the drawers. It was some time before he found what he wanted. Then he settled to half-an-hour of painstaking work.

Afterwards he rewarded himself with yet another scotch, and felt satisfaction, both with his achievement and his determination. He hadn't time to feel sorry for what he was doing. It was necessary. The decision having been taken, other things followed as a consequence. Nothing was going to stand in his way now. His mind was made up.

8

The meal with ex-Sergeant Bill Hunter was devoted almost entirely to reminiscence, and Hailston noticed approvingly that his guest looked in good physical trim. His fair hair was still cut short back and sides, the blue eyes were clear and calculating, the jaw still square and thrusting, the lips tight set. He looked what he used to be — a strong, tough man with a sharp intelligence. He had found the job with Hailston's old security firm lacking in action and, after a while, had left to disappear again somewhere in Africa. Hailston had heard rumours that Hunter had carried out one or two contract jobs as well as indulging in the odd mercenary activity. He had been a marvellous man to have alongside in the jungles of Borneo when, equipped with Armalite rifle and boots covered in sacking, they had penetrated deep and unseen into Indonesian-held Kalimantan to locate enemy bases and the kampongs where the Indonesian soldiers lived. The sergeant had had a marvellous facility for translating previously studied photographic information into a recognition of the rivers and ridges on the ground. Yet he was one of those few whom the SAS preferred not to know after he had left the service. He still looked as though he could not resist an adventure. Hailston was impressed.

When he asked Hunter what he was doing, the former sergeant answered, 'That's the hell of it. I'm not. Oh, I'm all right for money, sir. It's the action that's missing. I should never have got out, you know. Don't you miss it?'

'Sometimes. But I like what I'm doing. Besides I'm not as fit as I used to be.'

'You look in pretty good shape to me, sir.'

'I am — except for bloody diabetes.'

'I'm sorry.'

'That's all right. I cope. It doesn't interfere with my career.'

Only afterwards, when Hailston was driving Hunter round the outer circle of Regent's Park, did he refer to the reason for their meeting.

'We haven't met, Hunter,' he said.

'That's understood.'

'You're open for a job?'

'It has to be special. But for you, yeah.'

Hailston turned down Chester Road, then drove round the inner circle until he found a place to park. Then he took from his pocket four colour prints. He passed them over to Hunter.

The ex-sergeant studied them, then nodded his head. Hailston knew the man would not need to refer to them again, but he didn't take them back.

'That man,' he said, 'is a Czech. He's a member of the Czechoslovak Embassy staff.'

Hunter nodded. 'I've got him,' he said. 'It's a perfect photograph. You want him rubbed out?'

'No.'

Hunter turned to look at him with surprise. Hailston returned the stare, his eyes cold and determined.

'Early next week, most likely Monday, he will be going to a restaurant. The girl will be with him.'

'Which restaurant?'

'I don't know. You'll have to follow him from the Embassy — that's number twenty-five Kensington Palace Gardens.'

'So, what do you want me to do with him.'

'Nothing. The girl is your target.'

If Hunter was surprised this time he didn't show it. 'You

haven't got a frontal of her?' he asked, as he glanced again at the three-quarter back view.

A photograph from the family album would have been too risky. 'No,' Hailston answered. 'But the colouring is accurate, and she is certain to be with that man.'

'OK — that'll do.' He handed the photographs back.

'No, keep them. I don't want them,' Hailston said.

Hunter put them in the breast pocket of his jacket.

'Do you want to tell me anything about this? It doesn't matter if you don't. Probably better if I don't know.'

'Yes. But she's a spy.'

'So, it's just the terms, sir.'

Hailston got out of his car and opened the boot. He returned with a briefcase. He leant over, put it on Hunter's lap, and sprang the catches. The lid flew open to reveal neat bundles of twenty-pound notes.

Hunter's face was expressionless.

Hailston said, 'Twenty thousand pounds.'

'And the briefcase thrown in,' Hunter grinned. 'All right.' He snapped the case shut and left it on his knees. 'Is the girl a Czech?' he asked.

'No.'

Hunter shrugged. 'Any special instructions?'

'No. It's your operation.'

Hunter nodded. 'Suits me.'

'I'll drive you to your bank.'

The former sergeant shook his head. 'I'm not banking this lot. I shall leave after a day or so for Jersey, from some small airport, like Southampton. I'll take a holiday.'

'Good idea. Then I'll drive you home.'

Hailston drove round the inner circle and out the way he had come. As he turned out of the park towards Camden Town, he said, 'Don't be surprised by anything you read, Bill. This is necessary. It has to be done.'

'OK by me.'

* * *

David Rackham had suffered a few days of frenetic activity before he stood in the narrow file of people having their passports and visas checked by a khaki-uniformed and unsmiling immigration officer at Prague airport. A long and, he thought, very funny article for *The New Yorker* had been locked away in a drawer in his flat, and it would be some days before he could finish it.

He had discovered that the Association of Visual Arts Societies, AVAS for short, had arranged a weekend visit to Prague to see some of the city's artistic treasures. With such little time at his disposal that was likely to be his best cover. There was no point in trying to go officially, as a diplomat, to the British Embassy. That would only arouse suspicion.

The Secretary of AVAS, Miss Euphemia Norton, an earnest woman in her fifties with her hair taken back in a neat bun, was at first outraged, and refused any help whatsoever. Then, very reluctantly, she was understanding, and finally, patriotically co-operative. Rackham's easy charm had been ineffective, and had to be backed by what appeared to be government authority before Miss Norton began to appreciate the necessity of what was being proposed.

The party of thirty, which she was leading, was made up almost equally of men and women, photographs of whom had already been supplied in duplicate to the Czech authorities with the applications for visas. Rackham studied the tiny portraits of all the men with his fingers crossed. There was unlikely to be a perfect match, but as he went through them a second time he was beginning to despair of finding anyone remotely possible. Then he paused at the monochrome photograph of one man about his own age, but with a moustache and half-rimmed glasses — James Archibald Green. He checked the details of colouring — sandy hair and moustache, hazel eyes. Well, it was the best that could be done. Height was about the same.

'Who is he?' Rackham asked.

Miss Norton bridled slightly before giving way to a feeling of self-importance. 'An art dealer from Midhurst.'

'Wife?'

'No, he's coming alone.'

'Do any of the others in the party know him?'

'I don't know without checking records. Some might have been on trips with him before, but I don't recall seeing him myself. He certainly wasn't on our visit to Vienna a month ago, and he didn't come to Budapest before that. Wait a moment.' Long, narrow fingers flicked through a card index. 'No,' she said, 'he's only been a member for a year.'

'Oh dear,' Rackham smiled, 'he's going to be so disappointed.' Then turning on his charm, he added, 'Now, Miss Norton, what I must ask you very kindly to do is telephone Mr Green and tell him that, for some reason you just don't understand, the Czechs have at the last minute turned down his application for a visa. It has, I take it, already been granted?'

'Oh yes.'

'Well, you can never tell with these iron-curtain countries, Miss Norton, can you? Such a nuisance, but it has happened before on a number of occasions. No, they never give any reason. Just suddenly change their mind. It's quite useless protesting.'

Miss Norton didn't know whether to smile or look shocked.

'You are not going to get us into trouble, are you?'

'No, Miss Norton. I promise you that. Now don't forget that, from now onwards, I am James Archibald Green, an art dealer from Midhurst. By the way, any further information you have about him, I should be glad to have.'

Miss Norton jiggled her head uncertainly, and began to rummage in her old grey filing cabinet. 'What about your passport, Mr — ?' She hesitated, 'Mr Green.'

Rackham responded with a charming nod. 'Very good, Miss Norton, very good. Oh, a passport will be no problem. I just need this photograph, that's all, and your information pack, of course, with all the instructions that you have given to others in the party. And the next time you see me, I hope' — he held up the passport-size photograph — 'I shall be looking like this.'

When they did meet in Terminal One at London's Heathrow airport for the British Airways Friday flight, BA 700, to Prague, Miss Norton was duly impressed by the transformation, but played her role admirably by consulting her records, then stretching out her hand and saying, 'And you must be Mr James Green. I don't think you have been with us before. Well, I am sure you are going to enjoy the trip.'

Rackham rewarded her with a wink, undetected by other members of the party. The transformation, in fact, had not been difficult. Once he had altered his hairstyle and had the moustache expertly fixed, it only required the half-rimmed glasses to make him almost indistinguishable from the original photograph. He wasn't worried on that account. He only hoped that the other arrangements he had so hurriedly put together to get Beetle out would work once he had returned with the AVAS party to London. His only task was to explain them to Beetle in detail. His other anxiety was lest he, himself, was being set up. Did he know that Beetle was trustworthy? He saw the immigration officer glance up at him, then down at the passport. The man shuffled his papers until he came to the copy of the visa photograph. He looked up again, stamped the passport, handed it back with Rackham's copy of the visa. James Archibald Green had entered Czechoslovakia.

Rackham shared with the rest of the party an execrable lunch of tough meat in a tasteless brown sauce accompanied only by hard herb-filled dumplings, and eaten, as far as he was concerned, in a nameless restaurant in the Old Town, but the restaurant was housed in a building of the most exquisite proportions. Indeed, there were street after street, square after square, of staggeringly beautiful buildings, which had never suffered the ravages of modern wars. They had been left to grow older, even decay, with dignity. Fortunately, restoration had rescued them in time.

It was a day of warm sunshine, but with a certain crispness to the air that seemed to shimmer off the lazy surface of the Vltava river. Rackham was able to look down upon it from the height of the castle which, with the tower and spires of St Vitus Cathedral, dominated the skyline of the city that, on many levels of ridge and hill, still followed its medieval ground plan.

At the castle, in what was once the stables of a former emperor, Rackham looked at paintings by Titian, Tintoretto, Veronese and Rubens's *Council of the Gods*, and then, unnoticed, except for the sharp eye of Miss Euphemia Norton, slipped off to make his way down the steep drift of sixteenth-century steps towards Lesser Town Square, through the gateway with its Romanesque and Gothic towers, to the Charles Bridge. Its sixteen arches had borne every kind of traffic across the river since the fourteenth century. Rackham was grateful that now its rough setts were reserved for pedestrians only.

The bridge was lined with statues and Rackham, who had studied a detailed plan in London, made his way unerringly to the oldest of them, a statue of St John of Nepomuk. He looked at his watch. He was seven minutes early. He leant against the wall by the statue, while people walked to and fro, and occasional tourists paused with guidebooks in their hands. He would be approached and asked if he had seen 'The Excursions of Mr Brouček', and he would reply, 'No, it is seldom performed'. It was, in fact, the title of an opera by Janáček, and Brouček means beetle.

Rackham waited for twenty minutes past the appointed time, but there was no sign of Beetle. Well, provision had been made for the possibility that he might not be able to make the rendezvous, and a second meeting place had been arranged for the next morning.

Rackham got back to their hotel before Miss Norton and the others. The Inter-Continental was the national tourist agency's attempt to cater for the western tourist in a modern building with bars and lounges, dance floors and shops, and nearly four hundred air-conditioned rooms with colour television, and all of it, in western terms, ridiculously cheap.

When Miss Norton did return, he learned that they had only an hour to get changed and be ready for a concert of folk dance and song. Then they would eat in the hotel later.

'I don't think anyone noticed you go,' she whispered to him when they were alone.

'Good, they weren't meant to.'

'I feel,' she said, patting her bun nervously, 'that I'm part of some conspiracy.'

'Don't think about it, Miss Norton. Now, we're going to St Nicholas Church in the morning?'

'Yes, very baroque.'

Rackham smiled. He thought she looked a little baroque herself. 'Well,' he said, with a wicked look, 'I shall stay kneeling at my devotions. Please don't wait for me.'

'Very well. I understand, Mr Green.'

Rackham nodded his approval. 'Excellent, Miss Norton.'

'Will there be any other occasions when — ?'

'No. After that I shall be a most attentive member of the tour.'

'And will you be returning with us on Monday?'

'Of course.' Rackham sounded casual and confident. He hoped that he had reason to be. He was, in fact, somewhat disturbed that Beetle had failed to turn up, and as he had made his way through the narrow streets of the city, pausing now and again to admire its architectural wonders, he tried to keep a sharp eye for any evidence that he was being followed. As far as he could see, he wasn't, but how the hell could he be sure in a place like Prague?

'I think,' said Miss Norton, interrupting his reflections, 'that our meal should be rather better tonight. Stuffed green pepper garnished with lobster and salmon foam, followed by stewed leg of pork with mushrooms and something called ham rice.'

'My gastric juices are in a turmoil of anticipation.'

Miss Norton chuckled, then hurried away to prepare for their evening's entertainment.

It turned out to be an occasion of brilliant costumes, swirling skirts, delightful tunes and much stamping of feet. Rackham enjoyed it, and made sure that he was tucked insignificantly in the middle of the AVAS party, and as far away as possible from the young woman who was their enthusiastic Czech guide. It was uncharacteristic for him not to be noticed, but he resisted all temptations to wisecrack, and was a reluctant conversationalist with the doctor, accountant, solicitor, county councillor, Women's Institute president, and the mixture of retired men and women who were his fellow visitors. After tomorrow morning he would be able to evince a little more interest in them all; until then it was better to remain the obscure Midhurst art dealer.

Thus, the following morning, he made sure he was on the edge of their group and behind the ample proportions of the hearty county councillor and the Women's Institute president, while the young woman prattled on about this masterpiece of Bohemian baroque, as she gestured upwards to the brilliant frescos that covered the ceiling of the nave — more than one thousand five hundred yards of them, she said, all to honour St Nicholas. That was him — the statue dominating the high altar.

The building was richly ornamented, and there were frescos everywhere, including the huge dome itself. Rackham frankly found it overpowering, almost vulgar. As he craned his neck towards the dome, he reflected how it had taken the Czechs more than three years to repair the roof, and for no better reason than that it was opposite the Schönborn Palace, which housed the American Embassy. Hidden beyond those frescos were electronic listening devices.

He was, himself, being especially alert as he sidled into a pew and knelt down, hiding most of his head in his hands. He was sure the voluble young guide had not noticed. He remained there until the group had left. Then he got up and took a different position, the one which had been proposed for the meeting. Again he knelt as if in prayer. Beetle should be there within five minutes.

Rackham felt distinctly absurd, kneeling as though at his orisons. But when Beetle came and knelt beside him it would be the ideal posture for a full briefing. He looked up, then behind him, before apparently resuming his devotions, but this time he was peering directly ahead.

Rackham stayed like that, steadily getting more uncomfortable, for fifteen minutes. No one took the place beside him. He waited a further five minutes. Beetle had not made it. So either Beetle had himself been uncovered, and was now a guest of the STB, or he had deliberately not come and had betrayed Rackham's own cover. In that case Rackham might be at risk himself.

There was no one he could consult, nothing he could do. The operation had deliberately been set up as a one-man job. He shrugged as he got up from his knees, and realized for the first time that the interior of St Nicholas was decidedly cool, even when it was warm and sunny outside.

He ran down the steps of the church and began to cross towards Little Town Square. Even allowing for the fact that his instinct was to look left rather than right, he could swear the road was clear when he stepped out.

Then he heard the sudden fierce acceleration, the drumming of tyres on the setts, as the car hurtled towards him. Instinctively, he leapt ahead, catching on the rim of his vision the sight of a black saloon swerving towards him. Rubber squealed and screeched on the rough surface of the road. He saw a windscreen, hands pulling on the steering wheel. He leapt on to the pavement by the bollards and chains surrounding the Holy Trinity Column. The front of the car ricocheted towards him, then careened back to the road. He was left clinging to a stone bollard that was shaped a bit like an old milk churn. Holy figures and gilt crosses towered above him.

If the road setts had been wet, it might just have been an accident, but they were bone dry, and had there been only pavement, and not a monument in the way, Rackham had little doubt that the car would have careered into him. He made his way to the cool and shaded arcades on the northern side of the square. From there he looked out on a square lined with palaces almost unaltered since they were built in the seventeenth century. He saw nothing, however, to suggest that he was being kept under observation.

So it looked as though it was the second explanation — he had been shopped by Beetle. The bloody man wasn't trying to defect at all. Rackham wondered if the immigration officer at Prague airport would let him out of the country on Monday afternoon as easily as he had let him in. But on what possible ground could he detain a Sussex art dealer? Unfortunately, the Czech authorities did not need grounds. If they wanted to detain him, they would. Maybe he should have taken more time. Why had Sir Dick been in such a damned hurry? Beetle wasn't that valuable. Oh well, there was nothing he could do now. He wandered around, idly sightseeing until lunch time, when he met up with the AVAS party again in an allegedly prestigious restaurant just off one corner of the square.

Miss Euphemia Norton gave no sign of noticing his arrival. Only later when they were alone for a few moments did she say, with a sly smile, 'I hope your prayers were answered, Mr Green.'

Rackham winked. 'Ah, that depends on your point of view. I think St Nicholas and his buddies ignored me. On the other hand, but for the Holy Trinity monument, I might have been knocked down by a car.'

'Well, someone was looking after you.'

'Yes, I was. My leap must have been enough to qualify me for the Olympics.'

'What happened to the car?'

Rackham grinned. 'The driver regained control.'

Miss Norton gave a little pat to her bun and looked at him shrewdly. 'So it wasn't an accident?' she said.

'I expect someone was after that Rembrandt I keep wrapped round my body.'

'Anyway, it's all over now, Mr Green?'

'I profoundly hope so. I shall certainly be a most attentive member of the group from now on.'

Miss Norton looked at him with a mock frown. 'I've been wondering what on earth I shall do,' she said, 'if any of the members who are here meet the real Mr Green on another trip?'

The humour of that situation appealed to Rackham. 'Oh, I think you are clever enough, Miss Norton,' he flattered, 'to cope with almost anything.'

'And I think,' she replied with an admonitory smile, 'that you are a naughty boy.'

9

Former SAS Sergeant Bill Hunter inspected himself in his bathroom mirror, and decided he had done a good job. The short fair hair was now black with a dye that would wash out at the first attempt. He had a moustache of the same hue joining a well-trimmed black beard. The disguise was completed with a pair of grey-tinted glasses.

During the weekend he had planned his operation, but he had given little thought to the reason for it. Reasons were not his concern, never had been. He obeyed orders. If Captain Hailston wanted this girl rubbed out there must be a good reason for it. Spy was the only explanation the politician had given him, and that was good enough. He had no anxieties about the success of his plan either. He was a professional, and even on those rare occasions, like the affair in Angola, when the whole bloody thing had gone wrong, his professionalism had ensured his own survival. His escape route on this occasion was his disguise.

The 'execution' had either to take place at the restaurant or at the subject's own home. Hunter was not particular. He had provided for each eventuality. He only hoped that Monday was the right day because he did not like to hang about.

He rode the tube to Notting Hill Gate early, and made his way on foot to the Czechoslovak Embassy in Kensington Palace Gardens. He was there by eight-thirty, and took a position on the opposite side of the road. He was partly hidden by one of the plane trees. It was a dull day but, thank heaven, fine and dry.

He saw two or three people approach the Embassy on foot, and some others arrive by car and sweep down the slope to the left of the building to the garages. Each time he saw a car approach he crossed the road, and appeared to be walking back towards Bayswater Road, so that he got a good sight of the car's occupants. Shortly before nine o'clock a black Mercedes nosed its way through the raised barrier-arm towards the Embassy. As it drew level Hunter saw the subject of Hailston's photograph sitting in the back. The ex-sergeant memorized the car's registration number, and then continued his walk back to the Bayswater Road.

He returned at twelve-fifteen, this time in a taxi. They had been admitted to the road by the green-tailcoated figure when Hunter said they had an appointment at the Saudi Arabian Embassy. At his instructions, however, the taxi drew up on the other side of the road, some yards distant.

'Changed yer mind, guv?' the driver asked.

'No — I'm not going in, mate. That's all. I'm waiting for someone.'

The driver nodded, and Hunter reclined in a corner of the back seat.

It was twelve-thirty precisely when the Mercedes came out of the gates and, instead of turning out into Notting Hill Gate, swung round to go in the opposite direction along Kensington Palace Gardens. This gave Hunter the opportunity to catch a glimpse of the back-seat passenger. He leant forward and curtly instructed the taxi driver to follow the Mercedes and not to lose it.

As the driver let in the clutch and engaged first gear, he looked over his shoulder and muttered, 'What is this, governor?'

'I want to know where he's going to lunch, that's all.'

'You could have asked him, sir.'

'I don't like jokes. I haven't asked you to do anything illegal. And I shan't. You're getting paid, and what's more you'll find a bloody big tip at the end. That is if you don't lose the bastard.'

The driver said no more. He followed the Mercedes to the other side of Kensington Gardens and Hyde Park. In the crush of traffic in Knightsbridge, the taxi drew up immediately behind. Hunter saw the Czech lean forward and pick up a telephone receiver set between the backs of the two front seats. They had reached Hyde Park Corner before the man put it down and relaxed into his seat. The taxi followed on down Grosvenor Place to Victoria. The car with the CD plates stopped at the end of an alleyway. The taxi drew to a halt some way behind. Hunter thrust a bundle of notes into the driver's hand. 'Thanks mate,' he snapped.

Seconds later he was on the pavement, watching the Czech turn into the pedestrian way. By the time he had reached the corner, another car with a CD plate had drawn into the kerb where the taxi had so recently stopped. About half way along the paved alley, the Czech turned in beneath a canopy over which was scrawled, in a flowing red longhand, 'Traceys'. Hunter followed him, paused between the two tubbed bay trees to inspect the menu in the window, then walked in.

As the waiter approached, he noticed that the Czech had taken an isolated corner table.

'Can you manage one? I haven't booked.'

'Yes, that's all right, sir.'

Hunter was shown to a small table for two in the window. It was the length of the restaurant from the Czech's table. Hunter was glad to confirm to himself that the man seated in the far corner was undoubtedly the figure in Hailston's photograph. He consulted the menu, and ordered the soup of the day, and a steak. His tastes were basic and simple. He wasn't one for what he scornfully called messed-up restaurant meals. Moreover he liked his steak rare.

He was half way through his soup when the girl entered. As he was facing inwards, so as to keep the man under observation, Hunter got only a passing glimpse of the girl's face. It was enough to tell him that she was very attractive with red-blonde hair. She walked, with her back to him, towards the table. Hunter had no doubt. From the back she was the girl in the photograph, and there was certainly no doubt about the Czech. Hunter watched the man rise instantly and affably to greet his guest. Pity *he* wasn't the target. Still, Hailston knew what he was doing. And Hunter knew how to carry out orders, especially when they were rewarded with twenty thousand pounds. He was beginning to feel the excitement of impending action, only — and this is what had always fascinated him — it was a very controlled kind of excitement. That was what marked off the professional.

Hunter made sure that, in eating his meal, he was always slightly ahead of the couple in the corner. Between courses their conversation appeared to be serious and earnest. Apart from the handsome Czech's warm smile of greeting there had been no subsequent hint of humour from either of them. When they had finished their coffee and it was clear they were not having any more, Hunter called over the waiter and paid his bill, although he still had a second cup of coffee to drink.

It looked as though it was going to be plan two. Shame. He preferred working without weapons. Then, just as he had taken a mouthful of coffee, the girl said something to her host, got up, walked to the other corner and disappeared through the doorway marked 'Toilets'. Oh good, Hunter thought, plan one after all. He swallowed his coffee. Timing was important now. She would probably repair her make-up, or at least her lipstick, as well, but he didn't want to wait for that. After a couple of minutes, he got up and walked through the same door.

As he expected, the passage divided into two cubicles — one for men, the other for women. One toilet flushed as he walked in. He waited by the half-open door bearing the male symbol.

The lock of the other cubicle snapped back. The door opened, the girl stepped through. Hunter came out of his door, immediately behind her. This was the only dangerous moment, but it was no more than two or three seconds. Hunter's arm locked round her neck from behind, crushing the windpipe. Her arms flailed momentarily, desperately. He saw eyes bulge outwards. Hunter viciously tightened his grip. When this was done properly the victim had no chance even to scream. The only sound was a subdued gurgle of breath forced out of the windpipe, and then a sharp click. The legs gave way in an involuntary jerk, the body slumped, saliva trickled out on to her chin.

Hunter relaxed his hold, dragged her back into the lavatory and locked the door. He hoisted himself to the top, over the gap between the dividing wall and the ceiling, and let himself down into the men's cubicle.

He brushed down his clothes and walked out. He returned briefly to his table to check that he had left nothing there, and then left. As the door closed behind him, he noticed the Czech was still sitting at the table in the far corner.

Hunter felt now as he always felt after screwing a good woman — a proud and momentarily weary satisfaction. He did not see the man tailing him twenty-five yards behind.

He was, however, careful to make sure that no neighbours observed him entering his own house. Once inside he took off his glasses, went immediately to the bathroom and removed his beard and moustache. Then he shampooed the black rinse out of his hair. Only then did he pull the ring clasp of a can of beer and downed the contents with a feeling that it was well earned.

If Hailston's private secretary at the Ministry of Defence had been asked, he would have said that his Minister was just a little edgy that Monday afternoon. He did not regard it as significant because he knew that, although Hailston was an able, decisive and ambitious man, he was also a short-tempered man. So that afternoon the civil servant ignored his master's slight irritability.

Hailston had personally delivered to his daughter's address early that morning a list of names and addresses of British firms contracted for highly secret work under the American President's SDI programme. She had demanded them by

Monday, so presumably that was when she was meeting her Czech contact. In that event, by now he was probably free. Hunter would have completed his operation. Hailston did not reflect on it for long. Just as when he had commanded his small unit of highly trained, specialized soldiers, when the time came to act decisively out of necessity, he had accepted the responsibility. Once such a decision had been made, there was no point in analysing it further. The touchstone was necessity. That was an end of it.

Nevertheless, Hailston was aware of an incipient queasiness, a sweatiness of the hands and forehead. He tidied the papers he had been dealing with, locked them away. He would go down to the Commons shortly. He wanted to be with Jane. He needed her unknowing support. It was as though, subconsciously, he required the confirmation that her presence would give him. It was what, normally, he looked for in Esme. He needed them both — sometimes for different reasons, sometimes for the same reason.

He glanced at his watch. It was coming up to five o'clock. He switched on the portable radio on his desk, and waited for the jangling signature tune of the news magazine, PM, on Radio 4. The first two headlines were about international news stories.

Then the newsreader said: 'A young English woman, believed to have been the guest of a Czechoslovak diplomat, has been found dead in a London restaurant. The police are treating it as murder.'

Hailston waited patiently, taut as a wound-up spring, for the main news story. It did not contain a lot more information. The body had been found in the toilet, and the identity of the woman was not being released until next-of-kin had been informed.

Soon his telephone would ring, or a police officer would be shown into his office. 'Very sorry, sir,' he would say, 'but I'm afraid your daughter . . . '

The telephone did ring. Hailston didn't even jump at its repeated buzzing. Tense, a little sweaty, but calm, he picked up the receiver.

His private secretary said: 'Your daughter is here to see you, sir.'

Carolyn closed the door behind her, turned to face her father. She was aghast at what she saw. Hailston sat there, staring, the colour suddenly drained from his cheeks.

'Are you all right?'

He nodded, still staring.

'You look as white as a sheet.'

The sweat stood in beads on his forehead. He was feeling sick and dizzy.

'I — ' he began, but didn't get any further. Then suddenly he said, 'The drawer,' and reached out his hand towards the drawer on the right side of his desk. 'Quickly . . . '

Carolyn pulled it open. There was a box of sugar tablets. She gave them to him. His hands trembling, he opened the box, and they spilled on to his desk. Rapidly he put a couple into his mouth. Then he leant back in his chair.

'Do you need an injection?' she asked.

'No. No, you bloody fool. Do you want to kill me? I needed sugar. I didn't have any lunch. I've had damn all, it seems, for hours. And it's the bloody shock, too.'

She looked askance.

'I thought you'd been killed,' he said. 'The radio reported a young English woman, guest of a Czechoslovak diplomat, was murdered today in a London restaurant.'

'Well, I'm here — alive,' she said, smiling faintly. She felt confused. There was a piquancy in her father's shock, but what had happened, and where had it happened? And was Ivan the diplomat concerned?

By now Hailston had managed to acquire a veneer of control.

'You've been damned lucky,' he said. 'Don't you see, it was meant to be you? You'd have handed over the information, and then — they'd have disposed of you.'

'The meeting wasn't set up for today,' she said calmly.

'I thought you had insisted on Monday?'

'I wanted to be sure I would have the stuff in time. I was to see him on Wednesday.'

Hailston was suddenly furious. 'What the hell are you doing here?'

Carolyn smiled. She felt strangely elated, and didn't give too much thought to the reason.

'I've come for the rest — the report.'

'Here — ' he said, incredulously. 'You come here to — ?'

'Why, the place is not bugged, is it? Or is your PS listening at the keyhole?'·

Hailston slapped his hand on his desk in anger. 'You've no business to come here in . . . in these circumstances. Carolyn, I've had enough. You'd better understand that. You've had the list — that's an end of the matter.' He stared at her, uncomprehending. What the hell had happened? What had gone wrong? Now the bloody girl was smiling again, infuriatingly.

'We shall have to see,' she said.

'See? It's clear enough to me. I shan't protect you indefinitely.'

Carolyn looked stunned. '*You* protect me?' she scoffed. 'You're forgetting something. You're the one who's being protected — on my terms.'

Hailston glowered, his eyes cold with anger, but he had no chance to reply. The telephone on his desk buzzed. He snatched it up.

'Yes, yes,' he snapped impatiently, 'put him through.'

Hailston heard, at the other end of the line, the even tones of a senior police officer at Scotland Yard. 'Early this afternoon a woman was killed in the toilets of a restaurant in Victoria — '

'Yes, yes — I heard about it on the radio.'

'Well, I'm sorry to have to disturb you, sir — and with such distressing news. It appears that the deceased woman was your personal secretary, Miss Jane Bacton.'

Long after the police officer had finished speaking, Hailston sat there still holding the phone and staring ahead of him. For the second time, Carolyn saw the colour ebb from his cheeks.

At length he returned the phone to its rest. 'Oh, my God,' he muttered, 'oh my God.' He slumped forward on his desk, his head in his hands.

At Prague airport the immigration officer seemed to pay especial attention to the passport and papers presented by James Archibald Green. Ultimately he stamped them and, with a surly glance, handed back the passport. Rackham nodded politely and followed other members of the AVAS party into the departure lounge.

Twenty minutes later they were airborne, and the Boeing 737 had not long assumed its cruising height before the stewardess brought him a folded sheet of paper from the flight deck.

'A radio message for you, sir,' she said.

Rackham unfolded it and read, 'Jane Bacton, personal secretary to Stanley Hailston, was murdered at Traceys restaurant, Victoria, this afternoon. Murderer unknown. She was being entertained by Czech diplomat, Ivan Kubat. Palesworth meeting you at Heathrow.'

Rackham whistled quietly to himself to the astonishment of Miss Euphemia Norton who was sitting next to him and who, to her irritation, had failed to scan the message as he was reading it.

'Not bad news, I hope?' she ventured.

Rackham gave her a freckly grin. 'Could be,' he replied, disconcertingly, but offered no more information in response to her persistent probing. After a few minutes, she gave up trying, and Rackham was left pondering what it meant.

There was a further mysterious surprise for Miss Norton and the AVAS party when, on arrival at Heathrow, they saw a car speed out to the aircraft while it was waiting on the tarmac before proceeding to its arrival gate.

The rear door was opened, steps hastily swung into position. A stewardess called, 'Mr Green!' The AVAS members looked on in astonishment as the man some of them had even begun to call 'James' was hurried to the car and driven away at high speed.

As Rackham sank into the back seat he vowed that, the next day, he would send Miss Norton a monster bouquet of flowers. In the opposite corner was seated the round-faced, rotund Head of the East European Desk, the inaptly named Robert Palesworth. Rackham looked at his watch. It was not yet quarter to six.

'So what's it all about, Bobbie?'

'C insists that you handle it — whatever it is.'

'Do we know anything about Jane Bacton?'

'No. She was quite a stunner. You'd have liked her. Redhead. Well, blonde-red.'

'Strawberry blonde, I think it's called.'

'Of course there was that funny business in Prague with Hailston's daughter. Coincidence?'

Rackham shrugged. He profoundly hoped so. 'Palace of Uncertainties they ought to call Westminster. Hells bells and all the little fishes. If the Bacton woman has been feeding stuff to the Czechs — how long's it been going on?'

It was Palesworth's turn to shrug in his corner. 'Who knows? Or Hailston?'

'No. He's too ambitious. Wants to be Secretary of State for Defence. Unimpeachable record in the SAS — distinguished in fact. No, it's the Bacton girl. Or,' Rackham added reluctantly, 'Hailston's daughter.'

'The worst of it is,' moaned Palesworth, 'this bloody crime has brought it into the open. I mean if we'd found out that the Bacton girl had been spying, we could have quietly dealt with the whole thing. But, oh dear, the fuss those windbags in the Commons are going to make now.'

Rackham grinned. Palesworth approved of democracy so long as it didn't interfere with the overriding desirability of secrecy in all things.

The car, fortunately going in the opposite direction to the mainstream of traffic flowing from the metropolis, speedily threaded its way towards central London, while Rackham decided that, immediately he was in possession of the latest police report, he would pay a visit to Stanley Hailston and his daughter.

'I take it we still don't know who killed her?' Rackham asked. 'How was it done?'

'Strangled. Well, neck broken, windpipe crushed.'

'Oh.' Rackham sounded interested. 'That sounds professional — SAS professional.'

'A taxi driver has come forward. Told the police that he picked up a man who kept watch on the Czech Embassy for some time before following an Embassy car to Victoria. Tough, thickset fellow with dark hair, moustache, beard and tinted glasses. They've got a drawing for you to look at.'

'And what does Mr Kubat have to say — apart from pleading diplomatic immunity?'

'He's a slimy bastard. Mystified by the whole business. It was only the second time he had seen Miss Bacton. They'd met at a social gathering, and had been attracted to each other. He had offered to take her out to lunch — really their first proper meeting. Now he's taken refuge in the Embassy.'

'How sad.'

'Oh yes, David, sorry about Beetle.'

'Wasted trip.'

'I know. You were there before we heard. Beetle's convinced he made a mistake. They're not on to him. He's coming to London.'

'He's what?'

'Got a posting to their Embassy. So it's not all one way, old boy, is it?' Palesworth rubbed his podgy hands. 'Funny old world.'

Rackham sighed, and burst into a chuckle. The absurdity of the situation appealed to him, as he recalled his painful devotions in St Nicholas's Church. Then suddenly serious, he said, 'Oh, there's an inconsistency. The buggers tried to run me down — yes, in Little Town Square.'

'It's all inconsistency, David — that's the fascination. If you can still be fascinated at our time of life.'

'But someone must have known I was there and, presumably, why.'

Palesworth hung on to the roof strap as the car swung round a corner. 'The Hailston girl? The Bacton girl? Beetle? Or, heaven forbid, just intelligence?'

'I suppose the PM is demanding a full report?'

'Not yet. All in good time.'

In well under the hour the car was at Century House. Rackham took the lift to his office and immediately buried himself in the latest police reports, and all the relevant information that had been looked out for him. Then he phoned the Hailston residence in Chester Square, and ascertained that the Minister was at home. Yes, he had read the statement Mr Hailston had made to the police and, yes, he understood he must be very upset — an awful shock. But it was essential that he speak to Mr Hailston and Miss Hailston immediately. He would be round in half an hour.

10

Carolyn and her father were driven home to Chester Square in silence. Esme was superb — understanding, considerate, controlled. Carolyn admired the dignity with which her mother informed her affectionate sympathy. If she suspected that Jane had been Hailston's mistress she gave no sign of it. As for Hailston himself Carolyn had never before seen him so ineffectual, so bereft of self-confidence. She couldn't feel sorry for him. He made a statement about Jane to a solicitous police officer, but managed to summon only a few remnants of his usual authority.

By the time Rackham arrived Hailston had recovered a little of his composure. They were alone together in the small room that Hailston used as his study, the Minister in a half-reclining chair, Rackham sitting almost nonchalantly on the corner of the desk. Hailston clearly found it irritating.

'I don't see what the hell this has got to do with the FO,' he said.

Rackham grinned. Surely Hailston must, by now, have realized that he was SIS. Consequently he ignored the remark.

'Your statement to the police,' he said, 'is largely a character reference.'

'Well, what else do you expect? I can only speak as I know her.' He paused, again looking exhausted. 'As I knew her,' he corrected.

'And you never had the slightest idea she was working for the Czechs? Which is another way of saying the KGB.'

'I don't believe it — that's quite absurd.'

'Some years ago, Mr Hailston — 1972 to be precise — as I'm sure you will know, evidence was given to a House of Commons committee that more than a hundred MPs had contacts with the intelligence organizations of the Soviet Union and its East European stooges. I don't suppose it's much different now, and it would be naive to think that the KGB had not also managed to infiltrate the staff.'

'Not Jane Bacton — ridiculous. She wouldn't, couldn't.'

The impatience normally shown by Hailston arose from his own professional competence, but Rackham felt that the present impatience was due more to shock. The man looked awful.

'You would be a prime target.'

'For God's sake, man, she dealt with political things — my job as an MP. She had no access to ministerial matters.'

'Quite. It makes her role the less suspicious.'

Hailston let out a snort of indignation. He felt like picking Rackham up by the scruff of the neck and throwing him on the floor — something which, in fact, would have proved more difficult than he imagined. Rackham had undergone a not dissimilar training from his own.

'And,' said Rackham, underlining the point, 'this has been going on for five years.'

'I tell you it's an absurd idea. And if she was working for them, why should they kill her?'

'Did they kill her?'

'Well, who else did?'

Rackham shrugged and offered one of his irritating smiles. 'That's a mystery. Probably a thickset man with dark hair, beard and moustache. Know anybody like that?'

'No. Why should I?'

Rackham gave his annoying insouciant shrug again. 'The police tell you how she was killed?'

Hailston nodded, and winced.

'It's a technique taught in unarmed combat,' Rackham added. 'You would know about that.'

'What do you mean?' Hailston was fighting for control.

'Only that it was a professional job.'

Hailston did not reply, only twitched at his moustache nervously. He decided he didn't like Rackham, but the man was not to be underestimated.

Rackham shifted from one buttock to the other on the corner of the desk. 'It's very unlikely that the Czechs would want to get rid of her, especially in those circumstances — being entertained by one of their own diplomats. Doesn't make sense, does it? So, who would want her out of the way? We don't do that kind of thing — not here. And, to our shame, we didn't know anything about Miss Bacton anyway.'

Hailston got up, poured himself a scotch, looked inquiringly at Rackham, who shook his head. 'Nothing,' Hailston said, 'will make me believe that Jane was spying for the Czechs.'

'What was she doing with Ivan Kubat then?'

'In a restaurant — where anyone could see her?'

'Not unusual,' Rackham muttered wearily. 'You haven't answered my question, Mr Hailston.'

'I don't know. And I don't have to bloody answer your questions if I don't want to.'

'Sorry, but you do. You might, for one reason or another, refuse to give certain information to the police. But not, Mr Hailston, to me. Now look — of course I understand that this has been an awful shock, a terrible personal tragedy, when you have had her working so closely with you for so long, but — ' He paused, and did his best to look sympathetic. 'Not only do the police have to find out who killed her, but we have to find out exactly what's been going on, for how long, and what damage has been done. Mr Hailston, you must see that, rightly or wrongly, you immediately come under suspicion yourself.' Rackham held up his hand to forestall the Minister's anger. 'I'm afraid,' he continued, 'you are going to have to answer some very detailed questions about the work she has done for you over the past five years; about your own personal relationship with her; about things that may have been discussed between you; about what kind of material she might, with ingenuity, have had access to. A lot of work has to be done, Mr Hailston, and it has to be done quickly.'

'Oh, my God,' Hailston muttered, more to himself than to Rackham. His mind was a confusion: shock because of Jane's death, even greater shock at the way she had evidently used their relationship, anxiety about the implications of it all for himself. Hunter didn't concern him. That man would succeed in looking after number one. 'Oh, my God,' he repeated. He swilled the remnants of scotch in his glass and downed it quickly. He looked up at Rackham. 'This is all an appalling mess,' he said.

'So,' Rackham persisted, 'can you think of anyone who would want Miss Bacton out of the way?'

'No! For Christ's sake, no.'

Rackham swung himself off the desk and stood by the bookcase, built in from floor to ceiling. He looked at the titles on his eye level — books on military affairs, battles, campaigns, defence strategies, military biographies.

'We may have to spend most of tomorrow interrogating you and making a detailed assessment together, Mr Hailston. Meanwhile, I think I'd like a chat with your daughter.'

'Why? What's it got to do with her?'

Rackham smiled tolerantly. 'She was in Prague recently with a man we know. She had to confess to spying for us to get out. OK, we know she wasn't. But now we learn that your own personal secretary was probably spying for them for the past five years. Yes, there are things I have to talk to your daughter about.'

Hailston pulled at his moustache, gritted his jaw, but said nothing.

Rackham went to the door. 'No, don't get up,' he said, 'I'm sure I can find her.'

He did. Both she and her mother were in the drawing room. Esme asked anxiously, 'How is Stanley now?'

'Obviously very shocked. That's quite understandable, I think,' he said, catching Carolyn's unmistakably sceptical glance. Looking back at Esme, he added, 'I really wanted a word or two with your daughter.'

'Is that your white Porsche outside?' Carolyn asked.

'Yes.'

'In that case, you can drive me home.'

Esme looked surprised; clearly she had expected her daughter to stay.

'Well, I think it's better to leave the two of you alone, isn't it?' Carolyn said.

Esme acknowledged her understanding, as Carolyn led the way into the hall.

When she and Rackham reached the pavement, he opened the car door for her with a flourish and, with a boyish grin, removed from the windscreen the notice saying 'DOCTOR VISITING'.

'Did you know Jane Bacton?' Rackham asked casually as he turned into Grosvenor Place.

'Not really. Met her a few times. She provided me with my flat-mate, Toni. She was very attractive. I assume she was Daddy's mistress. That might account for him going over the top a bit.'

'I suppose so.' Rackham didn't sound all that interested. 'Same colouring as you,' he said, 'same hair, about the same build.'

He said no more until he was weaving his way past traffic in the Bayswater Road. Then, as if he had only just thought of it, he asked, 'Is it still Czech-mate? Or have you thought things over?'

'I don't know.'

Rackham didn't press the point. He waited until they were in her flat and she had produced a mug of coffee for each of them. He was lounging on the put-u-up almost as though he lived there, and she sat at the opposite end with scatter cushions propped behind her.

'Answer me one thing,' he said. 'Did you know that Jane Bacton was meeting Ivan Kubat today, or at any time?'

'No.'

'But he's your contact.'

She hoped she had not blushed. She said calmly, 'My only contact with him was because I was anxious about Josef. I told you about all that.'

'So you did. And I only partly believed you. Oh, I believe you fell in love with Josef Foerster, and that you're anxious about him. In those circumstances, who wouldn't be? But either you're trying to be clever — and I don't advise that, Carolyn — or you're being very naive.'

Carolyn looked at him. His freckly face was open and honest. She felt she could trust him, even wanted to tell him everything, but that wasn't possible — not yet. She dare not.

'You know,' Rackham continued, 'if you are being — ' he hesitated before giving a significant emphasis to his next word — 'being *indiscreet* it could be very damaging to your father's career — and that's had a pretty nasty blow today anyway — but it could also be dangerous for you.' He sipped at the hot, black coffee.

'I don't give a damn about his career.' The words had snapped out before she realized she had spoken them.

Rackham raised a sandy-coloured eyebrow. He said with a smile, 'If you weren't wearing those rather tight jeans, I'd say your slip was showing.'

Carolyn couldn't restrain a laugh. 'I think I meant,' she said, 'that my only interest was in Josef. After all he's on the right side — a member of Charter 77.' She took a longer drink of coffee before putting the mug down. 'Can you understand,' she continued, 'that I would do anything if it was going to help him? You see, I love him a great deal. Anything . . . '

'Except spy?'

Carolyn refused to meet his eyes, reached out for her coffee, and sipped at it again.

Rackham said nothing until he had finished his drink and put the empty mug on the nearby table. Then he resumed his rather carefree position, and said as though it were a matter of indifference to him, 'I think perhaps you are going to get rather cross with me in a moment, but that's your affair. I'm trying to help. Look — you probably don't quite understand how serious things are . . . '

'No? You must be joking? A woman — my father's personal secretary, probably his mistress — has been killed, and all the time she may have been a spy.'

'That's almost the sum of it. But the assumption that she was spying, also means that your father immediately becomes a security risk. He is at once under suspicion. Oh, I'm perfectly prepared to believe that he's as patriotic as they come, that he wouldn't dream of a spot of espionage. But the mere fact that the Bacton woman was at it means that now he'll be given the full treatment, before he's cleared.'

'While that's going on he's not likely to be made Secretary of State for Defence, is he?' Carolyn said with a faint smile.

'You're reading it right, baby.'

'More coffee?'

He shook his head. 'Now let me put an alternative, if painful, scenario to you. Jane Bacton had been working for the Czechs for several years. At some point recently she was given a specific job — to get certain information from your father. She failed. Whatever else she may have been able to provide from time to time, she was unable to come up with the goods this time. That wouldn't surprise me. Your father, with his specialist knowledge of intelligence gathering, would not be an easy subject. And she was probably in love with him — that would reduce her value. So the Czechs can't get what they want through Miss Bacton. How about through the Minister's own

daughter? She is conveniently in Prague. So, Josef Foerster — '
Rackham lifted his hand to fend off her interruption. 'No,' he
interrupted himself, 'I'm not saying this *is* so; I'm offering an
alternative explanation. Right? Josef is detailed to set you up. I
don't know what the plan was. But it would be Josef's job to
put you into such a situation that you had no alternative but to
get the information they wanted.'

Carolyn looked horrified. Her hands went to her cheeks.
'No . . . no, I don't believe it,' she said. 'No — that's impossible.'

'Wait a moment. You don't know if he was really a member
of Charter 77, or whether he had infiltrated the Chartists. You
don't even know whether the meeting you went to was a
Chartist meeting. The whole thing might have been set up.'

'It's impossible. I can't believe it. We . . . ' She paused,
looked down at her hands, gripped tightly in her lap. 'We were
lovers,' she said softly.

That didn't carry any weight at all with Rackham who, on a
number of occasions in his career, had willingly performed the
role of a lover — sometimes specifically to acquire information,
and on other occasions simply because the woman concerned
made him randy. Still, as he looked at Carolyn, he was
convinced that it had meant a great deal to her.

'Well,' he said, 'I don't know in what circumstances Josef
was able to make it imperative that you would get the
information Jane Bacton had failed to get. Presumably, the
Czechs would have been able not only to blackmail you, but to
ensure that you could also blackmail your father.'

Carolyn did not dare to think that Josef had arranged the
whole thing. No, that could only have been an accident. She
had seen him in that cell. They would have forced the
information out of him under torture — she was convinced of it.
He would never let her down. But about the rest, Rackham was
disturbingly right. She had been provided with the only possible
means of forcing her father to supply the information. She
looked at him, her eyes full of doubt and anxiety.

'I just don't believe that can be true,' she said, thoughtfully.

Rackham hid his surprise. He had expected a more vehement denial. 'I didn't say it was true — only another possible explanation.'

They sat silently looking at each other, Rackham sensing her personal dilemma.

'What is going to happen?' she asked.

'On one level, a police investigation to find the murderer of Miss Bacton; on another, a full inquiry into whatever Miss Bacton had been up to, and detailed questioning of your father. At some point, I suspect, the two inquiries will come together. I hope you're not involved — that's all.'

Carolyn wanted to be able to trust him, but now she felt more confused than ever. She was supposed to be seeing Ivan on Wednesday with the list her father had provided. It was going to be impossible for her to keep the rendezvous. Surely Ivan would realize that. Presumably he would not want to keep it either; he would want a different meet. She imagined that somehow he would get in touch with her.

Rackham sat silently observing her perplexity. He would dearly like to make her laugh, see her eyes sparkle blue and the little tilt of her nose twitch. That was what she was made for, not the tension of relationships caught in a complex web of espionage.

He swung himself off the put-u-up, grinned at her, and said, 'You've had enough to think about for one day. Why don't you go down to the country for a bit — clear your mind? You ought to persuade your mother to go as well.'

'I might.'

There was the sound of a latch-key and a door opening. Almost simultaneously Toni erupted into the room. She had been swimming, and the ends of her dark hair still showed traces of damp, in spite of the warm evening. The temperature was the reason why she was wearing very little beneath the shirt and the shorts that made her slim legs look longer than they were.

Rackham turned to face her with an immediately appreciative glance, but before he was able grinningly to declare, 'So this is Toni,' the latter burst out, 'Ah, the secret man in your life. Who is he?'

Carolyn introduced them, and Rackham beamed his approval. At least, he reflected pragmatically, Toni did not look like a girl with problems, whereas he was convinced there was something bugging Carolyn. He felt she was casting him as big brother, and that was not his kind of role. He looked from one to the other, marvelling at how desirable they both were. On the whole, he preferred Carolyn's colouring, but the vivacity of Toni suggested that she would be a far easier proposition. Suddenly he was aware that they were both looking at him.

'Ah,' he said, recovering himself. 'Carolyn needs cheering up.' It had been a fatuous thing to say, but they were the only words that immediately came into his head.

'I'll do my best. What is it — post Prague depression?'

It was obvious that she had not heard of the murder of Jane Bacton. Rackham glanced at Carolyn. Her eyes looked moist, as though tears were not far away.

'I think,' he said, 'it's time I left you to Toni.' He took out his diary, scribbled on the notepad at the front, and handed the page to Carolyn. 'That's a telephone number where you can always find me,' he said, adding, 'I'm on your side, you know.'

Carolyn puckered her brows. She wasn't sure what he meant. She no longer felt very sure about anything, but she murmured her thanks.

As he went out into the corridor, he looked back over his shoulder. 'Oh, don't worry if you see the odd policeman around,' he said. 'I've asked them to keep an eye on you.'

'And what did that mean?' Toni asked, as the door closed.

Carolyn shook her head. 'Jane Bacton's been murdered,' she said.

Toni looked startled. 'When? I haven't seen her at the House all day, but — '

'At lunch time — in a restaurant. She was with a Czech diplomat.'

Toni looked puzzled. 'I . . . I can't believe it. Jane dead?'

They went back into their sitting room, and Carolyn poured out cool fruit drinks from the fridge. 'You didn't know her that well — did you?'

'Not really, I suppose — just about the Commons. I liked her.'

Carolyn nodded. She said bitterly, 'She was Daddy's mistress.'

Toni gave a little shrug. 'Nobody knew. Was she a friend of yours?'

Carolyn shook her head. Reluctantly, she muttered, 'I've had a bit of a scene with him tonight.'

Toni did not know how to respond to that, because she was not sure what Carolyn meant. Presumably her father must have been pretty cut up. So what kind of a scene? Toni had to content herself with a simple, 'Oh.' She made up for it by putting an understanding arm round Carolyn's shoulders.

They sat for a few moments in silence, and then Toni chirped out, 'Who is he — David Rackham?'

'God knows. MI something or other, I suppose.'

'Really? He looks too much fun for that.'

'He's nice,' Carolyn said, distractedly. 'I think he's trying to help, but . . . '

She broke away, threw back her hair and paced to the other side of the room.

'But, but,' said Toni, 'there's always a but to a man.'

Carolyn didn't respond. She was looking past her friend to the abstract-patterned curtains beyond. At last she said, as though repeating thoughts aloud, 'He thinks Josef may have set me up — organized the whole thing. Nothing was real . . . nothing.'

11

Carolyn slept badly. Her mind was too active. Question after question fired into her consciousness. There were no certain answers — only doubt, suspicion, misgivings. There was also the worry of her own involvement. Her father had nothing to fear. She was sure that an investigation would find that he had not knowingly provided Jane Bacton with any information of the slightest use to an enemy. But what would happen when they came to investigate her? She had the impression that Rackham was trying to protect her, or perhaps at least reserve the full-scale interrogation for himself.

She turned, twisted, threw off the bed clothes. It was a close night. She got up, opened her window a little wider. The scruffy trees below smudged together like clouds. She walked round the room in bare feet, talking to herself, thinking aloud.

David Rackham's alternative scenario, as he called it, was plausible, even if to her it was unthinkable. She remembered those times together in her room at the Zlata-Husa — the wonder, the perfection. That was love. And recalling those moments, she yearned for him again. He was all she wanted. Josef couldn't be capable of such duplicity — it was not possible. No . . . no . . . no.

Yet still the questions came. Rackham had no reason to lie to her. But then he had told her that he was not saying it was true, only putting forward a different explanation. But then why should he even want to do that, unless he had some suspicion? Or some information? She could not bear the thought of it, and yet the thought recurred. She couldn't shut it out, not when she went back to bed and tried to bury her head in the pillow, as though trying to bury the doubts and questions.

In the morning, tired, exhausted, it was no better. Daylight, the bright daylight, made the questions starker, sharpened their capacity to hurt.

She was up at least an hour before Toni, and poured herself some orange juice from the fridge, then burnt herself some toast, which she had with honey and a mug of coffee.

When Toni did emerge from her room, looking as bright as day itself, she asked, 'All right? A new day, and things look different, don't they?'

It was hard to resist her enthusiasm, but with the shadow of a smile, Carolyn murmured, 'Do they?'

When Toni had left, Carolyn telephoned her mother. 'Are you going down to Sussex?' she asked.

'Daddy has been telling me to. I wanted to stay in London with him, while all this business is going on. He says I can be more use in the constituency, turning aside party workers' questions, I suppose. I might go down tonight, or tomorrow morning.'

'I'll join you there.'

'Oh, that'll be lovely, darling.'

So, she was doing what Rackham had told her to do. Now, having taken the decision, she began to wonder how it would help. She couldn't confide in her mother, not without disclosing the past, and she had no wish to bring that unhappiness upon her. Or could she suggest Rackham's alternative explanation without giving the reason for it? After all, he didn't know the reason himself. But then her mother didn't know Josef, could not know him. The thoughts tangled, disturbed and confused her.

It was in this dishevelled state of mind that she remembered the symbol of a violin on a pamphlet that Josef had shown her. It had come from London, printed by an organization that kept in close touch with the dissident movement in Czechoslovakia. She strove to recall its name. She remembered the story he had told her: a fifteenth-century knight, who befriended serfs escaping from oppressive and cruel masters, had led an uprising of peasants, been caught and then imprisoned in a tower. It was at the far end of Golden Lane. While he was in his cell, the knight learned to play the violin, and legend had it that the ghostly strains of the instrument could sometimes still be heard coming from the dungeon. His name was *Dal* something or other.

Carolyn fetched the first volume of the London telephone directory, turned to D, and began searching all names beginning with Dal. Slowly her finger slid down the columns. Ah — there it was: the Dalibor Press. That was the knight's name — Dalibor.

Almost without thinking, purely from the need to do something, she rang the number. A slightly accented voice replied, and she explained that she had recently been in Prague, had met members of Charter 77, and could she please come and talk to him, ask a few questions? The voice at the other end was cautious, but said he would be pleased to see her.

The offices of the Dalibor Press were in one of those small streets that network the area between Holborn and Fleet Street. Carolyn was received by a lean, alert-looking man in his middle thirties, with a high-domed, bald head. He introduced himself as Viktor Havel, and his handshake was firm. His eyes were dark. They reminded her of Josef's. He looked at her intently, as though he were judging her.

It would not have occurred to Carolyn to adopt anything other than an honest and straightforward approach, but she got no further than repeating that she had recently returned from Prague, before Viktor Havel, with a half-smile, said, 'Of course, you are Miss Carolyn Hailston. You had to tell them you were spying so that you could get out.'

She nodded with relief. 'The man who was arrested with me,' she said, 'was Josef Foerster. We . . . ' she hesitated, looking to Havel for understanding, 'we were friends,' she added.

'So?'

'Do you know him?'

Viktor Havel considered, as he leant back, and his swivel chair uttered a slight squeal. He stroked his chin, glanced round the comfortable disorder of his small room, lined with books, mostly in Czech.

Carolyn stared back at him, her eyes pleading. Why was he taking so long?

At length he said, 'H'mm. I know of him.'

'What do you know about him?'

Havel looked back at her, his eyes full of dark intensity. 'Why do you want to know?' he asked.

'He was my friend in Prague, we spent a lot of time together, he showed me the city, and I saw him in a cell at the STB headquarters. He'd been beaten.'

Havel gave her a sidelong glance, a mixture of surprise and scepticism. 'He was an active member of Charter 77, or at least he appeared to be. Then there were one or two arrests, always when Foerster was present. Recently, we've come to the conclusion that he infiltrated the Chartists and is working for the STB.'

He had spoken in a flat, matter-of-fact tone, and what he had said sounded all the more convincing because of it.

Carolyn felt cold, numbed, her brain refusing to react. She sat staring at him and beyond him, and said nothing.

The silence stretched, and he said, 'Are you all right?'

'What?'

'You look white. Feeling faint?'

She felt as though the blood had drained out of her, and she was cold and empty and weak. Her hands went to her cheeks. All she said, quietly, was, 'Oh God . . . no.'

Havel got up and left the room. He was gone about five minutes, and when he returned Carolyn was still sitting in the same position, still pale and staring and looking shocked. He handed her a cup of black coffee. 'Here, try this,' he said.

Carolyn looked up at him, as though awakened from a dream. 'Oh,' she said. 'Thank you.' She sipped at the hot, dark liquid.

At last she said, 'Are you sure?'

He nodded sadly. 'As sure as one can be, yes.'

It was worse because now she suddenly realized, with a numbing horror, that Viktor Havel had told her what she had expected to hear. The sleepless night, the kaleidoscope of thoughts, doubts, anxieties, had subconsciously convinced her. Only now had she become aware of it. She finished the coffee, gratefully.

'You see,' Havel was saying in the same matter-of-fact voice, 'that would explain the raid and your arrest.'

'Would it?' She didn't feel she was sure of anything.

'It was you they were after. That means they must have wanted to use you in some way.' He paused. 'Those stories about your father's secretary being killed — she was with a chap from the Czech Embassy, wasn't she? They must have been using her, and they wanted to use you as well.'

Carolyn didn't need telling that, but Josef . . . God, it was unbearable. Havel was staring at her again.

'They wouldn't have released you in Prague without some concession from you — a promise of help perhaps?'

Carolyn shook her head.

'How did you know about the Dalibor Press?'

'Josef had one of your publications. He told me.'

'So, what are you doing for the Czechs?'

The question had been uttered in the same flat, matter-of-fact tone, and it sounded like an accusation.

'I'm not. Would I have come here?'

Havel shrugged. 'Stranger things happen.'

'I wanted to know about Josef Foerster.' Even speaking the words had been painful.

Havel studied her. 'I believe you,' he said. 'I saw the way you reacted. You're not a good actress,' he added, smiling faintly.

'Maybe,' she said, dazed, 'they were just hoping to recruit me. Perhaps they knew what was going to happen to Jane Bacton.'

Havel nodded. 'Perhaps. But if you're not helping them, if they don't get what they want, you might be in danger, Miss Hailston.'

Carolyn walked back to the Underground at Holborn. From the kiosk she bought a selection of morning papers. As the train rattled her beneath central London towards Queensway, she looked over the front-page headlines, finding it hard to believe that they involved her and her family. WAS COMMONS SECRETARY RED SPY? . . . MYSTERY KILLING OF MINISTER'S AIDE . . . MINISTER'S SECRETARY SPYING FOR CZECHS? . . . SPY IN MINISTER'S OFFICE?

She read the stories in a daze, almost missing her station. She darted through the closing door, the papers tucked under her arm, and walked back to her flat. A couple of policemen were outside the block, and a group of photographers and reporters. Immediately they surged towards her. She heard camera shutters click. 'Did you know Miss Bacton? How long had you known her? Did you see her when you came back from Prague? You went to a Czech Embassy party — was Miss Bacton there?'

Carolyn looked at them, bewildered, confused. She said nothing, but glanced desperately towards the policemen. They came forward, pushing between the throng of newspaper men. 'Come on, Miss Hailston,' one of them said as he took her arm. Then turning to the reporters, he added, 'She doesn't want to speak to you, boys — you can see that.'

Carolyn was hurried to her flat. She slammed the door behind her, ran into the sitting room, threw herself on to the put-u-up, and lay still. She had a curious detached feeling, as though she could no longer believe in the reality of things about her. At last she began to cry.

* * *

By the next morning Carolyn was feeling calmer. It had not been an easy night, trying to face the reality of Josef's betrayal. When Toni had returned from one of her evening activities, Carolyn was already in bed, but awake. She dismissed her friend's anxious questioning and insisted that she was simply tired. She did not want to talk about anything.

At last she had found herself thinking of her mother, wondering how she would handle such a situation, indeed, how she was coping with what had already happened — the implied threat to her husband because of the murder of a secretary who might, all the time, have been spying for the Czechs. Esme would be calm, she would think about it coolly, and then she would make the best of things in that elegant way of hers. It had helped. Slowly Carolyn had forced herself to accept what had happened, and at last she had fallen into an uneasy sleep.

In the morning she stayed in bed until Toni had left, resisting her friend's urgent suggestion that she would bring her some orange juice, toast and coffee. When left alone, she eventually tumbled some cornflakes into a bowl and made some strong coffee herself. She looked out of the window to see the sun filtering through the trees. It looked like a hot day.

A couple of policemen were still at the entrance to the flats and, since she had a three-minute walk to the lock-up garage housing her red Ford Fiesta, she was grateful that there was no sign of reporters. Apart from her underlying anxiety she even enjoyed the drive down to her father's constituency.

The house, unimaginatively called 'Woodlands', was set in a clearing of birch woods among the narrow lanes of the undulating country south of Slaugham. The countryside gave the impression of being remote, but in fact the A23 road was conveniently close. The house itself was built of old stone with hanging tiles, and was reached down a narrow wooded drive which encircled an oasis of grass before a modest cottage-like doorway.

Her mother had obviously heard the crunching of tyres on the gravel because, by the time Carolyn had come to a stop, the front door was open and Esme was standing there, smiling. Resignedly, Carolyn noted two other figures nearby — policemen.

'I've got some nice cooling drinks on the terrace,' Esme said. 'I'm sure you could do with one after that drive.'

The terrace at the back of the house was south-facing, and seemed a natural culmination of sloping lawns and shrubberies. At the end the garden was bordered by woodland.

'Have you had the Press after you?' Carolyn asked as she sank into a floral-cushioned outdoor chair.

'Only the local boys. I don't think the nationals have found us here. Anyway, their real story is in London . . . unfortunately,' she added, and Carolyn saw a saddened cast in her eyes.

She wasn't sure what to say. She didn't care a damn about her father's career, but then she was not in love with the man. 'You mean it will finish Daddy?' she said.

'Oh no, because any inquiry will find that he's not involved at all, but obviously he won't get appointed to the Cabinet while the whole investigation is going on. It'll hit him hard, you know. In fact it has. I've been very worried about him recently. He's been edgy, preoccupied, and he's even been a bit slap-happy about his injections. And that's dangerous. I shouldn't be here really. But he insisted. Oh dear, I shall be glad when it's all over.'

'Yes,' Carolyn said distractedly, 'so shall I.' She took a long drink. It was a fruit cup with an alcohol base, and was very refreshing.

They were silent, sharing an unspoken understanding. Carolyn jiggled the swizzle stick, stirring the ice in her glass. She was beginning to relax.

'I told you about Josef in Prague,' she murmured quietly. 'They had him in prison.'

Esme nodded. 'Of course, darling.'

'It seems he was a bastard.'

'Meaning?'

'He set me up. He was really working for the Czech secret police.'

'How do you know?'

'An organization in this country — publishers. They keep in touch with Czech dissidents.'

'But why?'

Carolyn chinked her ice cubes. 'They hoped to recruit me. Get information out of Daddy.'

Her mother smiled tolerantly. 'My dear, what a hope. How could they, unless they could blackmail him? And I wouldn't give them too much chance then.'

Esme topped up her own long glass, then did the same for Carolyn. Her white cotton blouse and skirt added to the impression of coolness and self-possession that not even the dark red of her hair countered. Carolyn admired her — the handsome poise of the head that told you she was in control.

After a while Esme said, 'I suppose she was his mistress.' She added hurriedly, 'I don't blame him. I'm afraid I opted out. We had other things going for us. We're very happy.'

'I . . . I don't know. I'd assumed so, too.'

'Pillow talk wouldn't work with him.'

Carolyn said incredulously, before she realized what she was saying, 'You love him, don't you?'

Her mother looked up, surprised. 'Well, of course, darling.'

Carolyn didn't reply. She took a deep draught of the fruit cup. She felt close to her mother. It was comforting.

Esme interrupted her silence. 'You fell for Josef?'

Carolyn nodded. She attempted, defensively but unconvincingly, to be flippant: 'I suppose I write it down to experience.' Her mother patted her hand understandingly. 'Prague is a beautiful city, you know. I don't suppose I shall ever go back there now.'

'I believe Mozart felt more at home there than he did in Vienna.'

'Yes. He wrote most of *Don Giovanni* there. I saw the harpsichord he used. When he first went to Prague he stayed in what's now the British Embassy.'

Esme smiled. 'Do you want a damn good cry?'

'I had it last night. I'm not sure what I want now.'

'Get back to work, I should think.'

'It's time I did.'

'You haven't told me everything.'

Carolyn took her mother's hand. 'You're a very perceptive lady, Mother.'

'Well, why?'

Carolyn hesitated. 'I've told you all.'

'They why am I perceptive?'

Carolyn tossed back her hair and managed a laugh. 'Oh, you just are. No significance.'

'But if the Czechs hoped to recruit you . . . well, they must have been in touch.'

'I went to a party at their Embassy — just to find out about Josef. That was before I knew. I don't see how they can try to make use of me,' she faltered, 'now that I'm safely at home.'

'There's no point in hiding anything, darling.'

'I know.' But Carolyn thought to herself: If ever I told you, it would break your heart.

Esme nodded, and stared long and hard at her daughter. 'Who do you suppose killed her?' she asked suddenly.

Carolyn shook her head. 'Who knows?'

'And why?'

Again Carolyn shook her head. 'It's a mystery. I can't make sense of it.'

'No,' Esme muttered thoughtfully, 'neither can I. Who would want her out of the way? Unless . . . ' But she never completed the sentence. The sound of the telephone from the house interrupted them.

* * *

Toni had nothing arranged for that evening, and had rather assumed that, as she had left Carolyn in the flat, they might spend the time talking. She felt distinctly inquisitive. She was sure there was a lot her friend had not told her. Then Carolyn phoned her at the Commons to say that she was driving down to her mother in Sussex. As it turned out, both of Toni's MPs were away, and there was nothing to keep her at the Commons after about six o'clock.

Half an hour later, feeling disappointed and at a loose end, she let herself into their flat, still wondering what she might do with herself for the rest of the evening. At least she would get out of her dress. Not that there was anything wrong with it. It was a summer dress, fitted her figure nicely, and was smart. But it represented the working day and, even with nothing to do, she preferred to get into something more relaxing.

Thus it was that she breezed through the door into their sitting room — and stopped with a sudden gasp. Instantly she was alert.

'Who the hell are you?'

The man had been seated in a chair facing her. But he immediately rose politely to his feet, and bowed. He was a good deal taller than she was, slim, undeniably handsome, with black hair and liquid dark eyes. Suave was the word that instantly occurred to her, as she momentarily relaxed at the sight of his bowed head.

'Miss Toni Bright — yes?' he said in English that was intriguingly accented.

'Who are you?' she repeated. 'And how the hell did you get in here?'

He gestured expansively with his hand. 'Through the door, my dear Miss Bright. I hoped I might find Miss Hailston here too. Please,' he said, waving his hand back again, 'don't let me disturb you.'

'What are you doing here?'

'I came to see you — both of you. But I am — as you say — happy to see you, eh?'

162

Toni no longer felt apprehensive. On the contrary, she knew she was quite capable of dealing with him should he try anything. She was intrigued. What the hell was it all about?

'Why don't we sit down — yes? And talk.'

'You haven't told me who you are.'

'Oh, I apologize. It is remiss of me. You can call me Ivan.' He smiled ingratiatingly. 'It is spelt with an I, but pronounced like an E.'

He resumed his seat, looking thoroughly relaxed. Toni perched herself on the edge of the table, giving her a slight height advantage.

'You broke in,' she said. 'I could hand you over to those policemen outside.' Then, suddenly astonished, she added, 'Did they let you in?'

Ivan shrugged and smiled. 'They didn't see me,' he said.

Toni shook her head in disbelief.

'No,' he repeated, 'it is true. They are not the — how you say? — experienced kind. I don't think you "hand me over". We have to talk.' His voice had sharpened with a slight edge of menace. 'I was wondering why,' he continued, 'Miss Hailston had not kept her promise to meet me today.'

'No good asking me. You still haven't told me who you are.'

'You still haven't called me Ivan,' he said with exaggerated charm.

Toni had to admit there was something irresistible about him, but also something vaguely threatening. Perhaps she should return to the attack.

'What right do you think you have to break into my flat like this?'

Again he gave a little hunch to his shoulders, smiled disarmingly, and said, 'You must not look at it like that. I needed to see you, and that seemed the best way.'

'It might in your country, wherever that is. Not here.'

Once more his smile was meant to dismiss her objections.

'Let us not be unfriendly,' he said. 'We can help each other. Oh, and your friend.'

'All right. What is it?'

Ivan appeared to consider for a moment. Then he said, very smoothly, 'We should like you to help us.'

'Who the hell is "us"?'

'Czechoslovakia.'

'Very funny.' Toni swung her legs from where she sat on the table edge. 'I suppose you'll tell me that's why Carolyn was meant to meet you today?'

He smiled and nodded. 'You have — what you say? — got it in one.' He looked pleased with the expression, and even more pleased as he added, 'And you would make two.'

'Now look — you're very lucky I haven't thrown you out. I might yet. As for helping you: go take a running jump.'

Ivan pretended puzzlement. 'Jump?'

'You know what I mean. I'm not helping you.'

Ivan pursed his lips, considering. He took his time before he said, 'I had hoped that because your friend is helping us, you might as well. But — '

'I don't know what Carolyn's doing,' Toni interrupted, 'but I bet she wouldn't help you if she could avoid it. And I have no intention of helping. Mr Ivan, you can go.'

'Don't you want to hear what it is? And how much we would pay?'

'To spy for you bastards? Piss off.'

Ivan looked shocked, and then smiled. He put his long, elegant fingers together in a prayer-like attitude, and tapped the tips of them slowly and regularly, all the time staring at her. Then quietly he said, 'You do not have a choice.'

'Now, look here — '

'We want you to succeed Miss Bacton as Mr Hailston's secretary,' he interrupted. 'You already work at the House of Commons.'

Toni laughed scornfully.

Ivan ignored her mirth. 'It should not be difficult for you to persuade him,' he said. 'Perhaps Mrs Hailston would tell him that you are very suitable.'

Toni swung herself off the table. 'I'm fed up. You can go now,' she said.

He continued tapping his fingers together, a sardonic smile quivering about his lips. 'I said you have no choice, Miss Bright.'

Toni stood in front of him, aware of his charm; aware, too, of something more ominous in his manner.

'You see,' he continued patiently, 'you have been working for us already.'

Toni's eyes widened. 'Like hell I — '

'Oh yes,' he interjected. 'You have been far more helpful than you know. You came here at the recommendation of Miss Bacton — yes? And Miss Bacton told you that Mr Hailston was very worried about his daughter. She asked you to keep an eye on her, and to tell Miss Bacton if there was anything unusual, anything to cause concern — you remember — yes? One day she found you and a boy friend here, and you thought she behaved a bit irrationally — like there was something funny about her and men. So you told Miss Bacton about it. That information was very helpful to us when Miss Hailston came to Prague.' There was a small triumph in his smile.

Toni stared at him open-mouthed. 'That was just a father's natural concern. It seemed — '

'Innocent enough — yes? But Mr Hailston never said any such thing. Mr Hailston couldn't, as you say, care less about his daughter.'

'I didn't know.'

Ivan shrugged. 'We could make it sound a lot more important,' he said. 'There is a lot we could say you have done for us — if we cared to leak information to your Secret Service. So, Miss Bright, you see you have no choice. You will succeed Miss Bacton, and then you will be given new instructions.' He lifted a hand to silence her interpolation. 'Oh, you will be rewarded for such service,' he said.

Toni shook her head, and burst into laughter. 'I don't believe a bloody word of this.'

Ivan rose and stood close to her. The smile gone, he looked almost sinister. He said threateningly, 'Miss Bright, we could make life very difficult for you. Have a talk to your friend — she will tell you. There is no alternative. You must understand that. Then you will help us.'

'Get out before I kick you in the balls.' Her eyes lit up mischievously. She laughed at him.

Back came the charming smile, the ingratiating gesture of the hands. 'Just think about it,' he said quietly. As he turned to go, he added, 'If you are going to be troublesome, Miss Bright, we will frame you with your MI5 straight away. Now, don't forget that.'

With a little shrug he walked into the hall and let himself out.

Toni sank down on the edge of the put-u-up, feeling in spite of her laughing disbelief, a little apprehensive. Could they really blackmail her like this? And what about Carolyn — what was she doing? Were they blackmailing her as well — forcing her to co-operate? Toni's inclination was to regard the whole episode as preposterous, but she couldn't avoid a slight feeling of alarm. Beneath the suavity of Ivan's manner there had been an unmistakable threat.

As she sat thinking she suddenly realized that she was still wearing her House-of-Commons dress. A bath? That was a good idea. Then she would decide what to do with herself. She didn't like soaking — the weather was too warm for that — but briskly washed away the grime of the day, and afterwards spent a few moments wandering round her bed-sitter in the nude, debating what to wear. With only bra and bikini briefs beneath, she donned a turquoise T-shirt and white cotton skirt.

She was wondering whether to cook herself a meal or go out, when the doorbell rang or, to be more precise, made its customary burping sound. She opened it to face the freckly grin of David Rackham, and her expression brightened instantly.

'You're the one person I want to see,' she said spontaneously. 'Come in. But I expect you've come to see Carolyn?'

'No,' he replied as he followed her along the tiny hall into the sitting room. 'No, I imagine she's gone down to Sussex.'

Toni's eyes widened. 'How did you know?'

'I suggested it. Seemed sensible. So it's you I've come to see. And if I may say so, Miss Bright,' he added, deliberately pompous, 'you are very well worth seeing. And what a welcome I got.' When their mutual laughter had subsided, he announced, 'I'll take you out for a meal.'

Toni was about to say that would be marvellous when, unexpectedly, she replied, 'No. Let me cook us something. I've got some chicken pieces. Can turn them into a casserole. Come and watch me, and tell me why you want to see me.'

'Do I have to give a reason? Who wouldn't want to see you?'

Toni flashed him a smile and hurried into the kitchen. 'Look over our few bottles of wine and pick out the best,' she said.

That turned out to be nothing better than a Beaujolais Villages, but Rackham reckoned that would do nicely. Toni had already gone to work on the chicken pieces, some vegetables and stock, when Rackham said, 'I think Carolyn's holding out on me. That could be serious.'

'Meaning?' The word was flung smilingly over her shoulder as she chopped carrots.

'Has she told you about Josef?'

Toni made an affirmatory noise and continued with her chopping. She reached for an onion. 'I'll have you crying for mercy,' she laughed.

Rackham retired to the doorway. 'Well, I know she went to a party at the Czech Embassy. But I'm convinced they're blackmailing her.'

'They are,' Toni shouted. 'They've told me so. They call it helping them.'

'They — ?' Rackham began, astonished.

'The Czechs. I've had one of them round here tonight. Ivan somebody or other. Trying to blackmail *me*. Handsome bastard — full of charm and menace.'

'Tell me.'

'No, pour us a drink. There's gin and tonic. I'll tell you when I've got this in the oven. Go and look at naughty pictures in Carolyn's art books. The old masters liked a bit of flesh.'

'Who doesn't?' Rackham grinned, as he followed her instructions.

A few minutes later, gin and tonic in one hand, she came and peered over his shoulder. 'I can't believe all Renoir's girls had such big bums and bellies,' she laughed and then propped herself on cushions at the other end of the put-u-up.

'But beautiful boobs,' Rackham added, as he closed the book and darted an approving glance at Toni's turquoise T-shirt. 'Now, story-time, please.'

Toni embarked upon an exuberant account of Ivan Kubat's visit, not omitting her own role in telling Jane Bacton about Carolyn's strange reaction at finding a naked Harry in the flat. 'How the hell was I to know that Jane was working for those bastards? I just thought Carolyn's father was worried about her,' she said indignantly. Rackham nodded, and she continued with her story, leading to Kubat's proposition. 'He was a smooth cookie, that Ivan. I threatened to kick him in the balls,' she laughed.

'And did you?'

'No. He decided to leave.' She frowned. 'So how are they blackmailing Carolyn?'

'I wish I knew. I thought perhaps you might know something that would give me a clue.'

Toni shook her head. 'But something sexual, I suppose, if what Ivan said was true.'

Rackham gave a little grunt of acknowledgement. He was thinking that, whatever it was, it was presumably the reason for Carolyn's response to him, which was mostly characterized by a kind of sisterly affection.

Oh well, he thought to himself, if it wasn't to be Carolyn, it might be Toni. He caught her darkly glowing eyes looking at him, and he smiled. She had got disturbingly little on, and he saw that she knew he was admiring her body. Her reaction was a humorously knowing look, which Rackham interpreted as distinctly promising.

Over their meal and the bottle of Beaujolais they discussed Carolyn, Kubat and his demands, and finally themselves, which, since Rackham disclosed very little about himself, mostly meant talking about Toni and her interests. At the end of it, pleasantly mellowed with drink, Rackham announced with a grin, 'I should like to thank you for a delicious meal, providing you promise to keep your karate chops to yourself.'

She did not need to reply. Her eyes told him all he wanted to know. Nevertheless his kiss, although warm, was cautious.

'A bit diplomatic, wasn't it?' she laughed.

Rackham needed no further invitation. As he held her close, he murmured that it would be an awful shame to crease and crumple such a nice white skirt, and deftly he undid its zip and let it slip to the floor. He bent to retrieve it, looking breathlessly at the bikini briefs as he did so. As he straightened up, her hands reached inside his shirt, and then, as they kissed, skilfully unfastened his belt and trouser top.

They did not get to her bed-sitter until much later that night. The put-u-up was so conveniently close.

12

Camden Town — apart from having given its name to a famous group of painters led by W.R. Sickert — is a fascinating area of London. It is inhabited by a complex mix of nationalities living in anything from crowded council tenements to squares of gracious but unfashionable houses. For some years many a back street, square or crescent has been struggling to achieve something of the milieu of neighbouring Canonbury, but has never quite made it. In one such crescent, where crumbling stucco has expensive restoration as neighbour, lived ex-SAS sergeant Bill Hunter. He had bought it from the proceeds of an African adventure soon after he had left Stanley Hailston's security firm. The area, he decided, was slowly 'coming up', and accordingly he smartened the appearance of his own property. It also had the advantage of being the kind of area into which he could disappear. There was no great community interest, and his neighbours kept very much to themselves. So did he.

Since he returned home early on Monday afternoon, he had mostly stayed indoors. The radio, television and the morning newspapers had confirmed what he had confidently expected — that the police had not the slightest idea who had disposed of the person he now knew to be Jane Bacton. That first discovery had caused a slight whistle between his teeth. Hailston had said she was a spy but he hadn't said she was his own secretary. No wonder he had wanted to get rid of her — the bloody woman had been using his office to spy for the Czechs. Presumably

Hailston had not had enough proof to hand her over, or maybe there was some other reason. That kind of thing did not concern Hunter. He had been contracted to do a job, and he'd done it. The description issued by the police, and the reconstructed video-fit, bore not the slightest resemblance to his normal appearance. He had no anxiety. The most difficult crime to solve was the motiveless crime.

That Thursday he had booked himself a flight to Jersey from Southampton, and there was plenty of time for a leisurely drive. He was taking the briefcase of twenties to pay into his account in a Jersey bank. It was a bright sunny day and he felt well pleased, both with himself and the way of the world.

Early that same Thursday morning a green, high-sided van parked in the crescent some fifty yards from Hunter's house. The driver remained sitting in the parked vehicle. In due course he saw Hunter run down the steps of his home on to the pavement, and load a large suitcase into the rear of a car. A few moments later he emerged with a black briefcase, which also went into the back. Hunter unlocked the driver's door, got in and drove out into Agar Grove and on towards Camden Town and Regent's Park. Hunter's taste in cars was conventional. He was content with a red Austin Maestro.

The green van pulled out from the space where it had been parked for the past two hours, and followed at a discreet distance. At least the colour of Hunter's car made it easy to keep in sight as they made their way into the heavy streams of traffic in Marylebone Road and Westway. The van driver, assuming that the red Maestro was making for the M4, and accordingly keeping well out of sight behind, nearly lost his quarry when Hunter suddenly turned south leading towards Chiswick. The van closed the distance slightly until the driver was satisfied that the Maestro was making for the M3.

Hunter slipped in a music cassette of Frank Sinatra. Modern pop music was too noisy for his taste and, as he had never understood the classics, he preferred some recognizable tune that he could whistle. This he did as he drove at no more than a steady sixty on to the start of the M3 motorway. He had no reason to hurry, and he certainly had no intention of being booked by the police for speeding. He whistled and he sang along with the tones of Sinatra.

The green van closed the gap. Once both of them were on the M3 there was nothing suspicious about being followed for many miles by the same vehicle. The driver had only hired the van the previous day, having discovered to his annoyance that Hunter's house was too secure easily to make an entry. When later he abandoned the van, it would be found that neither the hirer nor his address existed. The present plan probably carried slightly more risk but the security of Hunter's home allowed no alternative. The driver realized that he was going to have to make his decision suddenly when the road conditions were just right. Moreover there was no point in forcing the red Maestro off the road after a long spell with the two vehicles racing neck and neck, side by side. That would only provide the Maestro's driver with valuable thinking time and the opportunity to take evasive action, and the car being faster and more manoeuvrable, he would probably succeed. So it would have to be a sudden action, so quick that the Maestro had no choice but to do the obvious, and that must result in his crashing. It was essential, however, to avoid a collision. That would prevent the van driver making a getaway.

The traffic thinned the further they drove west. They passed huge signboards indicating ways off to Woking and Guildford and Bracknell, to Farnborough and Aldershot. The van driver reasoned that the most suitable hazard would be an embankment, because that would give the Maestro driver less space for evasion. A rising embankment, however, might result in the Maestro careering back into the van. A falling embankment would be much better. The van closed until it was immediately behind the Maestro and, since both vehicles were barely travelling at sixty miles an hour, they were occupying the inner lane. Every time an embankment came into sight, however, there was a barrier at the road's edge.

Still they drove west. The sprawling development of box-like houses that was Basingstoke smudged the landscape on the right. Hunter had tired of Sinatra and switched off his radio-cassette player. The sunlight was flooding into the car, and he lowered the window on the driver's side all the way. A glance in his rear-view mirror told him that a green van was still behind him. At least that was one commercial driver who was probably obeying the law. He glanced at the clock on the fascia, then at his watch. There was no need to hurry. The speedometer needle was still hardly touching 60, but that was enough.

The road would soon be dividing, south to Winchester and Southampton, and further west to Andover. The van driver peered ahead.

There was an embankment — a falling embankment. And no barrier. He pulled into the second lane, as though he intended to pass the red Maestro, and drew level with the back of the car, giving the impression that he had not got quite enough speed to pass. It was going to be a risky manoeuvre.

They drew level with the embankment. The van pulled out even wider to the furthest limit of the second lane. The driver thrust his foot hard on the accelerator. The van surged forward — level, ahead. When almost past, from the far edge of the second lane, it lurched violently leftwards, right across the front of the Maestro.

Hunter's right foot jammed the brake to the floor boards. At the same time he swung left to avoid the collision. The two vehicles were rushing across the hard shoulder. The front of the van was bearing down upon him. Again instinctively, he swung the steering wheel to the left. The little red car rocked towards the edge. Hunter half saw the man in the van wrestling to spin the steering wheel to the right. The Maestro's nearside front wheel was over the edge. Hunter fought to pull it back on to the road. It lurched leftwards, half spun, tumbled on to

173

its side and over on to its roof as it hurtled down about twenty feet of embankment.

The van driver was breathing fast and heavily. That had been too near for his liking. He had only just managed to rock the van back to the right in time. Now, as his foot pressed hard on the accelerator, he came back into the inner lane and looked about him. The rear-view mirror showed four or five cars behind, and there were one or two immediately ahead of him. Some of them would have seen what had happened. It would have looked like an accident, but he knew that anyone who had witnessed it would now expect him to stop. He pressed harder on the accelerator, drew into the second lane and drove at the van's maximum speed to the next interchange. Then he swung back on to the eastward road of the motorway, and drove the vehicle towards London at the very limit of its performance. After only a few miles he was able to leave the motorway at exit 6 for Basingstoke. He followed signs to the railway station, parked the van, and bought a ticket to London.

About the same time that police were being called to an accident on the M3, Carolyn drove into Haywards Heath to do some shopping for her mother. She had hoped to park on the left side of the main street, but there was a continuous line of cars. So she turned right at the traffic lights and found a place in the National Car Park opposite Bejam's supermarket, which she had to visit anyway. First, however, she made one or two calls in other shops, paused to admire the classical cut of clothes in Country Casuals before going to make her main purchases in the supermarket.

When she returned to her car she was loaded with plastic carrier bags of food and various provisions. She redistributed them awkwardly while she fished in her shoulder bag for the car keys.

As she was trying to open the door, a voice said, 'Can I help?'

She recognized it instantly. Without even looking, she said, 'I don't think so.'

'But I think I can.' The tone was smooth, insinuating, faintly accented. She felt a hand grip her elbow, and turned to meet Ivan's deliberately charming smile. She put the loaded carrier bags on to the driving seat, and walked back to open the boot. Ivan followed with the goods and handed them to her.

'You drive rather fast in those narrow lanes,' he said. 'We had a little difficulty sometimes. Lucky we guessed your route, h'mm?'

Carolyn stood facing him by the back of the car. 'I've finished,' she said.

'Oh, I think there is some unfinished business.'

'There is nothing more I can do. That's the end of it.'

'I think not.' The charm had quickly given way to menace. He tilted his head. Immediately another man was alongside her. She saw the shape of a pistol in his jacket pocket pointing towards her. 'We need to talk, Carolyn.' The menace was still there in Ivan's voice. 'I think we take a little ride, yes?'

The other man jerked his head in the direction of the driving seat. The pistol twitched simultaneously. Carolyn met his gaze. He had not got the smooth, well-oiled charm of Ivan; his face was humourless, his body thickset. He looked a thug.

Ivan stood beside her, deliberately holding open the driver's door, while the second man went round to the other side of the car and got in. By the time Carolyn had settled herself in position, he was already seated in the back of the car. Only then did Ivan leisurely walk round and take his place in the passenger seat.

'Would you be so kind, Carolyn, as to take the Lewes road?'

For one impulsive moment, Carolyn thought she would drive to the nearest police station, but even as the thought came to her, she saw that the pistol had been removed from the other man's pocket. He leant forward, and she felt it poked insistently into her side. Without speaking, she started the car and drove out. At the exit the pistol was withdrawn. Ivan took the parking ticket from her and, with a smile, paid the attendant. Carolyn drove on silently. At Scayne's Hill, Ivan instructed her to take a small road to the left. After she had driven about a mile, he told her to pull in off the road beneath the shade of a tree.

When she had turned off the engine, he smiled and, the menace gone, he said, 'I think this will do very nicely for our little talk, h'mm?'

Carolyn was angry, but she determined to try to remain calm, telling herself that there was nothing they could really do to her now. Not that she trusted that ape in the back. She had to behave sensibly while he held the gun. But now that she had discovered about Josef, she felt that the balance was no longer tilted in their favour.

She said briskly, 'What is there to talk about?'

'You do not sound like yourself, yes?' Carolyn ignored him. He added, 'There is still the matter of the list. That is important. But more important, Carolyn, we think you are in danger, h'mm?'

'Only from that gun,' she said, tossing her head back.

Ivan smiled. 'Oh, I hope not. It seemed you needed a little persuasion, yes?'

'I think you've done enough persuading.'

He was unperturbed, graciously acknowledging her remark with a slow nod of his head. 'But I still think you are in danger,' he repeated.

'How?'

'I think you were meant to be the victim at Traceys, not Miss Bacton.'

'She was working for you,' Carolyn responded accusingly. The Czech shrugged. 'How long had that been going on for?'

Again Ivan shrugged, and offered an accompanying smile. 'I think Miss Bacton was mistaken for you. By someone who did not know either of you perhaps. Same build, same colouring, h'mm?'

'Oh, that's nonsense. Who would want to kill me?'

The look from the depth of Ivan's dark eyes might even have been mistaken for kindness. He hesitated before he said quietly, 'Your father?'

Carolyn didn't answer. She was thinking.

'You don't think so?'

'I don't know,' Carolyn said softly.

'Of course, not him personally, although he has the knowledge, the experience. He would not make that mistake, however.'

Carolyn considered. With that dynamic ambition of his, she could believe anything. He was used to removing obstacles — anything that got in his way. And she was sure he disliked her with an intensity that was close to hatred.

'Who did it then?' she asked.

Ivan looked enigmatic. 'We think we know. We are . . . er, dealing with the situation. We did not want to lose Miss Bacton.'

'I'm still not sure,' Carolyn said.

'You are a threat to him — don't you see? Blackmailing him for information. You have to do this. You have no choice, because of what has happened in the past — yes? But he needs to get rid of you, because you alone can verify all the allegations. No one else can. With you out of the way, he could deny everything. Just a Czech plot — hey? But you can ruin him. He knows that.' Ivan paused, looking confident and satisfied. 'And,' he said, the merest hint of menace returning to his voice, 'we have the power to make you do that. It is called Josef — no?'

'No. No it bloody isn't,' she said angrily.

Ivan looked surprised. 'Oh.' He pretended a gesture of dismay with his hands. 'Not fickle — you? You no longer love him?'

Carolyn resolved to keep her cool. 'Josef's an empty threat,' she said. 'He was working for you the whole time. He set me up.'

Ivan raised one eyebrow and gave a little shrug. 'So?'

'Well, it's no good using Josef to get my help,' she said patiently.

'No? You are forgetting one important thing, Miss Carolyn Hailston. You have been helping us. Secret meetings with the enemy, yes? We can hand you over to the British authorities at any time. That would make a nice scandal — eh? Minister's daughter a spy. What would Mrs Hailston think of that? And what about you? British prisons may be better than Czech prisons — I don't know. But I don't think you would find them very comfortable.'

He was smiling at her suavely. She felt like smashing her hand across his face, but controlled herself. There was no point. He was right, the bastard. Again, she felt trapped. Was there no way out? Everything she did seemed to involve her more deeply, and potentially more disastrously.

Ivan was content with the silence for two or three minutes. Then he said quietly, 'So we have a deal, Carolyn.'

'The list?'

He nodded. 'Yes, the proper list. And the report — not the unclassified version. We have that. The secret one.'

'You didn't expect me at Traceys after — ?'

'No. That is why we are here. Now, you do understand, Carolyn? Unless we have your co-operation, we hand you over. I should not like to do that.'

Carolyn nodded, feeling the anger pent up within her.

'When?' she sighed, resignedly.

'Why not Sunday? That should give you enough time. Your father is having some trouble, eh? But no mistake, remember. I think Coldfall Wood is still all right. Twelve noon. If I am not there you will know that you have been followed. In that case a message will be delivered to you.'

Carolyn was inwardly furious. She felt there was something she should be able to do. But there was no way out. She muttered her assent.

'Now perhaps we go back to Haywards Heath, yes?'

Glad to be doing something, Carolyn restarted the car, turned it round and drove briskly back to town. Half way along the main street he told her to stop. He got out, held the door for the man in the back, who had not spoken a word during the whole encounter.

As he was about to shut the door, with a gracious nod of thanks, Ivan said, 'Oh, Josef comes to London today. Joining our Embassy staff here.' He paused before slamming the door. 'You see, we keep our promises, Carolyn.'

Carolyn drove back to 'Woodlands' slowly, bemused. She had felt a quick frisson of excitement at the Czech's final words. Was she going to be able to see Josef, and what would happen if she did? For a few moments she was almost ready to believe that he had never betrayed her, and that there was some explanation that had so far escaped her. But no, that didn't make sense. He had deliberately provided them with information that made it possible for them to blackmail both her and her father. The more she thought about the whole affair the more trapped and the more desperate she felt.

'You've been a long time, darling,' her mother greeted her, when she carried the plastic bags of provisions into the spacious farmhouse kitchen.

'Traffic was bad,' she said casually. 'Had trouble parking.'

Then Esme saw her daughter's expression. 'Is everything all right, darling?'

'Yes, of course. Why?'

'You look a bit . . . well, strained. The Press haven't been after you, I suppose?'

'No, I — ' Carolyn bit her bottom lip, 'I don't know.'

Esme studied her. 'There's something, something important you haven't told me,' she said.

It was a statement, not a question, and Carolyn didn't know how to respond.

'Perhaps.' Disinterestedly, she began unloading the goods on to the kitchen table. She was thinking, and aware all the time that Esme was watching her. 'I believe I ought to see David Rackham,' she said. 'He's given me a number which he said would always find him. Would you mind if I asked him down, Mummy?'

'Of course not. I thought he was rather nice. Something of the little boy about him.'

'I didn't know you were such a romantic.' Carolyn's attempt at light-heartedness was not entirely successful.

'I wish you would tell me,' her mother said, suddenly serious.

'I don't know that there *is* anything to tell,' Carolyn muttered over her shoulder as she went into the hall.

She realized as she slowly punched out the number that she still had no idea what she was going to do. She was treating Rackham as a lifeline, something to hang on to in the hope that she might survive.

The number rang four times before a high-pitched voice squeaked, 'Ling Po Chinese Laundry.'

'I . . . I beg your pardon,' said Carolyn.

There was laughter at the other end of the line, and then the voice said, 'Rackham here.'

'Oh,' Carolyn breathed with relief. 'It's Carolyn Hailston.'

'Of course. Could I fail to recognize your strawberry-blonde voice?'

He made her feel better already. 'Are you never serious?' she asked, and then immediately answered, 'Yes, of course, I've *seen* you serious.'

'Ah, but I thought you'd ring sometime,' Rackham said, 'or rather, I hoped you'd ring.'

'You see, I took your advice. I'm down in Sussex.'

'Good.'

'But I need to talk to you.'

'About time if I may say so. In this sunshine the ice is getting thinner, you know.'

'You couldn't come down, could you?'

'Of course.'

'Do you know the address?'

'Again, of course. I'll be down for tea.'

13

David Rackham's white Porsche 924 scrunched to a stop on the gravel by the front door shortly before four o'clock. He showed his pass to the two policemen, but before he could reach the door, Esme Hailston had already opened it, and was standing there with a welcoming smile.

'Will Earl Grey do?' she asked as she led him through the hall.

Rackham had anticipated that it could only be Earl Grey, and so he uttered one word, 'Perfect.'

As they entered the drawing room, Rackham noted that Carolyn was already there. The room was a country version of its counterpart in Chester Square. The furniture was functional and comfortable, and covered in country prints.

Carolyn got up to greet him. 'Thank you for coming,' she said, as her mother went out to fetch the tea. 'I must talk to you alone. After tea we'll go for a walk in the woods.'

'Ah, "In the middle of the woods Lived the Yonghy-Bonghy-Bo". I'll look forward to it.'

Thus Carolyn was laughing when her mother brought in the tray with silver teapot and jug.

'That's better,' Esme said. 'I don't know what it is she wants to see you about, Mr Rackham, but there's something she won't tell me.'

Carolyn protested unconvincingly, 'No, it's not that. It's — '

She was saved by Rackham, who said engagingly, 'I'm sure there are no important secrets between you.'

'Have you,' Esme asked, 'seen my husband again?'

'This morning.' Then seeing her anxiety, he added, 'Oh, a full inquiry is necessary, it's inevitable, Mrs Hailston, but your husband is not involved in any way. It's the extent of the Bacton woman's activities we're interested in.'

'Do you yet know who killed her?'

'No. The police are handling that but, as yet, I don't think they have a clue.'

For the next half-hour they talked about the house, its situation, apparently so remote and yet so close to the main road, its convenience for the constituency, Esme's constituency activities, and the differences between life in the country and Chester Square.

Then Esme said, 'Well, I'll leave you two alone.'

'I think we'll go for a walk, Mummy.'

She led the way across the terrace, down the garden to the margin of the wood. It was still hot, and the frettled shade of the trees was welcome.

As they shuffled through the leaf-mould, he said, 'It's taken you a long time to realize that it's Czech-mate.'

'You were right,' she said. 'Well, it looks as though what you called your alternative scenario was right.'

He looked at her with a quizzical smile.

'Josef was working for them,' she said.

'How do you know?'

'Viktor Havel told me. The Dalibor Press — do you know it?'

'Yes.'

'I . . . I couldn't believe it,' she said, 'but I suppose I'll have to come to terms with it. You knew all the time?'

Rackham didn't answer her question. His expression seemed to her a mixture of the quizzical and the wise.

There was a fallen tree ahead of them. He took her hand, led her to it, and they sat down.

'You met Ivan Kubat at Traceys restaurant yourself,' he said. 'Why?'

182

'How did you know?'

'My job. You haven't answered me.'

'Only to try to find out about Josef.'

'You're treading on dangerous ground, you know. I told you the ice is getting thinner all the time.'

'I know,' she said softly, reached out to touch his arm for assurance, and saw his raised eyebrow.

'You're not doing anything for them, are you?'

She started to shake her head, stopped, and said, 'I don't want to. I don't, David. But — '

'Have you seen him again?'

'Yes, this morning — in Haywards Heath. No, it wasn't arranged. They — Ivan and another man — accosted me in the car park, forced me to drive out of town, down a lane and demanded that I should help them.'

'How?'

'Getting information from my father — about those firms that have secret contracts under the SDI.'

Rackham considered for a moment, and then said quietly, 'It is important that you tell me the truth. Have you handed anything over to them?'

'No.'

'Thank heaven for that. Were you going to?'

'Yes.'

'So your father co-operated?'

Carolyn shifted uneasily on the tree trunk. 'He didn't intend to.'

'So, they were in a position to blackmail your father?'

Carolyn nodded.

'How?'

She had asked him to come because events were moving too quickly out of her control and this had induced a feeling of desperation. He would be able to help her. But how could he unless she were utterly frank with him?

He interrupted the silence by reaching out and taking

her hand in his. 'It's better,' he said, 'if you don't hold anything back.'

She swallowed hard, nodded. 'I know.'

Rackham waited patiently. 'I expect they promised you Josef's release if . . . ' He purposely left the sentence unfinished.

She did not need to answer. She just looked at him and left her hand in his. That was understanding of him, comforting. He could have said something like, 'Better come clean; we don't want to have you arrested.' But he didn't. He merely waited, and she was aware of his patient understanding. That was helpful. Then she felt the gentle pressure of his hand, not firm enough to be called a squeeze. She looked at him and saw that his eyes were smiling reassuringly.

'They discovered something from Josef,' she murmured. 'Something I'd told him.'

Still he waited, nursing her hand tenderly.

'It was something,' she continued, 'that could ruin my father's career. His married life too.'

Even now he did not press her. He just went on cradling her hand in his, smiling understandingly. Need she tell him more? In the silence the flutter of a diminutive breeze in the leaves above them sounded deafening. She sighed. His hand pressed hers.

'I . . . I'm going to have to tell you, aren't I?' she said.

'H'mm.'

She gripped his hand tightly. She felt he was like a reliable brother. 'I was thirteen,' she said. 'My father and . . . It's called incest, I believe.'

The green-hazel of his eyes looked full of sadness and understanding. Her grip relaxed slightly, and she felt the reassuring pressure of his own fingers.

'I should think you could crush walnuts with that grip of yours,' he smiled.

Carolyn laughed, but she did not take her hand away. Nor did he. At last she said, 'Well, I've told you.'

'So you were protecting your father?' he said.

'No.'

He raised a sandy-coloured eyebrow.

'I've got to be honest with you, haven't I?' she continued.

'You're not doing badly,' Rackham smiled.

'Then, I don't care about his career — or him, for that matter. I was protecting Mummy. She doesn't know.' Carolyn lifted his hand and looked straight into his eyes. 'She must never know. You promise?'

Rackham knew only too well that it was dangerous to promise anything in his trade. 'She won't learn from me,' he said.

Carolyn sighed her gratitude, and then said, more brightly than Rackham might have expected, 'So now am I going to be arrested for spying too?'

'Not if I can help it.'

'Oh, David, what's going to happen? For God's sake, what's going to happen?'

'I'm not sure. I can't be more honest than that, Carolyn. But you haven't yet done anything, except behave rather foolishly. Oh, I know you thought you had a good enough reason, but the fact is — '

'I know,' she interrupted.

'Good. Then, from now on, do as I say. All right?'

She nodded.

'First, had your father provided the list?'

'Yes. I blackmailed him.'

Rackham smiled. 'Well, you should hand it to me. But I suggest that you burn it immediately. You certainly don't hand it to Mr Ivan Kubat. You don't see the Czechs again.' Then seeing that she was about to interrupt, he added, 'I'll see they don't get to you.'

'But if they don't get the list,' she said, 'they'll make sure that Mummy and the Press find out.'

'They'll only do that if they've got something to gain. But, without your co-operation, they haven't. Up to now, they've been able to blackmail you, too. But now that you know about Josef, they've lost that advantage also.'

'They could turn me over.'

'Is that what they told you?'

She nodded.

'But you've given them nothing, told them nothing. You could have behaved more sensibly, but you haven't behaved criminally.'

The reprimand was contradicted by the laughter in his eyes. She squeezed his hand. 'Thank you,' she muttered. 'I knew you'd be able to help.'

'Only just. You nearly left it too late, didn't you?'

'I'm sorry.'

'We just have to keep you safe now,' he said. 'I think I'd be happier if you came back to London with me. Will you?'

'If you tell me to.'

He pulled her to her feet. 'Perhaps we'd better go and explain to your understanding mother,' he said.

As they crossed the lawn to the terrace they heard the sound of a car driving rapidly on to the gravel and coming to a stop.

'Sounds like visitors,' Rackham muttered, and ran round to the front of the house with Carolyn following him.

He was in time to see a police inspector and a sergeant slam the car doors. 'Afternoon — no, evening, inspector,' he said, cutting off the policeman's route to the front door and, at the same time, taking his pass from his shirt pocket.

The inspector gave a nod of recognition. 'Not surprised to find you here,' he added.

Carolyn had drawn level with them as Rackham airily, almost proprietorially, said, 'Come in, inspector,' and led the way into the hall. There they were met by Esme, coolly poised against the hall table.

'Mrs Hailston?' the inspector questioned. 'I'm Inspector Hardy, madam, and this is Sergeant Trueman.'

Esme nodded, and led them into the drawing room. Rackham and Carolyn followed.

Esme showed neither curiosity nor concern, giving the impression that there was nothing unusual in receiving two police officers on a sunny summer evening. Her self-possession automatically put others at a disadvantage. It was evident that even the inspector was aware of it.

'I'm afraid there's been rather a strange development, Mrs. Hailston,' he began.

'Indeed?'

By now Inspector Hardy had recovered. He was a big man, looked a countryman, with a florid complexion. His sergeant, by comparison, was shorter, stockier, dark and rather pale.

'There's been a serious accident on the M3,' the inspector began. 'A car went over an embankment. The driver is in hospital with serious injuries. He's unlikely to live.'

Esme waited.

Inspector Hardy coughed. 'His name,' he said, 'was William, or Bill, Hunter. Do you know him, Mrs Hailston?'

Esme said without hesitation, 'No, inspector. Should I?'

'He had with him a briefcase containing twenty-thousand pounds in twenty-pound notes. From the serial numbers we have been able to trace the bank that issued them.' Inspector Hardy paused, not for effect, but because for him it was natural to do so. 'They were issued on a cheque which appears to have been signed by you, Mrs Hailston.'

Esme looked puzzled but maintained her poise. 'That would seem to be quite impossible,' she said.

Inspector Hardy coughed again. 'I imagined so,' he said, and then took from his pocket a photocopy of the cheque. He handed it to her.

Esme studied it carefully. 'It does look like my signature,' she said. 'But I haven't drawn twenty-thousand pounds from my bank, I assure you.'

'Yes, well . . . ' the inspector said inconclusively. 'Has anyone else access to your bank account?'

'No.'

'So that's not your signature?'

'It can't be.'

'You're quite sure, Mrs Hailston, that you've never heard of Bill, or William, Hunter?'

Esme thought for a few moments. 'Yes,' she said, 'I'm quite sure I haven't.'

'So how could he have come upon twenty-thousand pounds drawn upon your account?'

'I haven't the slightest idea, inspector. You haven't been able to ask him?'

'No, he's in a coma. Not likely to come out of it either. This is only a preliminary inquiry, Mrs Hailston, you understand. But we shall certainly need a statement from you later.'

'Naturally.'

'Meanwhile, would you be so kind as to let me have a specimen of your signature?'

Esme went straight to a bureau to the left of the window, took out a sheet of paper and signed it twice. 'There,' she said, handing it to Inspector Hardy, 'will that do?'

'Thank you,' he said, as he looked at it and compared it with the signature on the photocopied cheque. 'We'll get an expert on to this.'

Rackham and Carolyn had stood silently in the background. Now Rackham stepped forward. 'Do you know anything about Bill Hunter, inspector?' he asked.

'Not yet, sir. The Yard are really handling this.'

'Description?'

'Well, from what the local boys say, sir, he's in a pretty bad mess. But stocky, tough, fair hair, Army cut, blue eyes, square-jawed.'

'What identification on him?'

'Just a driving licence, credit cards. The driving licence had a

Camden Town address. That's being checked. You don't know him sir?'

'Not yet,' Rackham replied enigmatically.

Inspector Hardy gave his sergeant a nod, and he turned and unobtrusively left the room. 'I'm sorry to give you this additional trouble, Mrs Hailston,' said the inspector. 'We'll bother you as little as possible. For the moment, of course, the money is in police possession.'

Esme saw the policemen out, and when she returned Rackham thought how suddenly sad she looked.

'Well, what is one to make of that?' she said. 'I have a strange feeling, Mr Rackham, that I don't know what is happening.'

Rackham smiled. 'At least your twenty-thousand pounds is intact,' he said. 'Forgive me, but I take it you didn't draw the money?'

Her slightly bewildered expression told him that she hadn't, before she answered, 'No, I certainly didn't.'

'So who might have had access to your cheque book and forged your signature?'

Esme didn't answer. She looked pained.

Rackham uttered a little grunt. 'Would you mind if I took Carolyn back to London with me?'

Esme was grateful for the change of subject, and recovered her poise. 'Carolyn pleases herself,' she said, 'but of course I don't mind. But is this also part of whatever it is I don't know about?'

Rackham smiled engagingly. 'The world is full of mysteries,' he said. 'But I can tell you about this one,' he added with surprising candour. 'Since Miss Bacton's murder, the Czechs have made an attempt to talk to Carolyn —'

'Oh, darling, why didn't you tell me?'

Carolyn was momentarily disconcerted, and then hastily added, 'I was going to, Mummy, but I didn't want to worry you. Thought it better to consult David first.'

Rackham gave her a glance of approval. 'So you see nothing really very mysterious.' He scribbled a number on a pad taken from his pocket. 'You can always get me on that number, Mrs Hailston. And I'll see Carolyn is properly protected — don't worry.'

'And you're not to drive too fast,' Carolyn interrupted, 'otherwise I shan't be able to keep up with you.'

'Oh, you're coming with me. You can leave your car here.'

But before Carolyn settled herself into the front passenger seat of Rackham's Porsche, Esme suddenly hugged her close for a moment. 'Take care, darling,' she whispered.

For some minutes after they had left, Esme sat thinking. Then she went into the hall and rang the direct-line number of her husband's office in the House of Commons. She half expected there would be no reply. He could be in the chamber, or somewhere else in the House — the library, the tearoom, or one of the bars. So she was almost unprepared when a voice said crisply, 'Hailston.'

'Darling.'

'Oh, Esme. Are you all right?'

'*I'm* all right, yes. You?'

'I've had a long session with the security boys — most of the day. Suppose it's necessary, but it's damned tiring.'

'I expect so. Stanley, are your paired tonight?'

Hailston paused. 'Yes,' he said.

'Good. Then I'll see you at home. I'm driving up now — immediately.'

'Why? What's wrong?'

'That's what I hope to find out. We need to talk. No,' she cut in, sensing his interruption, 'not now darling. I'll be with you as soon as I can.'

She put down the receiver, went methodically round the house locking up, checking external doors, and then went out to the garage. She nodded to the two policemen by the front door. They watched her along the wooded drive and into the lane.

One of them, with a knowing glance at his colleague, extracted the personal radio from his tunic pocket, extended the aerial and called the station.

14

It was just after ten o'clock that David Rackham turned into the semi-circular drive in front of the small and expensively modern block of flats where he lived between Westminster and Vauxhall. That was not because he had driven back to London excessively slowly, but because he had diverted to a lovely Elizabethan manor, about five miles south-west of East Grinstead. It stood amid magnificent gardens, its walls brilliantly green with creeper. Within those walls the food and wine justified the expense. Carolyn was impressed and said so.

'Ah, I confess to liking the good things of life,' Rackham explained.

'I only hope this is not the equivalent of the condemned man's hearty breakfast,' she said.

'Not if I have anything to do with it. But life *is* too short not to be enjoyed.'

He nevertheless confined himself to one and a half glasses of wine, and refused to continue their earlier conversation, dismissively muttering, 'Not here.' Then as though she need have no care in the world, he talked to her about her job, and wanted to know why she had not returned to it.

'It's time I did,' she confessed, 'but the gallery is run by an especially dear cousin of Mummy's, and he seemed to think it would do me more good to have a break. I'm not sure that's right.'

'Are you any good?' Rackham asked.

'I think so. At least I'm improving.'

He intentionally kept the conversation cheerful, so that by the time they resumed their journey, Carolyn was feeling more relaxed, mellowed by good food and good company. She stretched back in her comfortably contoured seat. For the moment it seemed no problems were insoluble. As she watched him driving, confidently and decisively, she even began to feel there were no problems.

She was brought reluctantly back to reality, however, once they were in Rackham's flat. That, too, surprised her, with its evident luxury, for her to remark, 'The government — if they're your employers — must pay you very well, David.'

He grinned, a freckly, boyish grin. 'I can afford it — just. And why shouldn't I have a little comfort?'

It was dark, and she was standing by the large window, looking down on to the Thames slithering beneath reflected lights like an enormous snake. He came and stood behind her.

'It's a pity you didn't trust me earlier,' he said.

She turned her head to look at him, and Rackham found himself admiring the tilt of her nose and gazing into her very blue eyes. He would have liked to kiss her (to be honest, that's not all he would have liked) and he wondered why he didn't. Surely he wasn't starting to have moral scruples? Maybe, he rationalized, it was an instinctive realization that, for Carolyn, the security of their relationship was its platonic nature. He restrained himself to touching her hair that appeared to glow round her head like a red-blonde halo.

She turned away from the window to face him. 'I didn't distrust you,' she said. 'But can't you understand the difficulty I was in?'

'Yes.' He paused, looking at her. 'You know, even if Josef was on the level, and in jail, they wouldn't have released him — not if they didn't want to.'

Tactically, it may not have been a good idea to mention Josef, but Rackham thought she should come to terms with reality. He surprised himself by his own considerateness.

'I know that now. But perspective depends upon where you are standing.'

'And you've moved your position,' he said, being careful not to make it sound like a question.

'I've had to.'

'I hope things don't look too bad from where you're standing now.'

She laughed, gave him a sisterly kiss on the cheek. 'I feel a lot better,' she said. She was, indeed, surprised at how relaxed she felt with him, how safe. She took his hand and together they sank on to a modern but well-cushioned settee, from which they could still see the shimmering movement of the river below. Suddenly she asked, 'Do you know who killed Jane Bacton?'

'I didn't. I think I probably do now. But I'm damned if I can understand why.'

'Well?' She raised her eyebrows, pursed her lips.

'Mr Bill Hunter might be a fair bet, but — '

'Ivan Kubat says it was my father — not him personally. It was a mistake. He meant to kill me.'

Rackham had learned seldom to be surprised by anything, and he showed no surprise now. He began to see the pieces falling into shape.

'Were you going to meet Ivan in Traceys?'

'Yes, two days later — Wednesday.'

'You're the same build, same colouring. If the killer knew you were going to be there, and was relying on a description — it's a possibility, isn't it?'

Carolyn nodded. 'Mr Hunter, hired by my father.'

Rackham considered. 'Yes, and paid twenty-thousand pounds for the job. So, we just have to make the connection between Hunter and your father. That shouldn't take the police very long.'

'Well, that's him ruined, isn't it?' Her tone had instantly hardened.

'In one sense I can understand, but — you don't like him, do you?'

'Like him? I hate him.'

Rackham took her hand. 'Your mother is clearly devoted to him. She'll try to protect him in spite of twenty-thousand smackers.'

'It's Mummy I'm sorry for. I don't know how even she will bear this.'

'At the moment, of course, he's in the clear. There's no suggestion that he co-operated with Jane Bacton, except — ' Rackham gave a little cough, — 'except in bed, and no one knew about that. Not that he was ever really suspected, but when your own secretary has been consorting with the enemy . . . ' He did not need to complete the sentence. 'So the government is jolly relieved at the moment. Bacton is enough of a scandal. It doesn't want a minister involved.'

'You mean they might try to hush it up?'

Rackham gave a little shrug. He still held on to her hand, and was glad to feel her answering pressure. 'Sorry to be an old cynic. PM shuffling Cabinet before run up to election in eighteen months' time. Quite a motive for keeping things as quiet as possible.

Carolyn looked puzzled.

'This is a security matter,' Rackham explained, 'so the police are not releasing information except at the SIS's instigation. Now, supposing it becomes known that your father knew Hunter — the Press might even discover that — there is still nothing to connect him with Hunter over this business.'

'My mother's twenty-thousand pounds.'

'Who knows about it? The police and the intelligence service, and they won't issue anything to the Press. Privately, your mother will say that she wrote the cheque after all. Hunter must have stolen the money. Sounds ridiculous, I know. But if the government is determined to snuff it out, that's how it could be done. Then, after a little while, your father, because of ill health or some other excuse, will resign his seat.'

'I don't believe it.'

'Don't tell me you'd leak the whole thing?'

Carolyn smiled. 'Of course not — for Mummy's sake.'

'Your mother need never know that a mistake was made. For her, your father was simply getting rid of an enemy agent. Might just be the kind of thing an ex-SAS man would do, take the law into his own hands.'

'You're forgetting one thing. The Czechs.'

Rackham shook his head. 'No. But they could certainly mess up my scenario. Or they might not. They will do whatever is to their advantage. And that,' he said, holding up her hand and examining her fingers, 'needs thinking about. Would you like some coffee — a nightcap?'

She held his hand to her cheek for comfort. 'No thanks.'

'I'm afraid you're going to have to stay here tonight. I'll get things organized in the morning.'

'What things?'

'Well, not just a copper hanging around outside your flats, but a Special Branch man to give you personal protection. He'll stick by you like a leech.'

Carolyn looked surprised. 'Oh, am I that important?'

'You are to Mr Kubat — yes.' He paused, looked at her whimsically. 'Of course, it might be that I think you're important for other reasons.'

'I can't think what they are. Not as an art restorer — yet.'

'No — just as yourself.' Rackham was very aware of her closeness, and was struggling not to be aroused by it.

Carolyn, for her part, felt safe and tranquil in his company.

He took her by the hand and led her through the small hallway to the door of his spare bedroom. 'This is your room,' he said. 'Mine's opposite, if you hear any ghouls and ghosties.'

She turned to him, reached up and touched his face, then

suddenly she clung to him in gratitude. There was nothing more to it than that.

He was only slightly taller. He turned her chin up towards him, kissed her as chastely as he knew how. For a moment, she merely received his kiss, and then with another surge of gratitude, she hugged him.

Rackham hardly dare move apart from her lest he break the unifying tension, but at last he did draw away and looked into her eyes. They were bright, sparkling, but he was unsure of their expression. It was a situation which, even in a fairly wide sexual experience, he had not encountered before. He wondered if she was aware that he was sexually aroused. She gave no sign, and when she kissed him again it conveyed more thankfulness than desire. Reluctantly he ignored his loins, showed her into her room, planted a series of demure kisses on her forehead, and wished her goodnight.

Esme, not stopping for food, was in London long before her daughter. As she let herself into the Chester Square house, Mrs Drury came up from the basement into the hall.

'Oh, hello, madam,' she said. 'I wasn't expecting you. Mr Hailston is in his study. Is there anything I can get you?'

'No, nothing for tonight.'

Mrs Drury bowed herself back to her basement quarters, and Esme waited five minutes in the drawing room before making her way to her husband's den. She had reviewed the whole situation thoroughly during the drive back, and knew exactly how she was going to handle it.

As the study door opened, Hailston glanced up. He looked tired, strained. There was a large scotch beside him on the desk.

He got up, kissed her on the cheek. She gripped his arms affectionately. She still didn't want to believe what she suspected, what instinctively she knew.

He surprised her by taking the initiative, and yet she shouldn't be surprised. It was his nature to take initiatives, to explore ground, go on the attack. But she had seen herself asking the first question, in a detached, controlled way. Now already he was appealing to the integrity of their relationship.

'You don't believe,' he said, 'that I had anything to do with the Czechoslovaks, do you?'

'Of course not. I know you didn't.'

'I had no idea what Jane was doing — that's what's so . . . well, unbelievable, so hurtful, so — ' he broke off, turned back and picked up the glass of whisky. For a moment he looked into it, then took a long draught.

Esme watched anxiously. 'You're not drinking too much, are you? It's not good for you, Stanley.'

Hailston snorted. 'I've had a bloody day.'

'So have I.' Esme seized the chance to regain the ground she had lost by adding quickly, 'Who is Bill Hunter, Stanley?'

Hailston looked at her, his eyes slightly glazed. 'Hunter?' he asked. 'Used to work for me. You must know him.'

'No. I'd never heard of him until today.'

'Huh. He served with me.'

'Well, you've never talked much about those days, Stanley — part of the training, I suppose.'

Hailston went back to his desk, slumped in the chair, and looked up at her — a mixture of doubt and defiance.

'What about Bill Hunter?'

'He had an accident on the M3. He's probably dead by now.'

'How do you know?'

'The police told me, Stanley. Haven't they told you?'

'No. I don't suppose they know that I knew him.'

'They'll find out.'

Hailston looked sharply round, took another swig of whisky. He felt angry, not with Esme, but with events, angry with events that were escaping his control. What the hell was this about Hunter, what had been discovered?

'So?' he mumbled, wary not to commit himself.

'He had twenty-thousand pounds with him.'

'What are you getting at, Esme?'

'A few hours ago I saw a photocopy of a cheque for twenty-thousand pounds with my signature on it. Except, it wasn't my signature.'

'Oh Christ!' His glass was empty. And he was so bloody thirsty. He changed to beer, pulling the ring from a can, and pouring the contents into his tumbler.

'Why did you do it, Stanley?'

He slurped at the beer. 'They can't prove I did it, can they? Anyone might have forged your signature.'

She looked astonished. 'It doesn't matter if they can prove it or not. I want to know why you did it.'

Hailston pulled irritatedly at his short moustache, stared into his beer.

'Can't tell you.' He jumped to his feet. 'Esme, I can't bloody tell you.' He strode back and forth across the room.

'The date of the cheque was before Jane's death. It couldn't have been for her, and somehow Hunter got hold of it? Is that what it's about? Oh, Stanley, I knew she was your mistress. I think I've known for a long time. It didn't matter. You had reason. And it didn't interfere with our life together. We were still necessary to each other. I thought we always would be, that there was nothing else we didn't share. Stanley, what have you done? What have you done to us?'

Hailston stared at her, as though he were having difficulty focusing. He swallowed several mouthfuls of beer, shook his head. 'Wasn't for her,' he shouted.

'What was it for then?'

'Esme, I've already said — I can't bloody tell you. You don't want to know, d'you understand?'

She replied quietly, coolly, 'It's my money. I didn't think I'd ever say that, Stanley. If you needed it for some reason, why didn't you tell me? Instead of behaving like a criminal?'

Hailston stumped from one side of the room to the other, and then stood facing her. 'This is the end. It's the fucking end isn't it?'

He had never used that word in front of her; he had sensed that she didn't like it. But now he stared at her, as though still struggling to focus, and half shouting, half crying, he repeated it: 'The bloody fucking end.'

Esme wanted to take his head on to her breast, comfort him. She had never seen him like this before. Instead, she still kept her distance, maintained her dignity.

'Do you know who killed Jane?' she asked.

'Yes,' he mumbled. 'I know who killed her.'

'Shouldn't you tell the police?'

Hailston laughed, pulled at his moustache again, slurped back the last of his beer. 'Tell the bloody police? You must be joking? Ha. It was Hunter — that's who it was — bloody Hunter.'

Esme looked horrified. 'You . . . you weren't paying him to . . . ?'

Hailston thought he saw a way out — at least in his wife's eyes. But he had already told her that he hadn't known what Jane was doing. But perhaps he might have discovered. So he didn't reply, but looked at her as though she had hit on the truth. His voice was slurred as he muttered, 'You're very clever, Esme — always were very clever, you were. I'm a lucky bugger, aren't I? Having such a clever wife, eh?'

He staggered, shook his head. He began to sway, then fell back heavily into his chair. 'Oh God,' he muttered.

'Stanley!' She rushed over to him. 'It's the drink, the strain.' She moved aside the empty glass, and then held his head and shoulders close to her. 'Oh Stanley,' she murmured, 'what have you done?'

Hailston said nothing. He collapsed back against her.

Ten minutes later, feeling comfort draining from her, he was sitting in an easy chair and Esme was perched on the arm, cradling his shoulders.

'Somehow we'll get over all this,' she whispered. 'Don't worry, darling. We can deal with it together. But, Stanley, you must be honest with me. I'll help you. I always have. We'll think of a way.'

He wasn't really listening. He knew it was all over now. He'd even have to give up his seat, never be Secretary of State. It wouldn't take the police long to make a connection with Hunter. With Esme's help, the forgery could take a little longer, but in the end they would make the connection. And what had Carolyn said? What had she told the police, or Rackham? Perhaps he knew the whole Czech fiasco — not only Jane but Carolyn. She still had the list. That incriminated him. Rackham and the police between them were probably already tying the loose ends together.

He ground his teeth, setting his jaw hard, trying to control the desperate anger. Hell, he felt murderous. And why not? Esme was murmuring something, some bloody nonsense. Nothing made sense to him now except the inevitability of disaster. God, what was going to happen to him? Endless bloody years in prison? No, he couldn't face that.

'Come, let's go to bed,' Esme said. 'We'll talk about it in the morning. You'll feel better then. And please — easy on the drink, darling.'

He only half heard what she was saying. 'All right,' he muttered. 'You go on. I'll join you in a minute.'

Reluctantly she left, kissing him on the cheek. 'Don't be long,' she said.

Hailston was feeling weak. He poured himself another beer, and sat staring, seeing nothing, feeling only utter despair. He found he was muttering to himself, 'It's the end . . . the bloody end.'

The morning would solve nothing. It only brought the ultimate disaster nearer.

15

Hailston spent the next morning in his office at the Ministry of Defence. He was grateful that, but for routine matters, there was nothing of substance requiring his attention. Nor was there any occasion for him to go to the Commons. The order paper showed only the usual kind of uncontentious Friday business, which enabled most MPs to be in their constituencies. On the other hand he did not much want to return to Chester Square. It was painful being with Esme.

Breakfast had been difficult. He hadn't wanted anything to eat, but she had insisted. It was important — he knew it was — to have regular meals. He had tried to persuade her to return to Sussex, but she had refused to go without him. They would go down later together. Impulsively, Hailston had said that he had to remain in Town for the weekend. In those circumstances, he argued, it was sensible for her to be in the constituency. Then for once, she firmly maintained, she was not going to be sensible. They had too much to discuss together. Hailston did not want to discuss anything with Esme. There was no point. Even if she were to say that she had signed the cheque, he had drawn the money. By now the police would know that. If she went further and said that he had drawn it on her behalf, then how did Hunter come to possess it? The fact was — even now that he was sober and had taken some kind of grip on himself — he could see no way out. It was early in the evening before he returned to Chester Square.

Esme stood at the far end of the hall as he entered. Surprisingly her cool poise irritated him. It was, he felt, meant to convey normality, to suggest that she was in control of the situation, whatever it might be. That was almost more than he could tolerate. It was worse when, sympathetically, she kissed him on the cheek.

'Mrs Drury is getting the meal,' she said. 'You must be tired. You've had a long day for a Friday. I'll get you a scotch.'

'You didn't want me to drink,' he said antagonistically.

'Too much, darling — that's all.'

God, she was being so normal. And everything was so bloody abnormal. How long would it be before the newspapers were screaming: MINISTER CHARGED WITH CONTRACT KILLING? What did anything matter now?

The drawing room which, to him, had always been a restful place, now taunted him with her own good taste. When they were alone, she said to him with irritating calm, 'I want to be sure of one thing, Stanley, then we can decide how to deal with matters. Did you hire Hunter to kill Jane Bacton?'

Hailston ruefully twirled the whisky in his glass, took a slug. He said defiantly, 'I hired Hunter.'

'And you didn't take me into your confidence,' she said, matter-of-factly.

'Would you have coughed up twenty thousand to have someone killed? Of course not.'

Esme found it inconceivable that he should ever have considered such an operation, but it was a waste of time saying so now. She merely contented herself with, 'I can't pretend to understand why you did it. All that matters now is that the police should not find out that you hired him.'

'I drew the money.'

'Exactly — at my request. Hunter must have stolen it. Perhaps he robbed you of it on your way back.'

Hailston snorted. 'Damn funny we haven't mentioned it before.'

Esme knew it would not hold up. 'Nevertheless,' she said, 'they can prove the money was from my account and that you drew it, but they still can't prove that you gave it to Hunter. And have they yet any idea that Hunter killed Jane Bacton?'

Hailston peered into his whisky. It was no good snatching at these kind of straws. In time the police would make the connection. It was inevitable. He almost wished he had carried out the job himself. Then no money would have been involved. Only his own guts. Hadn't he the guts? Was that why he had hired Hunter?

His thoughts and their conversation were interrupted by the front-door bell, and a moment later Mrs Drury came in to announce that a police inspector wished to see him.

Hailston had seen the inspector before, and the sergeant who accompanied him. Esme ignored the inspector's glance that might have implied that he wanted to see Hailston alone. After she had greeted him, she sat firmly and erect on an upright chair.

Hailston enquired if the police officers would like a drink. Both declined.

'Shan't keep you long, sir,' said the inspector, as though his visit had no special significance. 'It's this man Bill Hunter . . . '

Hailston stood up, drew himself erect, adopting his commanding-officer stance. 'Is he dead — ?' he snapped.

The inspector hesitated. The question had been unexpected. He made his decision. 'He died this afternoon,' he said.

Hailston grunted. Esme was silent, watchful.

The inspector turned towards her. 'It's a pity, Mrs Hailston, that you didn't tell my colleague in Sussex that you knew this man Hunter.'

'I didn't know him,' she said with dignity, 'and that's what I told Inspector Hardy.'

The police officer nodded. 'But you knew him, Mr Hailston?'

'Yes, I knew him. I haven't been questioned about him, otherwise I would have mentioned it.'

'Quite, sir.'

'He served in the SAS with me,' Hailston continued. 'Worked for me briefly afterwards. I was helping to run a security firm. I think he found it very dull. He didn't stay long. I don't know what happened to him after that. Heard rumours, of course — something about mercenary jobs in Africa. Don't know how true they were.'

Hailston began to feel in control of the situation. Perhaps he could carry it off after all.

The police inspector nodded, apparently content with the explanation. Then, as though he had just thought of it, he said, 'There's this curious business of that twenty-thousand pounds of yours, Mrs Hailston.'

'Yes. I asked my husband to draw it for me.'

'What, on a forged signature?'

'No, it was my signature.'

'Oh — I see. It's being examined by an expert.' The inspector looked from Esme to Hailston and back again. 'That's not what you told Inspector Hardy.'

'Perhaps not. I was rather . . . well, disconcerted, upset.'

'Yes . . . yes, I can understand that,' the police officer said unconvincingly. 'So I wonder how Hunter came to acquire the same twenty-thousand pounds?'

'It was taken from my car,' said Hailston aggressively.

'Why didn't you report it, sir?'

'Because I didn't know it had been stolen — not immediately,' said Hailston.

'You in the habit of leaving twenty-thousand pounds in your car, sir?'

'No. But I did on this occasion.'

'Then, when you found it missing, sir, you still did not think it was worth reporting?'

Hailston was furious. It had been a bloody silly thing for him to say. Why had he thought it sounded convincing? The bastards knew everything. They were playing with him. He felt like smashing the bloody man's face in.

'I was going to,' Hailston growled. 'I wanted to discuss it with my wife.'

'Oh. You have spent rather a long time discussing it, sir. And at the end of several days' discussion, you decided not to report it?'

'That's right,' Hailston snapped. 'That's bloody right, officer.'

'Might I ask why?'

'You may. But all I shall tell you,' Hailston added irascibly, 'was that it was for private, family reasons.'

The police inspector muttered, 'Oh,' and turned to Esme.

Sitting bolt upright, she nodded.

'Do you want us to make statements?' Hailston asked provocatively.

'Not at this moment, sir. No need to bother you yet. There are a number of inquiries we have to make, I'm sure you'll understand that. But, yes, we shall be wanting both of you to make statements, of course.' He paused, and then as though irrelevantly, he added, 'There's still the murder of your secretary, Miss Bacton. That's giving us a bit of trouble, sir.'

Hailston had remained standing throughout. Now he turned his back on the inspector, muttering at the same time, 'Well, if that's all, inspector, I've got some work to do.'

'Yes, of course, sir.' At the door, he turned back, and added, 'We'll be seeing you again.'

Hailston felt like thumping him, but remained with his back to the policeman, controlling himself. He knew why they had not taken a statement there and then — they wanted discussions with the security boys first. That bloody man Rackham from MI6 was probably master-minding the whole thing. This was not just a police inquiry; it was a security investigation, and the net was closing. He could feel it. That inspector had been dropping hints like autumn leaves.

Only when they heard Mrs Drury close the front door, did Esme say quietly, 'There is still no connnection between Hunter and the murder.'

206

Hailston snorted and turned to the drinks cabinet. He poured himself a large scotch. 'There may not be proof,' he said, 'but they know it. That was bloody obvious.'

'But with Hunter dead,' she said calmly, 'they have no way of proving that you gave him the money.'

Even after twenty-seven years of marriage he was astonished at her composure, but he was too familiar with intelligence gathering to be impressed. They were just quietly, efficiently putting the pieces of the jigsaw together — the police and Rackham, Rackham and the police. There was no escape. What had been the first rule? Always leave yourself an escape route. He always had. That's why he had been so damned good. But this time? He had got to find a way out. He wasn't going to be ground down by years of imprisonment. He was finished, he was finished anyway. He had got to face it — bloody finished. So — there had to be a way out . . . some way he could still go on . . .

The thoughts tailed away in the blur of the amber whisky. He was aware of Esme's hand on his arm. He looked at her, taking a moment to focus. She was unreal.

He shook his head, turned back to the drinks cabinet.

'No Stanley, no more.'

Her voice came out of the distance. 'No more. No more.' He peered at her. She was blurring. He steadied himself.

She led him through to the dining room. They ate in silence. Several times Esme tried to return to the subject. For her it was urgent that they decide together and in detail what they were going to say. But Hailston was preoccupied. He thrust aside every attempt she made, until ultimately he shouted at her, 'For God's sake, Esme, leave it, leave it till tomorrow. I can't bloody take any more.'

So unwillingly she let the silence return. After the meal, he went to his study, muttering that he had some work to do. When he saw that Esme plainly did not believe him, he added, 'I want to think things out.'

He promised, as he closed the door, that he would have no

more scotch that night. Then he sat alone. He was going to make a real effort to be rational. He tugged thoughtfully at the bristled hairs of his moustache.

First, his political ambitions. Well, they were at an end whatever happened. Jane, curse her, had seen to that. Again he blamed himself for not carrying out his own operation. That's what he should have done. And Jane? How long would she have gone on using him? How long before he discovered? Would he ever have discovered? He thought of her body — it was unbearable. Meanwhile, Esme was playing with dreams. The signature was a forgery. The police would know that. A comparison with his own handwriting — there was plenty of it available — would show that he was the forger. Whatever Esme said would be of no consequence. Then, God knows what Carolyn had told Rackham. She had probably told him everything to protect herself — the little bitch. So the connection would be made. It would be made by Rackham, or the police, or both. The more he thought about it as coolly as he could, the more sure he was of it.

So, he was back to the escape route. Find the bloody escape route. An SAS captain ought to be able to do that. A way that would at least still give him some life.

He wondered how long he had got — probably not more than forty-eight hours. He thought over all the details again. Then he made his decision.

When Esme came in a couple of hours later, his head was slumped on his arms on the desk.

She roused him gently. 'You're over-doing it. Over-tired,' she whispered, as he peered up at her finely chiselled features and felt a sudden pang of regret. He shook it away even as he got to his feet.

'I'll have to go into the Ministry in the morning,' he said.

Hailston did go into the Ministry of Defence that Saturday — not to work in an almost empty building, but to think through the implications of his decision and, more than anything, to get away from Esme. That was painful, but inevitable.

First, however, he needed his daughter's help. The irony was lost on him. He told Esme he was going to walk to Whitehall. It was a fine, warm morning, and the exercise would do him good. In fact, he searched out a telephone box in a quiet part of Victoria. Phoning from the Ministry would be too risky. He was sure that, by now, calls from his office — and perhaps from his home, although that was less likely — were being monitored. He had to risk the possibility that Carolyn's line was tapped as well. His experience told him that there was a reasonable chance it might not be. He punched out her number.

Immediately she answered, he said with an urgent directness, 'I need to see you, Carolyn.' For some seconds there was silence, and Hailston repeated his request, adding, 'It's urgent.'

At length, she said icily, 'I don't need to see you. In fact, I don't ever want to see you.'

'I'll come round.'

'You won't. They won't let you in.'

'They?'

'I've got Special Branch protection.'

'You — ?' He might have guessed. Perhaps he had less time than he thought. 'All right,' he said, 'you come to me — the Embankment Gardens an hour from now.'

'No. I'm not seeing you.'

'Look, Carolyn — I need your help.'

'My help? You're being funny this morning. I'd watch you drown rather than jump in to save you.'

Hailston took a grip on himself. 'Where's your SB man — inside our out?'

'He's where I want him to be. At the moment he's in the kitchen having a cup of coffee. I've only just got back here — from David Rackham's,' she added threateningly.

Hailston grunted. Hell, the net *was* closing. For a moment he considered the possibility of going there anyway. He would be able to evade the policemen outside. The Special Branch man was different; it would depend on the element of surprise, and while he might not have all of Hailston's skills, he would be that much younger. Hailston had to be totally sure of success, or the situation would be worse, and he would find himself in a police cell right away. He decided it was not worth the risk. So he had to gamble on the line being untapped.

'I need to see your Czech contact,' he said.

'Why?'

Her disgust, her suspicion were obvious.

'For God's sake, Carolyn — it doesn't matter. I — '

'Ring the Embassy and ask to speak to Ivan Kubat.'

'Don't be stupid. Every call going in or out of the Czech Embassy is monitored — by us.'

Carolyn chuckled. 'I don't give a damn about what you need. You probably need to see the Archangel Gabriel, but I doubt if you will.'

Hailston took a deep breath, controlling his anger.

'Can that chap in the kitchen overhear this conversation?'

'Probably not.'

'All right, you don't want to see me. You don't give a damn about me. But what have you got to lose, giving me your contact? For God's sake, Carolyn, it's bloody urgent. If you want to help your mother . . . please, Carolyn.'

She didn't reply immediately. In fact there was such a long silence that Hailston had to ask, 'Are you still there?'

'H'mm. I'm thinking.' The silence continued. It was the two phrases, 'What have you got to lose?' and 'If you want to help your mother' that caused her to reconsider. She was not going to keep the appointment in Coldfall Wood the next day. What would Kubat do then? She had never been as sanguine as David Rackham about the Czech's reaction. What if her father went there instead? That should please them — get them off her back as well.

'It won't be a problem for you — or for your mother.' Hailston interrupted her thoughts.

'Do you know Coldfall Wood?'

'Yes, yes,' he said so quickly that, had it been a televisual phone, he would have seen Carolyn's eyebrows shoot up.

'There's a seat on the edge of the clearing near the wood. Twelve noon tomorrow, Sunday.'

Hailston noted that her voice had quietened to a whisper, and he assumed the SB man had not been able to hear. He repeated, 'Twelve noon, tomorrow. Thank you.' He rang off. He had no more reason to talk to her, and he was damn sure she did not want to prolong the conversation either. He strode out in the direction of Whitehall.

Hailston divided his time between the loneliness of his office and the summery paths of St James's Park. London's weekenders were strolling with their children, feeding the grey clouds of pigeons, and the ducks that waddled out of the water on to the grassy banks. There were girls in flimsy dresses, and some in bikini tops and shorts, sunning themselves on the grass. They made him think agonizingly of Jane.

He selected a deck chair and carried it well away from any others, took off his jacket, loosened his shirt collar, and sank into the brightly striped canvas. Slowly he was accustoming himself to his decision. He reviewed the whole sequence of events, considered the extent of the police inquiries, the nature of the SIS investigation, Rackham's coordinating role. The more that now, sober and rational, he thought about the affair, the more his experience told him that he was done for. His choice was stark: no life at all, or at least some kind of life.

When eventually he reached home, Esme was considerate and attentive, and he had to face her own review of events as she knew them. He only half listened, because the most important and the most damaging things of all, she did not know.

'So you see,' she was saying, 'it is not impossible to deal with this, and come out of it all right. Stanley, I have worked out our statements, precisely what we should say. Then, if we stick to it, I think — '

Hailston sighed. 'I think you're being optimistic,' he said.

That did not stop Esme going over everything in detail. There was a cool logic about it, except that it omitted the most important evidence, which only Hailston knew, and he could not tell her. She even produced draft versions of their statements. His only anxiety now was lest he should not have enough time. They obviously wanted to have their case complete before they came to him. They were not going to rely on events forcing a confession from him. They knew he was not that kind of man. They were going to be sure of being able to prove their allegations even before they took statements from him.

There was also the risk that Carolyn would now betray him, have him picked up at the meet. On the whole he thought it unlikely because of her consideration for her mother. The arrest would get publicity. So, probably, would his way, but there was always the chance that the government would avoid it. He knew he was on a knife edge, but there was even something exhilarating about it, something that appealed to his old expertise.

He got through the evening, convincing Esme that he approved her tactics. She went to bed confident that together they would win through.

'But you must never again keep anything from me,' she told him.

Hailston, knowing that this was another ending, lied to her that there would be no more secrets between them.

Carolyn received only one more telephone call that day. It was early in the evening and came from David Rackham. A cheery voice asked her, 'You all right?'

'Fine.'

'And Toni?'

'Yes, she's here.'

'That copper behaving himself?'

'Of course. We've never felt so important.'

Rackham chuckled. 'Like me to buy you both a meal?'

'I was going to spend the evening in.'

'Washing your hair?'

Carolyn laughed. 'Well, come over anyway, please. We'll decide then.'

When Toni bounced in from her own bedroom, half-clad, Carolyn announced, 'That was David Rackham. He's coming over.'

'Oh, super. Shall we buy a Chinese take-away, and eat in?'

'Why not? He did say he'd buy us both a meal.'

'Well, he can buy the take-away.'

That, in fact, is what Rackham did. When he arrived he was surprised to find both girls resisting a meal out.

'Places will be full around here on a Saturday night,' said Carolyn.

'And we're hardly ever in together,' said Toni. 'Let's make it a threesome here. It'll be fun.'

For one blissful moment, Rackham wondered if she had intended the phrase to have an erotic overtone, but sadly dismissed the idea. That was not Carolyn's scene. Perhaps it wasn't even Toni's. He wondered.

Carolyn said she would lay the table, find some wine, while they went out to get the take-away.

Rackham gave the Special Branch man outside the kind of look that said, 'Yes, I know I'm a lucky bugger.'

'How far is it,' he asked Toni as they came out on to the street.

'Oh, quarter of a mile.'

He took her hand, and she gave his a squeeze, as he looked down into two laughing brown eyes.

'I suppose you're skilled with chopsticks?' she teased.

'Of course.'

'I think we've got some. Oh, that'll be better still.'

As they approached the Chinese restaurant, Rackham became abruptly serious. 'We're being followed,' he said.

Toni pealed off a laugh. 'Is it Ivan the Gelical?'

Rackham smiled. 'I shouldn't think so. He's too important.'

'How do you know?'

'Experience. How good is your karate?'

'Good enough. Why, am I going to need it?'

'You might. I think they want to put the frighteners on you — just to encourage you to co-operate.'

As they went into the restaurant, Rackham noticed over his shoulder two men closing in behind them. But now the door was between them. Rackham was about to give the menu some thought when Toni knowledgeably reeled off a whole range of complementary dishes. He looked on in silent admiration.

The hot foil containers were piled into two plastic carrier bags. Rackham decided to test his theory, and told her to go on ahead while he paid the bill. He would follow with the other carrier bag.

Three minutes later he pushed through the door to see Toni about seventy-five yards away. The two men were immediately behind her, one each side. They quickened their pace. The one on the right reached out, grabbed her arm and swung her round towards him. Rackham began to run. Suddenly he stopped, marvelling at what he saw. Somehow Toni had slipped the man's grip, almost jerked his arm out of its socket and flung him on his back, at the same time causing him to collide with his colleague and knock him to the ground.

By the time Rackham reached them, Toni had pulled out of the carrier bag a container of chop-suey, and was plastering it into the face of the man who had attacked her. The other, however, was already on his feet. Rackham didn't conform to any of the niceties of the martial arts. He merely launched a hefty kick at the man's shins, saw him yelp with pain, and then immediately hooked his foot behind the fellow's legs and unbalanced him, forcing him to join his companion on the ground.

For the first time Rackham was aware of a group of passers-by. Some had slowed their pace, trying not to look;

others had gathered in a ragged line, and were looking on. No one offered to help. Rackham grinned at them, and then taking Toni's arm, he asked, 'You all right?'

'Painful wrist — that's all.'

'You're an expensive young woman,' he laughed. 'We shall have to go back and replace that chop-suey now.'

Toni grabbed his arm, clung to him, and shook him with a ripple of her laughter.

Only now the two men were painfully getting to their feet. Rackham turned and faced them. 'We don't want to spoil our evening running in these thugs, do we?' he chortled to Toni.

The men had not understood him. They glowered, but made no attempt to attack. Rackham turned away, and briskly led Toni back to the Chinese take-away. When they came out a second time the men were gone.

'You've been a long time,' Carolyn greeted them on their return.

'A slight contretemps,' Rackham answered, and then Toni — as she bustled about helping Carolyn unpack the food — launched into an exuberant account of their adventure.

'So who were they?' Carolyn asked.

'Some of Ivan's friends — not, I suspect, intending to do any great harm. Merely frighten Toni. But the pair of you had better take care — understand?'

'Yes, Uncle David,' Carolyn mocked.

She had covered the table with a red-check cloth, lit candles, and found some crisp white wine. So they spent an enjoyable evening in light-hearted chatter, with Toni periodically ensuring that the conversation darted off at inconsequential and illogical tangents. Rackham amused them with witty one-liners, and then launched into an hilarious impersonation of a maiden aunt who had disapproved of his way of life.

Carolyn had intended telling him about her father's telephone call, but there did not seem to be an opportunity.

For no very rational reason she felt that it was something to be shared with him alone, but it left her feeling a little uneasy.

Then when they were sipping coffee and some not very expensive brandy, which Rackham wrinkled his nose at, she said suddenly, 'Oh, there was something Kubat said the other day I forgot to tell you.'

Rackham gave her a mockingly reprimanding look.

'He said that Josef was arriving in London that day,' she added.

Rackham nodded. 'So he did. We watched him in.'

Toni looked up, surprised.

'Oh, he's joined their Embassy staff,' Rackham explained.

'That looks bad,' Toni declared.

Rackham said nothing.

Carolyn, more serious, said, 'I'm trying to accept it.' Then with a tilt of her head that reminded Rackham of her mother, she added, 'I haven't really any alternative, have I?'

He gave her an unusually solemn smile, and then with a brisk change of subject declared that he would help with the washing up.

At the end of it all, he announced, teasingly, 'After what's happened this evening, I wonder if I ought to offer you my personal protection tonight?'

Toni's glowing look was full of invitation, but Carolyn merely chuckled, and said she was sure the copper outside wouldn't approve. 'There'd probably be a demarcation dispute,' she said.

Oh well, Rackham thought to himself, there would be other times, other places. He bade them each goodnight with a kiss on the cheek, and sauntered out into the cooling night air, wondering when the next opportunity might come.

On Sunday morning, making a totally unconvincing excuse that he had to collect some papers he had forgotten from the office, Hailston drove off in his car about ten o'clock.

He made straight for north London, and then passed the time driving leisurely around Hampstead, Highgate, Hornsey and Muswell Hill until nearly twelve o'clock. Then he parked his car in one of the small residential turnings off Coppetts Road. He walked quickly back to the open ground north of the wood. As he approached across the uneven grass, he checked his watch. It was three minutes past twelve. He saw the seat by the edge of the trees. One man was sitting on it.

Two children rushed across the grass ahead of him and disappeared into the wood. Hailston went straight up to the seat. The man was tall and tanned with broad shoulders, dark hair, slightly curly, and dark brown eyes.

Hailston said, 'Are you Ivan Kubat?'

'No.'

The two men looked at each other. Hailston had to risk it.

'You were expecting my daughter,' he said.

He saw a sudden flicker of interest in the eyes that were watching him.

The seated man said cautiously. 'Then I think I know who you are. You are Stanley Hailston.'

Hailston nodded, and instantly produced the identity card that even he had to use to get into the Ministry of Defence.

'So.' The man got up from the seat, but pointedly ignored Hailston's outstretched hand. 'How, then, is Carolyn?' he asked. 'And why is she not here?'

'I'll explain,' Hailston said, already impatient. 'Who the hell are you?'

The man who stood by him was very considerably younger. He motioned Hailston down on to the seat beside him.

'I am not sure that I am pleased to meet you, Mr Hailston,' he said. 'My name is Josef Foerster.'

16

Hailston did not return to Chester Square until the middle of the afternoon, and for the rest of the day Esme found him edgy and irritable. She hoped he had been punctual with his injection, although she refrained from mentioning her concern because she knew he hated her fussing. Constantly she tried to reassure him: now that they had agreed precisely how they were going to handle events, she was confident everything would be all right.

Occasionally he looked at her strangely, almost longingly, and she even felt unaccountable twinges of guilt. Once he said, 'Thank you, Esme, thank you for everything,' and she thought that at last he was reconciled to their agreed plan. She went over it again with him, in detail, but she saw that it was difficult for him to remain patient.

Early in the evening he insisted on going to his own study to work, although she doubted whether there was any work to do. She took up a book to read but found her concentration wandering, and turned to the television set instead until, shortly before eight o'clock, she was interrupted by the police — the same polite, confident inspector and his taciturn sergeant. She was ready for them, quietly assured.

'Do you want to see me?' she asked. 'Or my husband, or both of us?'

'I really called to see Mr Hailston,' the inspector said solemnly.

'He's in his study, if you care to follow me, but first — ' she turned back from the door — 'there's something I should tell you.'

The inspector uttered a small, interrogative grunt.

'You were very concerned when you were last here, inspector, about why we had not reported the stolen twenty-thousand pounds.'

'Unusual, Mrs Hailston.'

Esme ignored the sarcasm. 'My husband said it was for family reasons. He obviously thought that was no concern of yours. But, of course, I can understand your interest.' She pretended not to see his nod. 'Yes, well,' she continued, 'it was for some investments for my daughter — to further her career. It was going to be a surprise. I regret I misinformed Inspector Hardy in Sussex. That was foolish of me. But my daughter was there at the time and, as I said before, I was very upset. I'm sure you will agree the circumstances were unusual — shocking.'

The inspector wore an amused smile. He looked utterly unconvinced.

'Certainly — unusual, too, to cash money for investments I would have thought. Anyway, what it amounts to, Mrs Hailston, is that you are quite sure the signature on the cheque is yours?'

'Yes,' she answered unhesitatingly.

'Oh,' said the inspector, stroking his chin. 'We have a handwriting expert who says it is not your signature.'

'Indeed. I think I'm the best judge of my own handwriting.'

'Yes,' he said sceptically. 'That's what you will say in your statement, is it?'

'Of course. Do you want me to make it now?'

'No.' Then noting her surprise, he explained, 'Normally, we would have taken statements by now, Mrs Hailston, but then this is hardly a normal case, is it? Other investigations are proceeding which, we are instructed, have to be taken into account. We are not, as you might say, wholly in charge.'

Esme gestured with her hand. 'Just as you say.' She opened the door and led the police officers to Hailston's study. 'Some

219

visitors to see you, darling,' she announced, as she tapped on the study door and opened it.

Hailston looked up abruptly, his expression a mixture of arrogance and anxiety.

Esme followed the policemen. The inspector turned. 'We rather wanted a word with your husband alone,' he said.

Esme stood her ground. 'I don't see that is at all necessary,' she said.

'With respect, Mrs Hailston, that's for me to decide. Now — if you wouldn't mind, please.' He held the door open.

Esme glanced quickly at her husband, but he wasn't even looking in her direction, and yet she was aware of the effort he was making to ensure that he did not respond with too short a fuse. The inspector closed the door behind her.

Hailston stood up. 'Well, gentlemen,' he began, affecting calm, 'can I offer you a drink?'

The inspector answered for both of them. 'Thank you, but no.'

'Then what can I do for you?' It was essential to appear as normal as possible. He had got to hold out until tomorrow. 'Have you found out yet who killed my secretary?' he asked.

'Not for sure.' The inspector motioned Hailston back into his desk chair, and he drew up a smaller chair and sat opposite. The sergeant bulkily hovered in the background. 'This money — twenty-thousand pounds — why did you draw it?'

'For my wife,' Hailston replied. 'We have both told you this before, inspector.'

'Yes,' muttered the policeman disbelievingly. 'The mystery is how it got into Hunter's briefcase.'

Hailston remembered that he had previously said it was stolen from his car, but he jibbed at repeating the absurdity. Instead, he made a little grimace which was meant to imply that he hadn't a clue.

'You told us that you hadn't seen Hunter recently. When did you last see him?'

'I dare say if I went through my diaries I could tell you. But I should think about a couple of years ago — at a reunion dinner.'

The inspector looked as though he was waiting for Hailston to continue. When the Minister said no more, the police officer allowed the silence to stretch a bit before he asked casually, 'You didn't see him the Friday before Miss Bacton was killed?'

The bastards. Hailston was instantly angry, but tried not to show it as he answered briskly, 'No.'

'You met him in a restaurant in Prince Albert Road — had lunch together.'

'No.' Hailston had got to bluff it out now; he did not need much more time. But the net was closing, and he was determined not to be trapped in it.

'You were seen, Mr Hailston. We have a statement to that effect.'

'To that effect,' Hailston mocked. 'People can make mistakes. I tell you, inspector, I wasn't there, and as far as I'm concerned that's the end of it.'

'Your face is well known, Mr Hailston. It's been in the papers a lot recently, with all the speculation about the Cabinet reshuffle — '

'Mistakes can still be made,' Hailston interrupted. 'Perhaps you've found out who killed Hunter, have you?'

'No. Not the person. But we know who was responsible. It was a revenge killing.'

'Who?'

The inspector smiled grimly. 'That's something I can't disclose at the moment. But you are denying that you met Hunter that Friday?'

'Yes.'

'And you will make a statement to that effect?'

'Certainly.' Hailston sounded and felt aggressive. 'Are you arresting me, officer? Taking me to the station to help with your inquiries?'

The inspector's expression made it plain that he would dearly like to. He said instead, 'No, sir.'

'Don't you even want me to make that statement?' Hailston was deliberately taunting the man, and even enjoying it.

'Not yet, Mr Hailston. I can promise that you will have your opportunity to make as full a statement as you like. I explained to Mrs Hailston that there are other important inquiries being made. You would probably know more about this sir, than I do. But . . . ' The inspector hesitated, clearly resenting that he wasn't wholly in control of the situation. It was obvious that he would have liked to bundle Hailston into a police car immediately. What is more he did not really see why he shouldn't.

'So,' said Hailston, 'You're wasting your time, officer.'

'I don't think so. I am sure we shall be meeting again very shortly, sir. Then I have no doubt that you will be able to help with our inquiries.'

Hailston resented the man's sarcasm, but it confirmed what he had suspected. They were being held back by the SIS, until such time as they were ready to move. They were out to prove something bigger. Well, the bastards weren't going to get the opportunity — not if he could help it.

He closed the door behind the policemen with a bang, returned to his desk, and poured himself a scotch.

Esme met the inspector and his sergeant in the hall. 'Can I be of any further help?' she asked.

The inspector's expression instantly softened. He looked almost compassionate as he answered, 'No, thank you, Mrs Hailston — not at the moment.'

She waited a while before returning to the study, hoping to persuade Hailston to have an early night. They could discuss matters in bed.

As she approached the door, she could hear him speaking inside — his voice raised.

'Yes, yes,' she heard, as she stopped, her hand on the brass door knob. 'I understand. What? De what? Bach? Never heard of it. Bach. All right, all right.'

She opened the door slowly, just as he slammed down the receiver. He looked up, startled, even, she thought, a little angry.

'Why not an early night, darling?' she said. 'It'll do us both good.'

'Yes,' he answered.

'The police didn't ask for a statement?'

'No. Only because it didn't suit them.'

'It's going to be all right, Stanley. There's nothing to worry about. Come on — bed.'

Hailston sighed. 'All right. You go on. I'll be up soon.'

It was half-an-hour later before he did follow her to bed, and she recognized the signs of anxiety and worry. He refused to discuss the visit of the police officers, or what he had told them. He merely muttered, disgruntled, that it didn't matter. He was still awake two hours later when, at last, she slipped into sleep.

Hailston appeared even more disturbed at breakfast. He only wanted coffee in spite of her badgering him to eat 'just a little something'.

'I know it's important,' he snapped, then instantly relented, and added, 'I know. But I really don't feel like — '

'Are you all right, darling?'

'Yes, yes, of course I'm all right. Stop fussing.'

When he left, he paused in the hall, stroked her red hair, looked into her eyes, smiled faintly, and kissed her, rather more warmly than she would have expected.

She let Mrs Drury clear away the breakfast things and wash up, and she retired to the drawing room with *The Times*, only to find that she sat there looking at the print, but not really reading the words.

It was ten o'clock when the telephone rang in the hall. The

voice, which she recognized as belonging to her husband's private secretary, asked to speak to the Minister.

'But he left at quarter-to-nine,' she said.

There was a pause at the other end. 'That's strange, Mrs Hailston. He hasn't come in yet. I was phoning to remind him that there is a meeting of ministers at ten-thirty.'

Esme was puzzled, worried.

'Did he say he was going anywhere else?' asked the civil servant.

'No,' she answered, preoccupied. 'No, I thought he was going straight to the Ministry.'

'Oh, well, I expect he'll be here.'

It was impossible to tell whether the private secretary was convinced; Esme was not. When she put down the receiver, she remained standing by the hall table, thinking, worrying, until she was certain that something unforeseen had happened. Then she knew what had to be done. Not the police. Instead, she took from her handbag the slip of paper Rackham had given her in Sussex. She rang the number he had written down, and was relieved to hear his voice answering.

To Esme's 'What ought we to do?' he answered confidently, 'Nothing.'

'But — ' she began . . .

'Leave it to me,' he interrupted. 'I will check with the Ministry, make sure nothing is done there. If he turns up, or I have any other news, I'll let you know immediately.'

'He hasn't been himself,' Esme explained. 'He's been preoccupied and irritable, and half the weekend he's been at the Ministry.'

'Are you sure?'

'Yes. Well, that's what he told me.'

Rackham made soothing noises, put the phone down, and immediately rang Hailston's private secretary who, after he had confirmed that Hailston had still not arrived, was told to take no action except let Rackham know at once if Hailston turned up, or if there was any other development.

Sooner or later — preferably later — the police would have to be informed. Rackham was still thinking about how to handle the situation when, on a different line, he received another telephone call, preceded by the code word 'Beetle'.

Half an hour later Rackham phoned Carolyn, and cheerily declared, 'Ah, so glad you're in. It's that copper keeping you there, I guess. Don't move. I'm coming to see you.'

The Special Branch man was outside the flat door when Rackham arrived, flashed his pass, and was let in by Carolyn.

'Don't I get a morning coffee? Or have your poured it all down old Flatfoot's throat outside?'

Carolyn laughed. He followed her into her tiny kitchen and watched her heap some freshly ground coffee into a stoneware pot. He approved the old-fashioned technique. It still made the best coffee.

'So what's this all about then?' Carolyn asked.

'Your father.'

She looked momentarily surprised, and immediately covered herself by saying, 'Should I be surprised?'

'The blue eyes are smiling, but the tone is frosty.'

'Do you wonder?'

Rackham shrugged. 'He's defected to the Czechs.'

She stopped in the middle of pouring out the coffee. 'He's what?' Not even she had imagined that was the reason he had asked her how to contact Ivan Kubat. And she hadn't told Rackham about it. She couldn't now — that was certain.

'Well, he's with them anyway.'

'How do you know?'

He had guessed she might ask that question, and he was equally determined not to tell her.

'An insect told me,' he said, his eyes brightly taunting.

'It's not the kind of thing he would do.'

'Normally, I would agree. But he hasn't been behaving very normally, has he? In fact, for one reason or another, he's been behaving quite irrationally.' He paused, took the mug of coffee

225

she had poured out, and led the way into her living room, where he seated himself on the corner of the put-u-up. 'But think,' Rackham continued, 'what was his alternative? To be arrested for conspiracy to murder. He knew it was only a matter of time. And time was getting very short, what with Hunter's death and the forged cheque. It was that, or a long term of imprisonment. At heart, Hailston's a man of action. Prison's not for him.'

Carolyn sipped at the hot coffee. 'So where is he?'

'At a safe house somewhere, I'd guess. Not at the Embassy. They know that's under constant surveillance.'

'What happens now?'

'They will want to get him away to Czechoslovakia. Once they've got him there, they'll announce his defection with a great flourish of propaganda.'

'I don't give a damn for him. But this is going to be hell for Mummy.'

Rackham nodded. 'Somehow they've got to be stopped.'

'You mean, we've got to get him back?' she asked, disbelieving.

'You're bright this morning.'

'David, for heaven's sake . . . '

Rackham laughed. In spite of everything he was enjoying the situation. Faced with the apparently impossible the adrenalin would start to flow. He rubbed his hands with enthusiasm.

'But how get him back?' she continued. 'I don't know that I particularly want to.'

Rackham took a long slurp of coffee, mockingly scratched his head, and muttered, 'Do you know, I haven't the slightest idea.'

'Didn't your "insect" tell you where he was?'

'No. He didn't know. That was suspicious in itself.'

He drained off his coffee, got up and put the mug down with a bang on the table. 'Come on,' he said, 'we're going to see your mother.' He thought for a moment, and then surprisingly serious, added, 'We don't have to tell her he's defected — not yet. That might be a bit much for her after everything else. There'll be no statement from the Ministry of Defence, in fact nothing from the government. So, for the present, no one need know that he's even missing.'

Rackham, driving his white Porsche with characteristic panache, briskly threaded his way through the traffic of Bayswater Road and Park Lane towards Chester Square. They were let in by Mrs Drury, who was efficiently banished to the kitchen, as Esme beckoned them into the drawing room.

She stood by the Adam-style mantelpiece, her head held high to show the fine line of her jaw, looking calm and elegant. Her smile at Rackham was both politely welcoming and interrogative.

'Yes,' Rackham said quietly, 'we have news of Mr Hailston. He's with the Czechs,' he added ambiguously.

'With them? You mean they've kidnapped him?'

Rackham didn't reply. He merely nodded his head, slowly.

Esme maintained her composure. 'But why?' she asked.

'I'm not sure I can answer that.'

'Something to do with Miss Bacton, do you suppose?'

'It could be.' He ignored Carolyn's sudden glance. He was wondering how far he could go without arousing Esme's suspicion. 'Was he here the whole weekend?' he asked.

'Yes — here, or at the Ministry.' Then, in response to Rackham's further questions, she gave him the times of Hailston's movements, and described his behaviour when he was at home.

'So, he was preoccupied, irritable, not himself,' Rackham confirmed, and Esme nodded. 'Did anyone call to see him, or do you know if he saw anyone?'

'The police called. No one else.'

'Phone calls?'

Carolyn interrupted: 'Aren't they tapped?'

Rackham made a tut-tutting sound. 'Not a respected Minister of Her Majesty's Government,' he said, but admitted to himself that, in the circumstances, they ought to have had a tap on.

'No, I don't think so,' Esme replied. She frowned. 'Wait a moment. He was speaking on the telephone about ten o'clock last night. He was in his study. I tried to persuade him to go to bed.'

'Did you hear any of the conversation?'

'He seemed snappy, angry. I think all I heard was something like "Yes, yes". Oh!' She paused, fingers to her lips. 'Yes, there was something — what was it? — he didn't seem to understand, or was questioning.' She bit the back of her forefinger, thinking. 'Bach — that's what it was. Or was it De Bach?'

'Like Bach, the composer?'

Esme nodded.

'Did he like Bach?'

'He hardly ever listened to music at all. It was one of my interests he didn't share.'

'You heard nothing else?'

She shook her head.

'You obviously don't know who he was speaking to?'

'No — except, as I say, he sounded annoyed, angry.'

'Thank you, Mrs Hailston,' Rackham muttered with a boyish smile. 'I wish I understood it, though. Would you mind if I had a look round his study?'

'Of course not.'

Immediately she had closed the door behind him, Rackham went swiftly and professionally to work — going through drawers, files of papers, books, but finding nothing that his instinct told him was significant.

When he returned to the drawing room, Esme and Carolyn sat facing each other, talking quietly, earnestly.

'Was that helpful?' Esme asked, knowingly.

'I don't think so. But there's something familiar about Bach. And I don't mean the Brandenburg concertos,' Rackham grinned. 'I mean just the name. Oh well.' He shrugged.

'Carolyn says they will want to take him out to Czechoslovakia. Is that right?'

'I imagine so.'

'Can't they be stopped.'

'I hope so.'

Esme was puzzled by Rackham's freckly grin; he hardly seemed to be taking the whole thing seriously and yet, in some irreconcilable way, she had confidence in him. 'What can we do?' she asked. 'What are you doing, or the police doing?'

'Not very much at the moment. But I promise you one thing, Mrs Hailston. They will not get him to Czechoslovakia if I can possibly help it.'

'I suppose it will be all over the papers tonight — and on the box?'

Rackham shook his head, and grinned again. 'Nobody knows it has happened,' he said. 'The government are not going to make any statements. And the Czechs certainly won't — not until he is safely out of the country. So at least you are saved the publicity.'

Esme returned him a wan smile of gratitude. 'Carolyn is going to stay the night with me,' she said.

'That's a very good idea. And try not to worry. We'll do all we can. I'll be in touch tomorrow.'

Carolyn saw him to the front door. She whispered to him. 'What are you going to do?'

'Kiss your pretty lips,' he said, and promptly did so in the most chaste and brotherly way he could manage.

'I mean — ' she began.

'I know what you mean. And the answer is: if I knew I wouldn't be telling.'

He waved as though he hadn't a care in the world, and ran out to his car.

It was mid-morning of the following day before Rackham returned to Chester Square and that, to be honest, was rather sooner than he had expected. Again it was a telephone call, coded 'Beetle', that provided him with the information he needed.

Carolyn saw the white Porsche draw to a stop outside, and just as he was about the press the bell button she opened the door.

He grinned. 'Such eagerness to see me — very flattering.'

'You're incorrigible.'

'I know. That's why I'm so endearing.'

'I hope this light-heartedness is justified,' she smiled.

'By Thursday afternoon it could be all over.' Then, as she closed the door behind him, he added, 'Your mother is in?'

She nodded, as she led him through into the drawing room and at the same time called out, 'Mummy! David's here.'

'I like this room,' Rackham muttered. 'It's a restful room.' He appreciatively studied a Paul Sandby of a ruined gateway with trees. 'It reflects your mother's excellent taste.'

At that moment, Esme walked in. 'Whose taste?' she asked.

'I imagine yours,' he smiled.

Esme looked tired. 'Stanley?' was all she said.

Rackham was immediately serious. 'The Czechs are planning to fly him out on Thursday,' he said.

'But how?' she asked.

'From Heathrow — scheduled flight of Czechoslovak Airlines, flight number OK seven double five, departure thirteen fifty-five.'

Esme shook her head. 'Isn't that a bit obvious?'

'Only because we know about it. It wouldn't be if we didn't. A well-known spy was once flown out as a double-bass player in the Czech Philharmonic Orchestra. Often the most obvious means are the easiest to use successfully.'

Esme still looked sceptical. Rackham smiled. 'Oh, he won't look a bit like Stanley Hailston,' he said. 'He will be thoroughly disguised — a new identity, a new passport, a member of the Czech diplomatic mission. If we didn't know about it in advance, there would be no problem. As we do know, and have the new name that he will bear, we shall be able to arrest him at passport control.'

'Arrest?'

Rackham gave a little cough. 'Well, I'm afraid that will be necessary, yes. It's the only way we can stop him being shipped out, isn't it?'

'Knowing Stanley, I would have thought that, once he was at the airport, he would create merry hell.'

'I think you can assume that they have ways of preventing that.'

'Drugs?'

Rackham said nothing.

Esme studied his blank expression. Then she said, 'I don't believe it.'

'Oh, I can assure you that is the plan.'

'I have no doubt,' said Esme precisely. 'That's not what I mean. I thought from your expression that I was meant to assume that Stanley was going of his own free will. That, I can't believe.'

Rackham shrugged. Carolyn looked at him, and then at her mother. 'I'm sure David is telling us all he can,' she said.

Esme didn't reply immediately. She looked thoughtful. She was remembering her husband's last kiss, the touch of his hand on her hair and, in retrospect, it almost seemed that he was saying goodbye. Is that what he had meant? Esme still found it difficult to believe.

She looked Rackham directly in the eyes. 'Is that what you were trying to tell me?' she asked.

'I'm sorry, Mrs Hailston. It . . . well, it just could be.' Then, in a lighter tone, he added, 'But by Thursday afternoon we shall know a lot more than we do now.'

Carolyn took her mother's hand and pressed it, but Esme seemed unaware of the gesture. After a few moments she recovered her poise. 'Can I get you some coffee?' she asked.

'No thanks, Mrs Hailston. I mustn't stay.'

Carolyn followed him out to his car, leant against the gleaming white coachwork.

'Mummy knows but can't accept it,' she said.

'She's a remarkable lady,' he muttered.

'I hope she need never know — the whole truth, I mean.'

'So do I. But if anyone could take it, she could.'

'He's a bastard,' Carolyn murmured.

Rackham raised a shocked eyebrow, took her hand. 'I'm not in the habit of picking up young women who lean provocatively against my car,' he said, 'but is there anywhere I can take you — like the Ritz for lunch, or something?'

She laughed, and shook her head. 'Will you go to the airport on Thursday?'

'No. I shall stay put in my office.'

'Can I be with you?'

'Wouldn't it make more sense for you to stay with your mother?'

'I might find it a little painful. And I think I might say something I ought not to. Anyway, can I? Am I allowed in your office?'

'Oh sure. Stranger people have been there.'

'Well — please!'

'I'm not sure I know why, but you're irresistible. It's where you'll get the news first anyway.'

'Thanks,' she said, and kissed him on the cheek.

'I think you want to gloat,' he said, as he walked to the other side of the car and let himself in.

She stood on the kerb watching until the Porsche turned out of the square.

17

The two men from the Czechoslovak Embassy, who were walking along the concourse of Terminal 2 at London's Heathrow airport, were sharply contrasted figures. One was dumpy, middle-aged with a squashed genial face; the other was over six feet tall, good-looking with slightly curly dark hair and deep brown eyes to match. The younger was undoubtedly the fitter, but he was the one whom a keen observer among the bustling air travellers might have decided was the more anxious of the two.

There were, in fact, a number of such observers, of whom the most significant was the Bunterish Robert Palesworth, head of the SIS's East European Desk. He was the one who made sure that the younger and taller of the two Czechs had noticed him. Palesworth also eyed the other figure with growing scepticism.

Soon one of them would go through passport control and then enter a special VIP lounge. In the meantime they had wandered into the large blue Skyshop in the middle of the concourse. While the dumpy one was picking over some English paperbacks, the other made an excuse to leave him for a moment, only to be restrained by a podgy hand and a flow of Czech which clearly indicated disapproval. The younger man appeared discomforted.

Palesworth observed this. It added further to his scepticism, and he decided to make a telephone call. In the open hoods by the tie shop his plump finger picked out the secure number that rang direct on Rackham's desk.

Immediately he recognized his colleague's familiar voice, he said, 'Unless I'm very much mistaken I think Beetle is rolling the wrong ball of dung and, judging by his expression, he knows it.' Then he rang off.

When the two men emerged from the Skyshop the dumpy one was carrying a couple of paperbacks. They walked left to the end of the concourse. Beneath the departure board were two brown-uniformed staff casually checking tickets and boarding cards. It was at this point that the two men shook hands, patted each other on the shoulders, and the older one walked through to passport control. There he was met by two officers who politely announced that they wished to ask him a few questions.

The other one, standing conspicuously near the desks beneath the departure board, opposite the covered way leading to the car park, looked about anxiously, and then made swiftly to the telephones. He also knew what number to punch out.

'Beetle,' he announced, adding in good English, 'It's the wrong man. It wasn't Hailston I brought to the airport. There was a last-minute switch. I don't know what they are doing.'

At that moment he sensed someone near him. He slammed down the receiver and swung round in one movement. Two heavily built men converged upon him. One had already reached out and grabbed his wrist. He flicked out of the grip in a way that would have sent a lesser man somersaulting on to his back. As it was it gave Beetle that momentary break to rush between them and run for the doors of the covered way leading to the car park. From where he was it was the only way out. Even as he lifted his head and charged forward, he caught sight of Palesworth's round face resisting the temptation to register surprise.

Beetle hurtled through the doors and flung them back on his pursuers. It gave him no more than a couple of seconds advantage, but that was enough for his long athletic strides to take him swiftly between startled returning travellers to the end of the corridor, past the pay machines and into the first row of parked cars. He sprinted to the far end before he saw the others force their way through angry travellers and pause at the first row of cars. Beetle crouched low, out of sight between two vehicles.

He had now to rely on his other senses. If he lifted his head he would be seen. Other people were coming, searching out their cars. He strained to differentiate the sounds. At least the presence of travellers would put his pursuers at a disadvantage, but he could not afford to rely on that. It would only deter them from the most extreme action. Anyway, they could afford to wait until the present batch of people had collected their cars and left. Indeed, that's what they appeared to be doing, for when he crept to the tail end of the car he was crouching behind and flattened himself to the ground, he could see one of the men standing at the beginning of the first row of cars, looking over the lot of them. But where was the other bastard?

Beetle resumed his crouching position, and waited. Two people carrying cases and plastic duty-free bags came along the row, obliging him to move round to the back of the car to take a position between the next two cars. Even as he was forced into the manoeuvre he knew it would make him visible to the man at the far end of the row. As he crept round, timing his movement so that the returning travellers should not notice him, he was grateful to see that the man was staring across the second row of cars. Quickly he slipped into the next space.

People were talking, calling to each other, shouting farewells. Cars started up. He could smell the exhaust gases. Another couple came towards him, coming to the very car that sheltered him. Again he moved swiftly round the back, but this time he had to go past the next car as well, otherwise he would still be visible to them. Twice the time, twice the opportunity to be seen. The man at the end was still not looking along the backs of the nearest row of cars, perhaps, Beetle hoped, because he considered it too vulnerable to offer good hiding. Then Beetle caught a brief glimpse of the second man. He was at a similar position at the opposite side on that level. Presumably they hoped that, between them, they would be able to see across the whole floor, and so be in a better position to note a movement.

More car engines barked into life. More exhaust gases swirled among the parked vehicles. Somehow he had to get out. He couldn't make a break for the next level because of the position of the second man. He waited, thinking, until the last of the present batch of returning travellers or visitors had left. For a few minutes the car park would be quiet, only the still lingering smell of petrol fumes.

He heard the first man moving along the back of the row of cars where he was. If he timed it carefully enough, and moved silently, that would still enable him to creep round the front of the next car and keep himself hidden. But then the bastard shouted across the echoing space to his colleague. Beetle realized that he had been thinking in English, and suddenly the familiar Czech language sounded ragged in his ears. The second man came running over. Now they were going to start systematically at the front of the row and work to the end. That made it impossible for him to creep between the cars. There would come a moment when they were level with him. But if he could get into the next row, it brought him nearer the exit.

He moved into a position where he could leap forward with the maximum acceleration. He couldn't afford to wait until they were nearly level. The sooner he made the move the better.

They were almost eight cars away when he shot forward, leaping across the space to the next row, then the next, and then he flattened himself on the ground to gain the most cover, before resuming his crouched position.

The two men had been taken by surprise, but they instantly rushed towards the second and third row of cars. Beetle knew he was not secure for more than a minute or so. At least they had not seen where he had ended up. Already they were working systematically along the back and front of the second row. As he was in the third row that gave him the opportunity to creep into the next. He timed it carefully when they could not command a horizontal view. It was then that he became aware of a quietly running car engine and he heard a faint peep on a car horn.

So did the other two men. They stopped simultaneously, stared about them. Beetle peered round the car that hid him, straining to see where the sound was coming from. The others now began to work along the rows horizontally. That enabled them to cover the ground more quickly. Beetle's time was limited. He would soon have to make a dash for the driveway down to the next level. At that moment there was the merest peep on the horn again, and a car drew out of the next line and began moving very slowly towards the exit ramp. Beetle leapt forward. The car would give him cover. As he ran to the other side of it, he saw the round face and figure of Palesworth at the wheel. The passenger door was flung open. He hurled himself in.

A pistol shot cracked in the confined space. It ricocheted with a scream off the roof of the car they had just passed. The pair of them ducked as Palesworth thrust the accelerator to the floorboards and the tyres screeched as he swung the car into the downward ramp. There was another crack of a shot. A sharp ping confirmed that it had splintered the concrete of a supporting column that offered momentary protection for the car. Palesworth was now careering it down the exit ramps.

'Oh dear, very naughty,' he muttered with a smile.

Rackham put down the receiver from Beetle's call, and looked up at Carolyn, who was sitting by a window which commanded a view of the Thames. 'They've outwitted us,' he said.

237

A few moments later another call from passport control at the airport confirmed that the Czechoslovak Embassy passenger aboard Flight OK755 was a bona fide Czech diplomat.

Carolyn's expression was of wide-eyed bewilderment. Rackham knew it had been a mistake to let her come to the office, and yet he couldn't regret it. Women, especially as young and fresh-looking as this one, were his weakness; except, he preferred to think of it as a strength. But this was not the time to be distracted.

'So they haven't tried to take your father out from Heathrow today,' he mumbled, more thinking aloud than talking to her.

'Another day?'

He shrugged. 'More likely a different plan altogether.'

'What happened?'

Briefly, he told her, and then in answer to a further question, he added, 'Either it means that our agent has double-crossed us and has co-operated in laying a false trail or, which is much more likely, that the Czechs have become suspicious of him as a double agent and deliberately misinformed him: told him that he would be accompanying a disguised Hailston to the airport in the knowledge that he would immediately tell us, and so we would be misled, while they got on with their real plan for getting him out of the country.'

'So what do we do?'

'We keep quiet while I think,' he said, and then uttered a 'Damn!' as the phone rang.

He heard Palesworth's voice, as rotund as his figure, saying simply, 'I've got Beetle aboard. It was the wrong ball of dung, but you know that now.'

'He still hasn't any idea what they're up to?'

'No. They rumbled him. By the way, they nearly shot him too. See you later.'

Carolyn looked up, a question in her bright blue eyes.

'Confirmation,' was all Rackham said. Then he sat alternately

238

staring straight past her and doodling on the pad in front of him. Earlier he had written on the top of the pad, 'Bach', followed by 'De Bach'.

Once he got up and stood by her chair, looking along the Thames towards Westminster. She glanced up at him, her eyes brimming with questions, but neither spoke. He paced back to his desk, slumped into his chair, leant forward with his hands propping his chin. He was systematically reviewing every piece of information relating to Hailston that he could remember.

It was half-past two when he said, 'There is something familiar about that name.'

'What name?'

Rackham was about to pronounce it, and then stopped. Instead he showed it to her, written on the top of the pad.

'It's not Bach,' he said. 'It's something else. That's what's familiar about it. Bach and not Bach.' After a few more minutes of silence, he suddenly brightened. 'I've got it,' he exclaimed. 'There's a fellow at the American Embassy can tell me. I had his father here — actually staying in this flat for a night or two. He was over here visiting wartime airfields. It was a reunion of some kind or other. It's an airfield, I remember seeing it written down.'

The American was, in fact, part of the CIA's London station — a Jew by the name of Ben Chomsky, with a Durante face and a humour to match. Rackham pressed the numbers on his telephone, and prayed the man would be there.

Soon he was rewarded with, 'Hi! — Chomsky.'

'David Rackham.'

'Say, where have you been hiding? Don't tell me — Czechoslovakia. Well, what do you know? Saved by the Holy Trinity, I was told.'

Rackham laughed. 'They have reckless drivers in Prague.'

'OK, so you want Ben's help?'

'Two or three years ago your father came over here with some other wartime pilots visiting old airfields — remember?'

'Sure, you put him up, David.'

'Was there one spelt B A C H, or maybe D E B A C H? I seem to remember seeing it printed.'

'Sure there was — Debach. Not used now, but not so very far from our present stations at Woodbridge and Bentwaters.'

'De — what? Say it again.'

'Yeah — the locals call it Debbitch, accent on the first syllable.'

'Debbitch,' Rackham repeated. 'They wouldn't know that.'

'Who wouldn't know what?'

Rackham ignored the question. 'Ben, you're marvellous.'

'My dear old mother, God rest her soul, always said so. Now the old man — well — '

'Is he still going strong?'

'Sure he is.'

'Then give him my love. And tell him I like Bach too, pronounced Bitch.'

The American chuckled. 'I don't know what the hell this is all about, but good luck. Let me know if you want Ben's help again.'

All Rackham's freckles appeared to be grinning with him when he put down the receiver.

'Debbitch,' he exclaimed again. 'Those Czechs wouldn't know it wasn't pronounced Debach.'

'You mean that's where they're taking him?'

'From,' Rackham explained. 'It's a long shot, but it's worth it.'

'Where?'

'Suffolk,' Rackham enthused, as he picked up the telephone receiver again and, from the crisply issued instructions, Carolyn learned that he was ordering a car and a helicopter.

'Now, a few more calls then I'm airborne,' he smiled.

This time he punched out the number of the Suffolk Constabulary's headquarters at Martlesham Heath, and asked to speak to the Chief Constable, Paul Grantham. Rackham had met him on a previous operation and they had taken an instant liking to each other. Grantham was a modern policeman with an alert but amused expression that creased the corners of his eyes in a way that signalled to Rackham that he was another man with a sense of humour. He was also, as Rackham had reason to remember, a no-nonsense, efficient officer.

The greetings over, Rackham asked, 'Is there still an airfield at Debbitch?'

'Ah, you know how to pronounce it. Disused.'

'Could an aircraft land there?'

'Don't know without checking. Doubt it.'

'Blast!'

'Well, there's some light industry there now. Too many obstructions, I would think.'

'Are you sure a light plane couldn't get down?'

'The chap who farms the land round the place has got a grass landing strip there. It's used by crop-spraying aircraft.'

'That'll do. Paul, I'm coming to see you — as quickly as possible. By helicopter. Meanwhile, I want the whole area around the farmer's airstrip staked out. It's a covert operation. I've got full authority.'

'I understand. When?'

'Immediately. We haven't a minute to lose. Unmarked cars, unmarked men, too. Armed.'

'So, what are we expecting?'

'My guess, Paul: a car, and a light aircraft. I'm sure no flight plan will be filed, at least not until he's in the air, and then he's unlikely to be going anywhere more controversial than, say, Jersey or Guernsey.'

'What is it? You're not concerned with drugs.'

'If I'm right, it's the Czechs flying someone out that we want to keep in the country. Somehow your cars have got to be hidden, and so have the men.'

'All right. By the time you're here the whole thing will be organized.'

'Oh, if *they* arrive before I get there, you'd better arrest the lot, Paul. And, needless to say, be ready for violence. And, I repeat, the whole thing is a secret operation. If there are to be any Press releases, or information of any kind, it will come from 10 Downing Street.'

Before he put down the receiver, Rackham said, 'There's one other thing, Paul. Book me a good secure room in an Ipswich hotel, please. If we get our man I shall want him to myself. The rest of them you can keep secure until it's decided what to do with them. But the chief character I shall want for a little private questioning before he's taken back to London for security debriefing.'

'And, I presume, to enable our masters to decide how much is to be published?' Grantham said.

'You're an old cynic — but that's about it. See you, Paul.'

Once Rackham had put down the receiver, Carolyn asked brightly, 'So where are we going?'

'I'm going to Martlesham Heath in Suffolk. You're going back to Chester Square.'

Carolyn shook her head determinedly. 'I'm coming with you.'

'Listen Goldilocks, by now your mother will be wondering what the hell's happened. She expected us to have the whole thing wrapped up, and your father on the way home. You're going there to explain.'

Carolyn looked up over her brows at him, still slowly shaking her head. Rackham found her manner irresistible, even enticing.

'Give me one good reason,' he said, weakening.

'I'll give you three: he's my father; I like to be where the action is; you need looking after.'

Rackham laughed. 'The one thing I'm good at is looking after myself. So we can chuck that one out. On your own admission, you don't give a tuppenny damn for your father. That's another one gone. You have been rather careless about being where the action is. So that's not a justification either. Back to Chester Square you go.'

As he got up from his desk, she went and stood close to him, looking straight into his eyes. 'No,' she said, simply, 'I want to be with you.'

Normally he would have taken advantage of her proximity and kissed her, but he knew that was not what she expected, or the reason why she wanted to be with him.

'All right, you can come,' he said slowly, 'providing you do as you're told when we get there.'

'I promise.'

'I've got a couple more phone calls to make. Go into the next room, phone your mother and tell her that the Czechs have had a change of plan. We'll be in touch as soon as we have some more news.'

Ten minutes later she was sitting in the back of a car with Rackham, heading for Battersea heliport.

18

The headquarters of Suffolk County Constabulary is a modern cube of dark red brick and glass set among silver birches in a green clearing in the woods and heathlands a few miles north east of Ipswich. The helicopter came in low over other outlying buildings and car parks to settle on the lawn in front of the headquarters.

Rackham and Carolyn jumped down from the aircraft, its flailing rotors drowning the pittering sound of the fountains that lifted sunlit showers of water from the moat flanking the entrance to the building. The pair of them hurried beneath the projecting canopy into the spacious glass entrance hall. On their right a police officer leant over the reception desk, behind him a large glass display cabinet of silver trophies. He was ready for his visitors, because immediately Rackham snapped out his name, he and Carolyn were led to the lift and taken to the third floor.

Paul Grantham was waiting for them, sitting casually on the corner of his curved teak desk. He was a bit older and taller than Rackham, but had the same athletic figure. In a light-check lounge suit he looked both smart and sharp. He came forward, his hand outstretched.

'Carolyn Hailston,' Rackham introduced. 'It's her father, Stanley Hailston, we are interested in.'

Grantham's amused expression denoted his immediate understanding. 'We are in position,' he said. 'There is radio contact with this headquarters. The result of radar surveillance by any of the bases in the neighbourhood will be reported to us immediately from RAF Watton. So far there has been no unauthorized light aircraft in the area. I've booked you accommodation at the Marlborough Hotel in Ipswich.'

Rackham grinned. 'Splendid. Let's get out to Debach.'

'And you're taking charge of Hailston?'

'Yes. I'll take full responsibility for him. I want to do a little debriefing at the Marlborough, before the full-scale job in London. Whoever else we snaffle you can hold in custody until you get further instructions. I imagine we shall take them back to Town and they'll be shipped out of the country pronto. Undiplomatic activity,' he grinned.

Grantham sighed. His eyes twinkled. He led the way out of the room to the lift.

'Oh, can we drop Miss Hailston off at the Marlborough on the way?' Rackham asked.

'It's not on the way. But I'll see she gets there.'

Carolyn started to protest. Rackham raised his hand.

'You promised. Remember?'

Carolyn sighed with resignation.

In the entrance hall, the Chief Constable snapped to the police officer behind the desk, 'Lay on a car to take Miss Hailston to the Marlborough Hotel, Ipswich.'

'See you soon — I hope,' Rackham smiled as they strode through the glass doors to a waiting car.

When they turned right on to the A12, he asked, 'How far?'

'Oh, six to seven miles.'

A few minutes later they turned left at the Woodbridge roundabout on to a B road and were heading north west. In under fifteen minutes the car was going along a concreted drive with a low building ahead of them, plainly labelled 'Debach Enterprises'. Behind this stretched the disused runways.

The car slowed, and swung to the rear of the building.

'No, that's not an old hangar,' Grantham said, anticipating

Rackham's question. 'I know it looks like it, but it's been put up since. Houses various light industries, not part of Debach Enterprises.'

The car drove between a mixed collection of buildings and out on to the old runway. The surface was badly broken, and impeded by a variety of constructions.

'A light aircraft might just get down at the far end,' Grantham said, 'but it could be tricky. I've got one man here just in case, with radio contact. If it should come in here, we'll have to tear over like blue-arsed flies. But I imagine the pilot has been instructed to use the grass landing strip. He'll see a windsock at the end of it, and he's got five hundred metres of good firm grassland there.'

They drove back the way they had come and turned left into a side road, evidently one of the service roads of the old airfield. It had an uneven concrete surface leading between fields that were high with green wheat. They passed modern farm buildings on their right and, soon after, a short side-road sheltered by trees in full leaf. The trees served also to hide a couple of unmarked police cars. A few yards further on was a wide clearing and a long swathe of grass cutting through the wheatfields. On the edge of it a windsock filled out in the breeze.

The driver swung round and returned to the tree-lined roadway. Rackham and the Chief Constable got out and walked back to the windsock.

'Presumably,' said Grantham, 'the aircraft will taxi up to the edge of the strip, and the car will meet it on this bit of open ground.'

'Then the plane will have to taxi back along the strip to take off into the wind,' Rackham muttered.

'That's what we have to prevent. This is my plan: if the aircraft arrives first, we've no alternative but to let it turn ready to taxi back along the strip for take off. When the car arrives we wait until the passengers are out of it and making for the aircraft. At that moment, our three cars dash forward. Two of them take up positions immediately in front of the aircraft. That will stop it moving forward. We will drive to a position immediately behind it.' He turned to Rackham with a half-smile. 'A harder target,' he said. 'If anyone remains in their car they will be looked after either by three chaps lying in the wheat, or by some other fellows we have handy in the farm sheds back there. Of course, if the car arrives first, it's a fairly simple job of moving in and arresting the occupants.'

Rackham took a final look round the scene. As they walked back towards their hiding place in the car, Grantham asked, 'So the Czechs are removing Hailston — voluntarily or forcibly?'

Rackham grinned. 'Guess.'

Grantham nodded, a discreet amusement tweaking the corners of his lips.

'And the weapons?' Rackham asked.

The Chief Constable produced a familiar .38 Smith and Wesson from his jacket pocket. 'The chaps in the wheat have got the five point five-six Heckler and Koch. And in one of the blocking cars there's an officer with a Remington pump-action shot gun — just in case we want to put a heavy slug into the aero engine.'

'H'mm, very satisfactory,' Rackham mused as they got back into the car. After half-an-hour of waiting, he uttered a deprecating little chuckle. 'Of course, if I'm wrong — '

'You'll have wasted a lot of policemen's time,' Grantham cut in.

'And ensured a big enough kick up the arse to propel me out of the service I should think.' Rackham grinned to himself at the thought of devoting all his time to his humorous pieces for *Punch* and *The New Yorker*.

'What about the pilot?' Grantham asked.

'You'll have to take him in, I suppose. But I should think he's innocent enough. Probably find it's a small company, and he's simply been chartered to make a private trip from here to Jersey. That's where they'd make the connection to Czechoslovakia.'

'Do you expect a shoot out?'

Rackham shrugged. 'They shouldn't be armed. But who knows?'

It was five o'clock before the radio from Martlesham Heath headquarters told them that RAF Watton was reporting a small unidentified aircraft heading in their direction. Ten minutes later they heard the sound of its engines.

Rackham got out of the car and stood in the shelter of the hedge. Through his binoculars he watched a twin-engined high-wing monoplane circle once and then make its approach to the far end of the airstrip. It had plenty of grass to spare, and the pilot taxied slowly towards the windsock on the edge of the open ground.

'It's a BN-2B Islander,' Rackham announced through the open window of the car. 'It's a popular aircraft. Can take nine people as well as the pilot. I don't imagine he will have more than three passengers though — Hailston and two others.'

Rackham watched as the pilot brought the aircraft to the very edge of the landing strip before turning it ready to taxi back to the far end. He stopped about ten yards in, engines still running. Drivers in two of the police cars immediately started their engines.

Rackham had only just resumed his seat beside the Chief Constable, when they heard a car approaching at speed. A black saloon hurtled past their slip-road and on to the open clearing.

Two of the police cars accelerated from their cover, and swept out each side of the open space. Their tyres screeched on the rough surface. Rackham and the Chief Constable followed, taking a central course between them. The Czech vehicle had turned on to the grass landing strip and was coming to a stop at the rear of the aircraft. There were two doors on the port side, one forward of the wing, and the other at the back of the cabin. The rear doors of the black saloon flew open. Hailston and two other men bundled out. The two police cars swung round in front of the aircraft, blocking its path. Rackham and Grantham drew up slightly to the left behind the black saloon.

Hailston was being rushed towards the forward door when, through a loud-hailer, the Chief Constable yelled, 'Stop — all of you!'

The group momentarily hesitated. As yet, they clearly had not appreciated what was happening.

Grantham shouted again. 'You are all covered. Drop any weapons, and come this way.'

At that moment three policemen rose out of the green corn holding their Heckler and Koch self-loading rifles. Other police cars which had been further back in the farm buildings now came to a stop on the open ground, officers leapt out and approached the two men remaining in the front of the black saloon.

The other men crouching with Hailston near the port side of the aircraft looked up startled. Then one of them heaved open the door and forced Hailston in, almost falling in behind him. The third man scuttled back to the rear, but before he could get in he was grabbed by two policemen.

Rackham smiled. 'One in the bag anyway. And the others can't get far.'

The forward door was slammed shut. A single pistol shot rang out from the front of the aircraft, aimed in the direction of the three police officers. They did not return the fire, but kept the aircraft covered.

The Islander's engines were cut. The single door forward of the wing on the starboard side flew open, and the pilot jumped down on to the grass. The sound of another shot came from the other side of the aircraft. The pilot was ordered to get back into the plane or he would be killed. He did as he was told.

At Rackham's suggestion they made no response. The armed police officers took cover again in the wheat, and for fifteen minutes there was silence. Then the Chief Constable addressed them through the loud-hailer: 'You can't take off. Please leave the aircraft, drop your weapons on the grass, and come forward. We are prepared to stay here as long as necessary.'

There was no reply. Another five minutes passed before a face appeared at the cockpit's open window. It shouted: 'Clear the path, or we shoot the pilot.'

Rackham and Grantham exchanged glances, and Rackham slowly shook his head.

The Chief Constable hailed back: 'Those terms are not acceptable. The cars stay where they are. Without the pilot you can't take off anyway. Please leave the aircraft and give yourselves up.'

Two shots were instantly fired at the forward police cars. Rackham heard the shattering of glass. Over the car radio Grantham gave instructions for the cars to be abandoned and the men to take cover in front. Then, using only the officer's name, he summoned the policeman with the Remington pump-action shot gun to join him. Rackham and Grantham's car was sheltered by the abandoned black saloon.

Through the loud-hailer the Chief Constable reasonably argued that, as there was no possibility of them getting away, it really did make sense for them to leave the aircraft and give themselves up.

It was another five minutes before there was any response. Then the man at the window shouted, in a coarsely accented voice, 'Take away the cars or Mr Hailston will be killed. Leave the way clear for take off, or we shoot him.'

'Play for time,' Rackham whispered.

Grantham replied unemotionally through the loud-hailer: 'I don't think that is a good idea for you. If you come out of the aircraft and give yourselves up, the worst that is likely to happen is that you will be sent back to your own country. If you kill Mr Hailston you will be charged and tried for murder in this country. Now don't you see it would be much more sensible to leave the aircraft and give yourselves up?'

The reply was immediate. 'No. Clear the cars or we kill Hailston.'

Grantham added factually, 'We have three of your colleagues in custody, you know. I must ask you again to leave the aircraft. It is your best hope.' Grantham realized that they knew their colleagues were in no danger whatsoever, but he hoped it might keep them talking.

Their reply was to show Hailston at the next portside window with a pistol pressed to his head.

'You have not much time,' a voice shouted from the aircraft.

'We would like to consider the matter,' the Chief Constable called back.

'There is nothing to consider. Move the cars, or he's dead.'

Over his car radio Grantham called in one of the officers armed with the Heckler and Koch rifle. He was risking the possibility of the communication being overheard in the Islander's cockpit, but its radio was unlikely to be tuned to the same frequency. Indeed, there was no response to his instructions, and within seconds the officer had crept round under the cover of the two cars.

With a half-smile at Rackham, the Chief Constable again addressed himself to the loud-hailer. 'I need your assurance,' he said, 'that my men will not be fired on when they return to the cars.'

'They will be safe,' came the immediate shout from the Islander.

'Thank you,' Grantham replied and then told his men to return to the two forward police cars and await instructions.

'What instructions?' came the shout from the aircraft. 'Move the cars.'

'I need to tell my men where to go,' Grantham replied.

Hailston could still be seen at the window with the pistol against his head.

Grantham turned to Rackham. 'I think this is one for me,' he muttered. 'Check: there's no aisle in the aircraft?'

'That's right,' Rackham answered. 'Rear seats fold forward as in a two-seater car.'

'Good. That means I'd get some protection from the seats. They're all sitting forward. We'll blow the catch of the rear door with the Remington. Simultaneously the Hecklers will open up, firing over the top of the aircraft, one man moving forward to the portside front door, and the other to the starboard door. The noise will be a distraction. By then I shall be in the rear of the aircraft, covered by the third officer. I'll make up my mind when I'm inside if it's necessary to fire.'

'Sounds fine.'

The Chief Constable picked up the loud-hailer for the last time. 'I'm going to tell my men to move the cars,' he shouted at the aircraft. Immediately he had switched off the loud-hailer, he used the radio to instruct the drivers to take the cars slowly straight down the airstrip. Quickly he outlined the plan to the rest of his men. Then, hidden by the black Czech saloon and his own car, he moved to the rear of the aircraft just as the police cars began to drive slowly ahead. He was reckoning that the man threatening Hailston would now have turned his attention to the pilot, ordering him to restart the engines.

The sound of the Remington shattered the brief silence as it blasted the rear door of the Islander. Rackham saw two men firing above the aircraft as they hastened to the forward doors.

By the time Grantham was in the back of the plane, an officer beside him with a menacing Heckler and Koch pointing at the occupants, the other officers were threatening the forward doors.

As Grantham had expected, Hailston was temporarily unguarded.

'All right,' he shouted, as he jerked up his Smith and Wesson, 'drop your weapons. We'll fire.'

The pilot looked round, scared. The Czech on the starboard side was unarmed. The other turned back from the pilot, still holding his pistol to confront the much superior fire power of the Chief Constable and his officer.

'Come,' Grantham commanded impatiently. 'Throw them out.'

The Czech looked ruefully at his gun, then at Hailston, and threw the weapon out of the window on to the ground.

The two police cars driving slowly down the airstrip, turned, and quickly made their way back to the aircraft.

The three men got out of the portside forward door to be met by a group of armed police officers. Standing among them was David Rackham.

'All right, Mr Hailston,' he said, 'you're coming with me.'

The two Czechs, who had now been joined by the pilot, were led away. Rackham took Hailston's arm and steered him towards the Chief Constable's car.

Grantham soon joined him, an amused expression twitching at the corners of his lips. Rackham nodded. 'Nice job, Paul. Oh, this is Mr Stanley Hailston. The Chief Constable.' Rackham grinned.

Hailston drew himself up. He looked shaken, but angry. He made no reply, but got into the back of the car with Rackham.

Grantham gave a series of crisp instructions to one of his inspectors, and then took his seat in the front of the car with the driver. As they drove back along the concrete roadway, the driver said, 'I thought, sir, it might be a good idea to take a back route to Ipswich through Grundisburgh and Tuddenham.'

The Chief Constable grunted his assent, and then turned round to ask if Rackham needed any assistance at the Marlborough Hotel.

'One police officer and a car to get us back to Martlesham to pick up the helicopter later this evening. It need not be an unmarked car this time,' Rackham smiled.

Grantham reached for the radio-microphone and gave some curt instructions to his HQ.

Hailston said nothing. Rackham was surprised by his appearance. While he looked like a man containing anger, he also looked shocked, nervous and almost exhausted. Rackham had thought the man's training would have stood him in better stead.

At length Hailston muttered wearily, 'What are you doing with me? Does Esme know?'

'Not yet. We're going to the Marlborough Hotel at Ipswich. Rooms have been booked there. I want to question you first. Then we shall return to the Suffolk Police headquarters, where a helicopter will take us back to London. By then we shall know what is to be done with you.'

Hailston muttered, 'I should have thought that was bloody obvious.'

'Perhaps,' said Rackham. 'You look pretty knocked up.'

'So would you if you'd been . . . Bloody hell, I haven't had any proper food — bits and pieces any old time. And I haven't got my pee-testing kit with me. I might even have been giving myself too much insulin . . . I don't know.'

'So what do you want to do?'

Hailston grunted. 'I could do with a lie down.'

'That's possible — while I'm talking to my boss, and to Downing Street.'

The last two words appeared to send a shiver through Hailston. 'I'm bloody tired,' he mumbled, and he looked as though he had no idea what was happening.

The car moved swiftly through the narrow and twisting country lanes until it emerged on the Colchester Road of the old Ipswich by-pass. A few minutes later it turned into the forecourt of the Marlborough Hotel in Henley Road. It is an elegant nineteenth-century building with modern extensions at the back.

Rackham helped a slightly trembling and bemused Hailston from the rear seat, as another police car swept to a halt beside them.

'Your man and transport,' Grantham smiled.

Rackham led Hailston through the glass doors into a large entrance lounge, tastefully papered with a design of huge poppies, and liberally provided with armchairs and settees.

Rackham grinned his approval at the girl behind the reception desk, and declared, 'Adjoining rooms booked in the name of Rackham.'

'Yes, sir — number 23. It's a large room, and there is a small room adjoining.' She handed him the key, adding, 'It's at the top of the staircase, sir.'

With a brisk, 'See you later,' Grantham turned to go.

'Sometime this evening,' Rackham acknowledged and, supporting Hailston's weight with both arms, he turned towards the wide staircase. At that moment Carolyn rose out of the depths of a brown armchair nearby.

'My God,' groaned Hailston.

Rackham grinned at her. 'See — I keep my promises, too,' he said.

Father and daughter looked at each other, but neither spoke. He even appeared to be looking beyond her.

'I'll be with you shortly,' Rackham added, as he almost carried Hailston up the stairs.

The walls were hung with magnificent sailing photographs, and at the top, Rackham turned the key in the door of number 23. It was a tall and spacious room in the old building, all green and pink with buff-coloured satin wallpaper. On the wall to the left was an attractive floral print, signed Mary Ford, with a bust of the artist on a table immediately below it. The windows looked down upon well-maintained gardens at the back.

Hailston sighed and threw himself on to the bed.

Rackham saw that he was trembling. He looked grey-faced and sweaty.

'You all right?' Rackham asked.

'Fucking tired.' The words came out slurred.

'OK — rest for a bit. I've got calls to make first. Is there anything you want?'

Hailston looked confused. 'No,' he muttered, trembling.

Rackham inspected the adjoining room. It was small and narrow, clearly meant as part of a family suite. He noted to his satisfaction that the communicating door was locked.

Downstairs, he told Carolyn, 'Your father doesn't look too well. Seemed a bit chilled, but sweaty too.'.

'I'm not surprised, are you?'

Rackham shrugged. 'He's resting. Perhaps you'd better go up and see him shortly — see if there's anything he needs.'

Carolyn raised her eyebrows. 'If you say so.'

Rackham told the police officer at the bottom of the stairs that his task was to keep a watch on Room 23; the occupant must not be allowed to leave.

'What happened?' Carolyn asked.

'Tell you later,' Rackham replied infuriatingly. 'I've work to do first.'

He then sought out the manager and borrowed the privacy of his office for half an hour, so that he could report direct to Sir Dick Randle, who undertook to brief the Prime Minister immediately. Subject to advice, it would be for the PM to decide how the whole thing should be handled, and Downing Street would deal with the Press.

Sir Dick's austere tones added, 'You'd better get Hailston back here as quickly as possible.'

'There's a helicopter laid on,' Rackham answered, 'but I don't want to move him yet, sir. He's not feeling too good. As soon as I can.'

Well, that was true, Rackham reflected, but he also wanted to get at Hailston himself.

He met Carolyn coming down the stairs. 'How is he?'

Carolyn smiled. 'He's sleeping,' she said.

'Damn. I suppose we'll have to let him have a rest. There are a few questions I want to ask him, and we've got to get him back to London as soon as we can.'

Carolyn lingered on the last stair. 'You . . . want to wake him up?' she asked uncertainly.

Rackham looked at his watch. 'We can't delay too long. I suppose we might fit in a meal — say one course only. Time for that,' he grinned. 'Give him a bit of a sleep.'

'Hedonist, aren't you?'

Rackham thought to himself that he could wish she were, but all he said was, 'I enjoy good things.'

The dining room, with its green carpet and rose-coloured wallpaper, and with flowers and crystal glasses on all the tables, had that touch of relaxed style that appealed to Rackham. They were shown to a corner table in an alcove overlooking the gardens. Carolyn ordered steamed salmon with cucumber fondue, and he settled for paupiettes of sole with lobster mousseline. He chose, expensively but delightedly, a 1982 Puligny Montrachet. Then, as they ate and he rolled the dry but full white burgundy round his mouth, he gave her an edited account of what had occurred at Debach.

He thought she looked a little unsettled, so much so that at one point he asked, 'Aren't you enjoying your salmon?'

'Oh yes,' she said distractedly. 'Yes, it's lovely.' Her eyes brightened. 'And your sole?'

Rackham pursed his lips and brought his fingers together. 'H'mm, perfect,' he muttered. More seriously, he added, 'I'm not sure what we're going to tell your mother. Depends a bit on what Downing Street decides.'

'What will he be charged with?'

Rackham shrugged. 'Again, that's for the PM. Perhaps nothing at all.'

Carolyn's blue eyes widened.

'Well, the Czechs are hardly likely to want to advertise their own cock-up, are they? Who knows that Hailston was defecting? They might have been trying to kidnap him against his will. A whole lot of them are going to be sent packing to Prague. So they've got nothing to shout about.'

Carolyn looked thoughtful. 'In which case, Mummy need never know.'

'Except,' Rackham added, 'there's still the twenty-thousand pounds paid to Hunter. But only the police know. If the PM decides that, in the interests of security . . . ' He left the sentence unfinished.

'All very tidily hushed up,' Carolyn murmured. 'Do you really think so?'

Rackham answered with one of his characteristic grins. 'Who knows? But it is one way Downing Street might decide to play it.'

Rackham looked at his watch. 'Do you mind if we skip everything else?' he said. 'There are those questions I want him to answer first. Then we ought to be getting back to London.'

He ordered her coffee, and then made his way to Room 23. The policeman was sitting on a chair at the turn of the staircase, thus giving himself a view both of the door of No. 23 and of the lounge downstairs. Rackham unlocked the door.

Hailston was sprawled on the bed, but Rackham had already decided that resting time had come to an end.

'Hailston,' he called, 'wake up, man. We've got a helicopter trip.'

Hailston didn't reply. At the same moment, Rackham realized there was something unnatural about the man.

Stanley Hailston was dead.

Rackham looked at the body. One shirt sleeve was rolled up. On the bedside table there was the outer wrapping of the disposable insulin-hypodermic. He found the syringe itself in the bathroom wastepaper basket. A moment or two later he returned to the door and beckoned the police officer. He nodded at the body. 'Our man's dead,' he said quietly. 'It's either insulin — he was a diabetic — or a heart attack. Get rid of him will you?'

Rackham used the telephone in the bedroom to report this new development to Sir Dick Randle, whom he traced to 10 Downing Street. At least the Prime Minister would know immediately.

When he put down the receiver he remained for a few moments, thinking. Then he hurried downstairs. Carolyn was drinking coffee in the lounge. She looked up as he approached.

'Your interrogation didn't take long,' she said. 'Are we off now?'

'No. Your father's dead, Carolyn.'

Carolyn stared at him, silently. At last she said, 'How?'

'I don't know for sure. It might be a heart attack. It might be insulin.'

Carolyn shook her head, but all she said was, 'Mummy.'

'I'll tell her,' said Rackham. 'I'll phone her now.'

19

The morning papers carried headlines like CZECH KIDNAP PLOT FOILED : MINISTER DIES. The stories beneath told how a disused wartime airfield in East Anglia was the scene of a daring attempt made by Czech agents to kidnap a British Minister and fly him to Czechoslovakia. They were thwarted when police cars screamed on to the runway and armed officers rescued Minister Stanley Hailston seconds before the aircraft was due to take off.

Other facts were comparatively scarce, and reporters filled out the story with background information about the operation of Czech agents and speculation about why they wanted to kidnap Stanley Hailston, the father of the girl who had recently been jailed in Prague. Reporters were, however, provided with the information that Hailston had been taken to the Marlborough Hotel at Ipswich to rest before returning to London. He had died at the hotel, presumably from a heart attack. Police also disclosed that the pilot of the aircraft had been innocently engaged to fly from Debach to Jersey. British intelligence sources claimed that the plan had been to fly Hailston from Jersey to Prague.

An inquest some days later, however, was told that Hailston, who was a diabetic, had died from insulin poisoning. A hypodermic syringe had been found near the deceased. The ordeal that Hailston had suffered, together with irregular feeding and incorrect dosages of insulin, had caused him to go into a hypo-glycaemic coma. In these circumstances he should have been given glucose but, in his deteriorating state, he had clearly injected himself with insulin. This had caused his death. The Coroner who could find no reason why, in those circumstances, Hailston should take his own life, recorded a verdict of death by misadventure.

This was also the information that had been given to Esme Hailston before the inquest. Rackham had gone to Chester Square himself and had admired the controlled and calm way she had listened to him. She had sat erect in her chair, and had shown no sign of the emotion she obviously felt. At the end she had said, 'There is one thing I still don't understand, Mr Rackham. Why Stanley should have forged my signature to acquire twenty-thousand pounds to pay to that man Hunter?' She paused and then forced herself to ask, 'Was he paying him to kill Jane Bacton because he knew she was spying for the Czechs? Surely there were simpler ways of getting rid of her?'

Rackham was solemn. 'I'm afraid, Mrs Hailston,' he said, 'that is something we shall never know. I realize that's painful, but you have to set against this one little mystery your lifetime knowledge of your husband.'

Esme nodded reflectively. 'Yes, I suppose so.' Then disconcertingly, she said, 'Have you told me all you know?'

Rackham could have replied, 'All I'm allowed to tell you,' but he decided it was much kinder to lie, and he answered simply, 'Yes.'

'Oh well,' she said, and then looking directly at him, she added, 'You'd probably like a cup of tea.'

The funeral service was held at St Mary's Church, Slaugham, in Sussex, a week later. It was conducted by Esme's elder brother.

The church, built of stone, has a squat thirteenth-century tower and a long nave. Opposite is a green mound with brick and tile-hung cottages grouped about it and, Rackham noted, a welcoming white-painted pub called The Chequers.

The day was heavy and humid. The sun came only fitfully, and Rackham was glad of the stone-chilled coolness of the church. He stood immediately behind Esme and Carolyn, and found himself staring at the halo of strawberry-blonde hair and envying Josef. But beside him was Toni, and her vivacity, he reckoned, was sufficient compensation. On the assumption that Carolyn would stay with her mother, perhaps he could drive Toni back to Bayswater in his Porsche. He was still planning out the evening when, now seated, he was aware of the gentle pressure of Toni's leg against his own. He turned to look at her. They smiled briefly at each other. He thought, blasphemously to himself: Oh well, in the midst of death . . .

But the priest was saying: 'Stanley Hailston may have been an ambitious man, but his ambition was always put to the service of his country and his fellow men. We think not only of his work in one of the most elite, and secret, of Her Majesty's services, but also his decision to enter politics, not only for his own fulfilment, but as the most constructive way he could serve the community. All those who knew Stanley were impressed by the great energy and enthusiasm that he brought to every undertaking. Those who have known him in government have been aware of the benefit of this energetic devotion to his task, whatever it might be. His own constituents, irrespective of party, know how he has served them unstintingly, and in all these things so loyally supported by his loving and devoted wife. There are few students of current affairs who would not have predicted for Stanley Hailston the highest offices in the land. This is the man . . . '

The heads of a number of the deceased's political colleagues nodded sagely. Rackham, however, found he was not listening any more. He was becoming too aware of Toni beside him, and he hoped he might become even more aware of her beside him later that evening.

When they processed along the path to the far side of the huge grassland of graveyard, the sun sidled out from behind a bank of cloud and blotted the grass with the shadows of yews. Rackham found he was looking in sheer admiration at Esme Hailston. Her poise had not deserted her. She remained an elegant figure by the graveside, her emotions under control. Carolyn, by contrast, looked lovely, but strangely abstracted.

'We have entrusted our brother Stanley to God's merciful keeping,' he heard the voice drone into the humid air, 'and we now commit his body to the ground — earth to earth, ashes to ashes, dust to dust — in sure and certain hope of the resurrection to eternal life through our Lord Jesus Christ, who died, was buried, and rose again for us . . . '

In spite of the sun, the warm damp air, Rackham felt an involuntary shiver run through him. They were all walking back, disorderly, towards the church, towards the waiting cars. Ahead of them, at 'Woodlands', would be that incongruous scene that followed all funerals — a mixture of custom and feast, celebration and grief. Carolyn was beside him. She looked up with a fleeting smile, difficult to interpret.

'Well, that's that,' she said.

Most of the others — some members of the government and of the opposition, local party officials, family and friends — seemed to be ahead of them. Carolyn was deliberately slowing her pace, pausing.

They had come round the back of the church, and there, on the east wall, was a long marble inscription to various members of the Matcham family, including Catherine Matcham, the sister of Lord Nelson.

Carolyn looked around her. No-one else was near them. The air was heavy.

'So Mummy need never know,' she said. It was half a statement, half a question.

Rackham took her hand. 'No,' he said. 'It's better that way. Sometimes illusions are valuable.'

'Yes.'

'Of course,' Rackham continued, 'the government don't

agree with the Coroner, but then the Coroner didn't know that Hailston had defected.'

'So,' she said uncertainly, 'what do the government think?'

'Oh, they think he committed suicide — knowingly injected himself with insulin.'

He turned and looked straight into the bright blue of her eyes. Her lashes lowered over them. She bent her head as she muttered, 'Oh — not an accident.'

Most of the funeral party were now near the lich-gate. Rackham took her chin gently in his hand, and forced her to look at him.

He said quietly. 'We both know it was not an accident — or suicide. You really did loathe him, didn't you? But you shouldn't have thrown the hypodermic away in the bathroom. I had to put it back near the body.' He took his hand away. She paled, gave a little shrug, as he added, 'But no one will ever know that either.'

There was no breeze. The air was still, oppressive.

'They'll wonder what has happened to us,' he said prosaically, 'paying our respects to Nelson's sister.'

She didn't speak. She just let him lead her along the path. Suddenly he stopped.

'Oh, I nearly forgot,' he said. 'Someone who we know as Beetle — we're busy debriefing him — handed me this to give to you.'

Rackham carefully extracted from his jacket pocket a small, golden-budded rose. 'He said you would know if I told you, "Patience brings roses".'

THE

DIRTY DUCK

A Richard Jury Case

MARTHA GRIMES

Stratford-on-Avon is more renowned for its Shakespeare than its slaughter. And, despite its name, The Dirty Duck pub had enjoyed a blameless reputation until an innocent American tourist took her last drink there before being brutally murdered.

Superintendent Richard Jury, visiting friends in the neighbourhood, finds himself at the centre of the hunt for the killer. The only clue is a blood-stained theatre programme, left on the victim's body.

With the welcome assistance of the aristocratic Melrose Plant – and the very unwelcome attentions of Plant's formidable Aunt Agatha – Jury must track down a murderer who intends to kill, and kill again, until he has achieved his deadly ends . . .

'It is hard to overpraise this book . . . Miss Grimes may come to be regarded as the Dorothy Sayers of the 1980s'
New York Times

FICTION 0-7472-3004-8 £2.50

More compulsive fiction from Headline:

The explosive novel of abuse and betrayal

Silk & Satin

MARCIA WOLFSON

They are known as 'The Sisters' – five charismatic women who seem to enjoy every luxury and privilege money can buy. But beneath the glossy surface, each one hides a dark secret – a secret that Mark Saunders' murder threatens to reveal . . .

Darleen – is she really the grieving widow?

Joy – she chooses to celebrate Mark's death in a provocatively sensual way.

Deborah – the councillor whose public respectability conceals dark appetites.

Aida – actress and drug addict.

Samantha – her Oriental fragility masks her ruthless ambition.

Combining the sensuality of LACE with the hedonism of HOLLYWOOD WIVES, SILK AND SATIN is the pulsing novel of power and revenge.

FICTION 0-7472-3007-2 **£2.95**

On a Far Wild Shore

Young, beautiful and newly widowed, Elizabeth Troy travels to her late husband's Cornish home hoping to find comfort in its fertile hills and valleys. But she is shocked to discover the vast, decaying acreage of Pallas is now solely her responsibility – a legacy as unexpected as it is unwelcome.

Elizabeth's plans for her inheritance provoke the bitter hostility of her sister-in-law, Morwenna, whose word has been law at Pallas for thirty years. To bring the troubled estate back to prosperity Elizabeth must look for help elsewhere. And there are many very willing to be more than a friend to the widow – David Troy, a poor relation whose sober exterior hides some disturbing secrets; Courtenay Rodda, the sensual newspaper proprietor; and James Troy, the rich and worldly wise American cousin who begins a thrilling but dangerous liaison with Elizabeth . . .

'The book is beautifully written, the characters depicted with a passionate realism that held me entranced. I simply loved it!' Patricia Wendorf, bestselling author of *Larksleve*.

FICTION   0-7472-3001-3   £2.95

Roberta Latow

Three Rivers

A SENSATIONAL WOMAN.
A FABULOUS MAN.
TOGETHER THEY EXPLORE THE WILDER
SHORES OF LOVE . . .

Isabel and Alexis – rich, beautiful, successful – and
obsessed with each other.
This is their story.

AN INTOXICATING NOVEL THAT GOES
RIGHT TO THE HEART OF EVERY WOMAN'S
FANTASY OF EROTIC LOVE

FICTION   0-7472-3045-5   £2.50

Headline books are available at your bookshop or newsagent, or can be ordered from the following address:

Headline Book Publishing PLC
Cash Sales Department
PO Box 11
Falmouth
Cornwall
TR10 9EN
England

UK customers please send cheque or postal order (no currency), allowing 60p for postage and packing for the first book, plus 25p for the second book and 15p for each additional book ordered up to a maximum charge of £1.90 in UK.

BFPO customers please allow 60p for postage and packing for the first book, plus 25p for the second book and 15p per copy for the next seven books, thereafter 9p per book.

Overseas and Eire customers please allow £1.25 for postage and packing for the first book, plus 75p for the second book and 28p for each subsequent book.